La Sorellanza (The Sisterhood)

"It's over Lu," said Pat. "All that crap is over and we have survived. You know in a way we were all victims, victims of centuries of garbage. The Mafia, the Mob... you know what I am speaking about. It was always there, always a part of our lives but we never said anything about it. We never said anything about the octopus in the living room. It was just part of our lives. We tiptoed around it, but we could never tell anyone it lived in our house. I've done a lot of thinking. I had plenty of time to do so. Think about it. We lived together. Thank God we liked each other because life would have been very lonely."

Wings

La Sorellanza

(The Sisterhood)

by

Barbara Wilson Wright

A Wings ePress, Inc.

General Fiction Mainstream Novel

Wings ePress, Inc.

Edited by: Dianne Hamilton
Copy Edited by: Marilyn Kapp
Senior Editor: Marilyn Kapp
Managing Editor: Dianne Hamilton
Executive Editor: Lorraine Stephens
Cover Artist: mpmann

All rights reserved

Names, characters and incidents depicted in this book are products of the author's imagination or are used fictitiously. Any resemblance to actual events, locales, organizations, or persons, living or dead, is entirely coincidental and beyond the intent of the author or the publisher.

No part of this book may be reproduced or transmitted in any form or by any means, electronic or mechanical, including photocopying, recording, or by any information storage and retrieval system, without permission in writing from the publisher.

Wings ePress Books
http://www.wings-press.com

Copyright © 2004 by Barbara Wilson Wright
ISBN 1-59088-643-7

Published In the United States Of America

February 2004

Wings ePress Inc.
403 Wallace Court
Richmond, KY 40475

Dedication

To The Women who were ...ill are a part of my Sisterhood, ...k is dedicated with thanks and love.

Alice, Andrea, Anne Marie, Barb, Brandy, Connie,
Doreen, Eleanor, Emily, Florentina, Helena, Jean, Karen,
Linda Beth, Lucy, Mary Alice, Maxine, Olga. Pat,
Sue-Pu, Silva and especially Carrie, Laura, Wanda,
Marlys, Nana, Annie and Sasa

Fran
Chears to all the
women in your Sisterhood!
Enjoy the book

Sincerely
Barb Wright

Prologue

Queens, New York, October 1949

Mrs. Reilly knocked once on the principal's door and without waiting for an answer opened it.

"Sister Mary Martha, come quickly. We've got a fight on our hands outside in the playground."

"Who is it this time," asked Sister Martha, quickly heading for the door. "Is it Bernie Golewski against the Schmidt boys again? He still hasn't gotten over who started the War in spite of how many times we have talked about forgiveness." She paused and grabbed a sturdy yardstick from Rappaport Bros. Fabrics, which was kept in the corner for just such occasions. In truth it was more for show then actual use. Somehow the picture of Sister Martha, the principal, wielding the "stick" and bearing down on a recalcitrant youngster was enough to encourage instant cessation of hostilities and immediate repentance.

"No, Sister it's worse. It's some Eye-talian girls beating up on a few others!"

"A girls' fight?"

Both women hurried down the corridor leading to the playground. Ahead were two more nuns walking swiftly toward the exit.

A scene of chaos presented itself as most of the student body of grades four through six had formed a circle and were yelling encouragement to the girls tussling in the middle.

"Sister, go immediately and ring the bell," the principal ordered one nun and, with the other nun, waded into the melee, pushing students aside until she reached the center.

Both nuns grabbed the girl closest to her and ordered her to stand aside. In a few seconds all nine girls were standing, eyes downcast except for an occasional glare at the opposing side. The bell blared and the children ran extra quickly into line where they ignored the no talking rule and whispered among themselves about the fight that they witnessed.

The principal spoke, "There is no fighting at school. This is a place for learning. Your recess will be cut short and you will all walk in quietly to your classrooms."

A few groans were heard but obediently the student body walked in. The nine walked in and headed straight for the principal's office.

"Alright, let's hear it. Who started it and why?" Sister Martha asked sternly. "Miss Donovan?"

"They did, Sister, they pushed and I fell then when my sister came to help they pushed her, too," the girl replied, sneakily sticking out her tongue.

"That is a big fat lie! You and your sister started it with your name calling."

"Did not!"

The ruckus, which was about to begin again, was halted by a loud crackling WHACK! Sister banged her yardstick against her desk. That was enough to bring about instant silence as each girl pondered the fact that the stick could land on her bottom.

"Catherine, Pat, Regina, Celestina, Luisa—outside. You will wait in the hallway."

The girls paraded out and sat on the bench. The next group of students was on its way to lunch, then recess. From some of the boys, there were thumbs-up signs, while the girls giggled.

After what seemed like forever, the other combatants came out and returned to their classrooms, not before smiling smugly at the waiting girls.

Sister Martha called them in her office. "Mrs. Reilly is notifying your parents. They will be here after school. I can't tell you how disappointed I am with all your behaviors, especially you, Miss Damato, and you, Miss Perrini, of all people. In the meantime, you will go into the library, sit at separate tables and write two hundred times, *I will not fight at school*."

It was five fifteen that afternoon when Reno Roccollo drove into the schoolyard. He parked his car, got out and was headed inside when he spotted Sylvia Ferrara coming toward him.

"What's this about, Sylvia? Jesus, Rosa calls me at work with the story that the girls were fighting."

"I don't know Reno, I got the same call. Joe has the car so I walked."

Both entered the building and headed for the office. The five girls were sitting on the bench outside the door to the principal's office. Reno looked at them and motioned them to go inside.

"Thank you for coming. I'm sorry you had to leave work and come down here for this sorry matter." Sister Martha was very business-like.

"Yeah, well, I'm here for my daughter and I'm here for Mrs. Damato who is working. What was the problem?" Reno Roccollo asked.

It seems these five girls were fighting other classmates in the playground. That is a behavior we don't tolerate."

"That true?" Reno looked at the girls sternly.

None of the girls answered at first then Cathy spoke up. "Yeah, Mr. R., we were fighting."

"Which one of youse started it?"

"I guess I did," admitted Cele. "I started it."

"No, I jumped in," said Cathy. "That was after they pushed Reggie first."

"Reggie? Who pushed her?"

Sister Martha interrupted, "It doesn't matter. What does matter—"

Reno raised a hand. "In a minute, Sister. It does matter who started it. Cele?"

"I was telling two other girls about my birthday party next week and the Donovan girls came up out of nowhere and started saying stupid things about my party like we have PUS-ghetti cake with meatball candles. She said she would never go to a party with all those garlic-eating guineas. Those were her words. I told her she would never be invited anyway. Then she says she wouldn't come because we're all related to Al Capone and Lucky Luciano and everybody would be murdered because we're all Mafia. Cathy comes up and Kathleen Donovan calls her another garlic-eating guinea and how she should go back to Italy where she belongs."

"So whadda you do?"

"I breathe on her. I went OOOOO." Cathy imitated the sound.

Reno looked at the clock on the wall, trying to keep from laughing out loud.

"That's when Reggie came over and said let's leave from this spot. Eileen Donovan shoved her. No one shoves my friend Reggie. So I shoved her back, then Maureen came running over and she calls us Mussolini-loving WOPS. Then it started."

"What did you do, Lu?" Reno asked his daughter.

"Nothing, Pa. I didn't do anything."

Celestina and Cathy looked shocked at her reply. "Did too" they mouthed at her.

Lu went on. "I was trying to get away and Maryanne O'Shea bumped into me and tripped over me and sat there yelling that I pushed her down."

"So!" said Reno, "you didn't start it, huh?"

"That's not what we heard," Sister Martha stated. "We heard quite the opposite."

"Where are the other girls? Where are their parents because I want to talk with them and if it's true then these kids will have to apologize."

"The other girls have been dismissed and are home."

"Wait a minute—you mean their parents aren't here either?"

Sister nodded.

Reno took a deep breath. "Why don't you girls wait outside? Sylvia, will you please make sure they behave themselves? Sister and I need to talk."

As soon as the office was cleared Reno launched in. "That doesn't seem fair, does it? I mean two groups of girls slug it out and only one group is here after school and the others have been sent home and no parents around. Something's not right!"

"I interviewed the other group. They all stated that it was Cathy and her friends who started this nonsense."

"How about witnesses?"

"I'm not going to make a federal case out of this, Mr. Roccollo. There was a fight and your girls started it"

"Yeah, well, it seems my girls were provoked. They were goaded into defending their nationality."

"You can defend your nationality without shoving."

"Oh, yeah? Well, Sister, if I were to call you a *mick* and tell you to go back to Ireland and eat rotten potatoes, you'd want to shove me, too, nun or not. I think the kids were justified and I don't know what punishment is in store but it had better be distributed evenly over both groups."

"Your girls will apologize to the entire student body at Mass tomorrow morning and they will write and read their composition about not fighting in school in front of their classmates."

Furious, Reno struggled to control his voice and language. "I don't think so, Sister, not unless both groups do it. I want to speak to the priest, to the pastor. Get him here!"

"I most certainly will not! It's almost five thirty and Monsignor is probably getting ready for supper."

"Well these kids haven't had their supper either and they've been here for over two hours. You tell that priest to call me at home tonight. I want to talk to him about this and you tell him if he doesn't then I'm gonna pull my two kids out of this school. So will the Ferraras and Clara Damato and the Perrinis. And if I do, Sister, I will also pull out my collection envelopes. Tell the priest to check how much I put in each Sunday and how much he's going to lose. These kids aren't going to take the whole rap themselves, that's for damn sure." He pointed his finger at the nun and walked out of the office.

"What's going to happen, Pa?" asked Luisa, his daughter.

"Nothin'! Sister and I worked this thing out. I don't want to hear about no more fighting and neither do the other parents or it's not going to go so easy next time, ya hear?"

Just then Vinnie Perrini walked into the building. "I got here after my wife called all in tears. What's up?"

Reno took Vinnie aside and talked with him in Italian. Vinnie covered his mouth to keep from laughing. Reno put on a stern face and returned to the girls.

"OK, it's already five thirty. How about I take youse guys out for pizza since you gotta be hungry? That okay, Sylvia?"

The girls piled into Reno's car and began to relive the afternoon's events triumphantly this time.

"Cathy really showed them. Boy, she jumped right in after they pushed Reggie."

Lu said proudly.

"Yeah!" Cathy beamed. "I did but they don't push us around!"

"Like a fox, huh?" laughed Reno. Then he turned serious. "Now let this be a lesson to youse . Youse stick together. Youse don't need anyone from the outside. Youse are like family—like sisters. You keep together! *Sempre come sorelle*" Reno said .

"Yeah !" came the response from the five girls. *Always like sisters.*

One

October, Queens New York 1959

Reno Roccollo walked up the stairs to his daughter's bedroom. He could hear the commotion, the twittering of voices and peals of laughter coming from her room. It was her wedding day and it was time for the wedding party to leave for the church. There was just one more thing he had to say to her. He knocked on the door and went in.

"Hey Mr. R! Hi!" Assorted voices greeted him.

"Ah, jeez, look at youse. You're beautyful, all of youse . Hey, Reggie, you look great. Patsy, how are you? Cathy, behave yourself today," he said, pointing a finger at her. "Celestina, you're gorgeous! Are you gonna be next?"

"Sure thing Mr. R, as soon as I find someone as good-looking as you!"

A chorus of OOOOO's arose from the girls.

"God's sake, Cele, he's my father. Knock it off!"

"Hey, never mind. Celestina knows a good-looking guy when she sees one," Reno answered giving Celestina an approving look.

"All I can say is youse are the most beautyful bunch of girls ever gathered under this roof and there's not an eggplant among you."

He winked at his daughter, Luisa, the bride. Several months ago when the wedding was still in the planning stage, Luisa and Rosa, her mother, had a heated discussion about the wedding attendants.

"But why won't you ask Anna Marie? She's your cousin, your own blood. Why can't she be in your wedding instead of strangers?"

"Strangers! Ma, how can you call the girls strangers? For Christ's sakes Reggie's father was in your wedding. Pat's mother and you shared the same baby doctor. We were born in the same hospital. Cathy and I took dancing lessons together since we were four and Tina and I were partners when we made our First Communion. I didn't exactly pick them off the street. I'm not having Anna Marie as a bridesmaid and that's that!"

"But she's family. What am I going to say to my sister?"

"I don't care what you say. I'm not having her. She's big and fat and in the purple bridesmaid gowns I've chosen, she's gonna look like an eggplant. I want this wedding to be the most beautiful ever and I don't want to look at the pictures in ten years and say everything was great except for the eggplant in the front row."

Rosa was screaming now. "Well, how is she supposed to find a husband if not at your wedding?"

"Anna Marie is in high school for God's sakes. She shouldn't be thinking of a husband, she should be thinking of passing her Regent exams first. Jesus, Ma!"

That's enough, both of you!" Reno roared from the den. "All I want after a hard day's work is my supper and some peace. Rosa, it's Lu's wedding—if she doesn't want an eggplant in it she doesn't have to have her. That's it! And you, young lady, I don't want to hear God's name mentioned unless you're praying. What the hell's the matter with you? Didn't those nuns teach you anything in that school? Now I want supper and I don't want to hear nothing more."

Rosa had wiped her eyes and went back to the kitchen and noisily began to bang pots and pans around. Lu had retreated to the dining room where she began to set the table, slamming down plates and utensils.

Lu smiled at her father as they shared this memory.

The photographer came up and asked for one picture of the bride and her father alone before church. Reno stood next to his daughter as she adjusted his boutonniere.

"You're beautyful, Babe." Reno always said *beautyful* in his Italian accent which after all these years hadn't quite disappeared.

"Hey," yelled Cathy, "one more time for our cheer. Come on!"

Giggling, the girls gathered in a circle around the bride.

"Holy Smokey, Crimin' Crokey!

Watch out world while we do the Hokey.

Shake those boobs, shake those booties,

In all the world, no sweeter cuties! La Sorellanza! The sisterhood! *Sempre come sorelle*! Always like sisters! YEAH!"

This was the cheer the girls had made up while they were still in junior high school. It was used for all sorts of celebrations. No birthday, Confirmation, graduation, or other achievement was complete without the five of them getting together for *their* cheer.

Reno laughed at the antics. "Hey, where's that fag of a photographer? I want a picture of this. Get in here and take a shot of all of them!"

The photographer obliged as the girls gathered for a group hug.

A knock on the door and the wedding coordinator popped her head in.

"All the cars are here. Ladies, please, mother of the bride also. The bride and her father in the last car."

Reno turned serious. "OK, all of youse out. Downstairs everybody. Rosa and I want to spend a minute with Lu. Everyone out!"

Grabbing their bouquets the bridesmaids obediently left the room.

With his wife standing next to him, Reno faced his daughter and cleared his throat. "Lu, your mother and I want to give you our blessing. You've been a good daughter. You were raised good and now we want you to be a good wife, a loyal wife, a good mother." He stopped as he felt his emotions getting the best of him. Leaning over he made the Sign of the Cross on Lu's forehead and kissed her on the cheek. Rosa for her part was already tearful and said nothing but blessed her daughter. She started wiping her eyes.

"Ma, don't cry cause you'll ruin your mascara and there's no time to fix it."

That stopped the tears quickly and Mrs. Roccollo looked in the mirror to check for smudges.

"Mother of the bride please," a voice called from the bottom of the stairs.

"I guess it's time, let's go."

~ * ~

The limousines pulled up to the church and the purple-gowned bridesmaids got out and came to attend to the bride. Reno got out and looked around. He frowned. Leaving his daughter to the ministrations of her attendants, he motioned to his driver.

"Mickey, see that guy over there? He's a cop or FBI. He's taking down names of who's here. I want you to go up to him and tell him to get the fucking hell out of here right now or I'm personally gonna grab him by the neck and stick his goddamn head in the holy water font until he drowns. Ya get that? And tell the same thing to his partner, the guy on the corner. Go on!" Having taken care of that piece of business he took his daughter's arm and walked up the stairs to the church.

Inside, the wedding coordinator was giving last minute instructions. She was being paid a lot of money and everything had to be perfect... or else!

"All right, little flower girls don't squeeze the rosebuds too hard otherwise they will be clumps and they are supposed to float. Little ring boy, don't wave the pillow around like an airplane. We don't want to lose the ring. Ladies, remember, count ten pews before the next girl starts down the aisle. We want everyone to get a good look at each of you."

A young altar boy appeared at the back of the church and announced that Father Dominic was ready. Then he ran back. The great doors opened to a flower-festooned main aisle. A quartet was playing and the wedding coordinator gave the signal that Mrs. Cianci, the groom's mother, was to be escorted to her seat.

Mrs. Cianci, in her beige mother-of-the-groom gown and wearing a double orchid corsage, made her way down the aisle, smiling to her friends and family. Then Mrs. Roccollo, dressed in lavender lace and wearing a four gardenia wrist corsage, like a Queen Mother, made her way down the aisle, smiling and inclining her head to both sides. This was as much her day as it was her daughter's. No expense was spared as heaven and earth, as well as a good bit of Manhattan and Queens, were turned upside down to find the perfect accessories, decorations, and flowers for this day. Even the murderous glance from her sister who still smarted at the snub her daughter received by not being asked to be an attendant did not spoil this moment. A bell in the sanctuary rang and Father Dominic, along with two other clerics and six altar boys, came out. They genuflected and, turning, faced the congregation. Father Dominic nodded to the organist. The music swelled. It was time.

"All right," the coordinator excitedly whispered, "this is it. First lady, remember right, left, slowly."

Regina "Reggie" Perrini began her walk. Reggie was practically family. Her father had been in Reno and Rosa's wedding some twenty-two years ago. Petite and sweet, that best described Reggie. Always pleasant to everyone, she was the Pollyanna of the group.

"Seven, eight, nine, ten. Next please."

Cathy Ferrara moved down the aisle. She first met Lu when they took tap dancing lessons together. She, like the rest of the girls, had gone to grade school and high school with Lu. If there was fun around, Cathy found it. Her nickname was "Foxy" and she earned it. Fun-loving, a prankster, she could make people laugh just by saying "Hi."

Celestina Di Benedetti was next in line. Cele faintly resembled Maria Callas, the opera diva. Dramatic looking with smoldering dark eyes and a flair for fashion that set her apart from the other pretty girls, she moved like a cat without waiting for the go-ahead signal. She first met Lu when they were partnered together at Annunciation Grade School for their First Communion. They were to walk together behind Bobby Burns and some other now forgotten boy. Sister Lucy's instructions were that the partners were to walk together slowly. Bobby took Sister's instructions too literally.

"Jeepers," whispered Celestina obviously not afraid of defying the no talking in line rule. "A crippled snail can walk faster." With that she walked right up close behind Bobby and goosed him with her First Communion purse. This made Bobby jump and Lu laugh and Cele became a new friend.

Pat Damato was Lu's oldest friend. Both their mothers had used the same baby doctor and both girls with birthdays close together, had practically grown up in the same house. Pat was the studious one, the conscience of the group, the one who never studied but got the best grades and she always shared answers. Pat was the sister that Lu never had so of course when the time came for Lu to choose a Maid of Honor, who else was there but Pat.

Pat turned around and gave Lu an okay sign, then she too went slowly up the aisle until she reached the altar and turned to face the back of the church. With a fanfare, the organist began the Wedding March.

"Pa, it's time now," said Lu.

Reno was peering out the church door to see if Mickey had followed his instructions regarding the two cops. He quit frowning and returned to his daughter's side.

"Sure, Sweetheart, I'm ready. Now you're sure you want to go through with this. We can still change our minds."

Lu shot her father an exasperated look. Reno offered his arm to his daughter. Luisa, or Lu, was the prettiest girl in the group with Italian movie star looks. She was also the group princess because of her father's position in the neighborhood as "a man of influence."

Clearing his throat, Reno and Lu began the trip up the aisle. By the tenth row, tears had begun to well in his eyes. By the fifteenth row, tears poured down his face and by the time he got to the foot of the altar, Reno was sobbing.

"Take good care of my baby," he said to Jimmy Cianci as he handed his daughter over to the beaming groom. Then he turned and wiped his eyes and wept audibly and in that church so did every other self-respecting Italian male.

Two

Pat limped painfully to the bar.

"A large water with lots of ice please." She winced as she slipped off her purple satin high-heeled shoes. The orchestra had played the spirited Tarantella twice since the dancing began and twice she joined in. Now her feet hurt.

"Yo, maid of honor," a voice said, "hey, *bella ragazza*, there's something wrong with your dress."

Pat looked down...nothing was missing, nothing was ripped. She looked around and found the source of the voice, a cute brown-eyed, brown-haired guy in a Navy uniform.

"There's nothing wrong with it."

"Yeah there is! The dress goes in and out and in and out." The guy traced a woman's figure with his hands.

"The dress goes in and out because I go in and out."

"That's what I thought. Ricky Campione, Third Class Petty Officer.

"I guess I'm impressed. I'm Pat Damato. Are you bride or groom side?"

"Well, I guess I'm both. I could have sat right in the middle of the aisle. I played softball with Jimmy and I'm a cousin of Francine Tomasino who as we know is related to everyone. Actually I met you once before. It was a couple of years ago at the Roccollo's house. I think it was a joint graduation from high school party."

Pat nodded. Every celebration, be it a birthday party, or graduation, or Holy Communion, was always a joint celebration at the Roccollos. Years ago, her father who was an associate of Reno Roccollo's, had died and Reno adopted Pat and her mother as members of his family. Not that she complained of course. He was incredibly generous and there was little that she lacked. If the truth were told, her father had been a small time hood who was to drive the getaway car in a robbery that went bust. The cops had been tipped off and were waiting. There was a shoot-out and Pat's father was severely wounded but he managed to drive for a block or two before he died, thus giving two of the robbers a chance to escape. For this loyalty Pat's family was rewarded. When Lu got a bicycle, there was one for Pat. When Lu and Cathy went to camp, Pat was sent right along. When it came time for high school, Pat along with Lu, Cathy, Reggie, and Celestina went to Mother Cabrini High. No mention of this was ever made to Pat. Pat's father got more respect in death than he ever had in life.

"Yeah, that was quite a party. Half of the Bronx and Queens came. I don't remember you there."

"I stayed long enough to pay my respects, then I had another party to go to. Actually, it was my last night of freedom before I left for boot camp the next day so my buddies and me had to celebrate." He smiled at the memory.

"And did you?"

"Hell yes! It was at least six weeks before I sobered up. I graduated near the top of my class and it wasn't because I was smart or anything like that. It was because if I sat down I'd never be able to get up so I just kept going."

Pat giggled. "So what do you do now?"

"I'm stationed in Naples, Italy. I'm in procurement."

"Procurement? What exactly do you 'procure'?"

"Oh, lots of things. When ships come into port they have to be reprovisioned, so I get them what supplies they need. Vegetables, meats, spare parts... whatever."

"Women too I suppose. Do you 'procure' them too?" Pat asked teasingly.

"Well, not exactly, but I give them a few suggestions."

"I bet you do! What was the most exciting thing you had to procure?"

"Hmm, let's see. Uh, probably some teak paneling for a frigate."

"Teak? Like the wood?"

"Yeah, there was a captain who came in and wanted to get some teak paneling for his wardroom so I made some connections and we got some."

"How?"

"Promise you won't tell? There was a Greek yacht that docked at a marina near Naples and the deck was pure teak. Beautiful! Anyhow, I guess everyone was happy. The captain got his paneling, my connections got paid, and I got a letter of commendation for my 'resourcefulness' and an early promotion. I got my crow. It's called that because the chevron has an eagle on it." Jimmy laughed. "The only ones who maybe weren't happy were the Greeks. They found their yacht with no decking on it."

Pat laughed skeptically not quite sure whether she should believe this story but she had to admit it was quite a line.

"Are you patriotic?" Ricky asked.

"Oh, yes. Why?" Pat responded, puzzled.

"Because it's time to do your country a favor and dance with a poor sailor."

"Sure, why not, as long as it's not another Tarantella. My feet are killing me."

"Give me your shoes," and taking the high-heels, Jimmy tucked each one in his side pockets. Then he led the way to the dance floor.

"Hey, Jimmy," yelled a voice from the bar, "you're out of uniform."

"Not now, but maybe I'll get lucky later."

Pat blushed furiously as she trailed Jimmy past some of the tables.

"Hi, Patsy," said one of the girls.

"Patsy, huh. Is that short for Patricia?"

"No, it isn't"

"Pat, Patsy and you're not a Patricia? What's your name?"

"Just call me Pat, that's fine."

'Well no, if I'm going to dance with you I want to know your real name. Let me see. P—uh—Petra?"

"No!"

"Paola?"

"No again. What is this? Rumplestiltskin? If you guess my name, I have to give you my first child/"

Ricky laughed. "Jesus, this is a little early for that but..." He paused, grinned, then continued. "How about Pasqualina?"

"God, who told you?"

"I was sitting behind two old ladies when you came down the aisle and I asked who you were. They said that was the Damato girl, Pasqualina."

"Nobody calls me that except little old ladies who remember my grandmother. I was named after her."

"Okay, Pat! Let's dance."

~ * ~

Celestina had just walked back into the main ballroom and was looking around.

"Hey, Cele, how come you're not with all these good-looking guys around here? You could be next you know? I could fix it so Lu would throw her flowers right at you."

"Thanks, but no thanks, Mr. R. Someone else can catch the bouquet."

"What? You given up on guys?"

"No! I'm just not in a hurry to get married. I'm young and smart and besides I've heard all their lines times ten. I'll get married when I find the right guy—someone smart and savvy." She looked up to him.

"Now wait a minute. Stay right here. Don't move. Some cousins came down from Buffalo for the wedding and there's a young guy I want you to meet. I'll send him over. His name is Sal and he's smart, so they say."

"Smart like you?"

"Hmm, close enough. Wait here."

Celestina waited and before long a young man came over and introduced himself. A pleasant looking guy, kind of quiet and they talked for a while. For Cele, there was no magic.

~ * ~

Cathy was table-hopping, visiting with friends but she had this uncomfortable feeling that someone was staring at her. She was right. As she moved on to another table someone came up behind her.

"Ya wanna dance? I'm Nicky Torino."

When she turned around, she found herself face-to-face with a porcine-looking guy. Small piggy eyes, thin lips, sort of a perpetual sneer on his face. Actually he reminded her of a portrait she had seen of Henry the Eighth when she did a paper on him. She swallowed hard, trying to resist the urge to throw up on his shoes.

"Gee! Thanks but I've had a little too much wine and I have to go to the Ladies Room. Maybe later?"

Without waiting for a reply, she dashed off to the bathroom where she remained for a half-hour talking animatedly with anybody who came in. Finally she peeked out to check if the coast was clear. It was and she scuttled out quickly to the main ballroom.

"Where the hell have you been?" asked Celestina. "We've been looking for you. It's almost time for the cake. We've got to have more pictures taken."

"I've been in the john trying to fake constipation." Cathy looked around anxiously.

Cele laughed, "Who are you hiding from?"

"Some guy, he kind of looks like an Italian Porky Pig. You know who that is?"

Cele broke up laughing. "Yeah I sure do. That's Carmine Torino's son. You said 'No" to him? Oooh, that's going to get you in trouble. Come on, put on a happy face, let's go. Jimmy is anxious to cut the cake, leave and get started on his honeymoon like they haven't jumped the gun before this. Thank God Lu got the curse a week ago 'cause she was really sweating it."

The cake, a gift from a baker, had six layers decorated with bells and doves. It had been cut and was being distributed. The dancing began again when Reno appeared next to Celestina.

" Hey, Cele, didn't Sal come over and talk to you?"

"Sure he did and we talked for about twenty minutes during which time I told him all I knew about Reggie from Grade Two onward."

"Reggie? Our Reggie?"

"Yup. If you look over there you can see they are having quite a long conversation."

Reno looked a little embarrassed. "What can I say?"

"Nothing but you could ask me to dance. Maybe you're better at dancing than you are at matchmaking."

Reno Roccollo led a smiling Celestina to the dance floor.

~ * ~

The wedding was over. The last of the gifts were brought to the Roccollo house to be kept until the newlyweds came back from their honeymoon. Rosa made a pot of coffee and she sat down with Cathy and Celestina to review the events of the day.

"It was a great wedding, Mrs. R. Really! You planned everything so beautifully and it all went so well."

Rosa flushed with pride. "Yeah it did go well, didn't it? Was there enough food? I know there was plenty of liquor and the cake is almost gone. Even Jimmy's mother came over to me and says how great everything was. You know we had three hundred seventy-two people." She said this with awe. "And they all had a good time."

"Yup, they sure did and who knows? Maybe we'll get to do this again soon. Did you see Reggie and Mr. R's cousin? She did catch the bouquet after all"

"Yes but I'm worried about you two. You should have found someone. Each of you. There were lots of nice boys there. You could have had your pick."

"Don't worry, Celes-TINA and I each got a piece of wedding cake and we'll sleep on it tonight." Cathy always kidded Cele by calling her Celes-TINA.

Cele snickered, "Cathy may be next. Somebody was ogling her I hear."

"Really, our Cathy? Who is it?" Mrs. Roccollo was immediately curious.

Cathy stuck her tongue out and put her finger in her mouth.

"Some jerk! I'd rather be an old maid. Thanks a lot, Cele."

~ * ~

Later as Cathy drove Cele home she asked, "Do you believe in sleeping on wedding cakes?"

"What? And get frosting in my hair? Hell no! I'm not going to. No, I know the man I would want and sleeping on wedding cake isn't going to get him. How about you?"

"I don't know Cele. I just have this feeling it's not for me."

Three

Queens, July, 1960

Cathy and Cele walked arm in arm across the hall. They sang *"Wedding bells are breaking up this old gang of ours."* They joined Lu, Pat, and Reggie. Cathy leaned over Lu and gave her a hug and began to massage her neck and shoulders.

"Ohh! God, that feels good. I didn't know pregnancy gave you a backache. Down lower Cathy."

Mrs. Tomasino, carrying a plate of cookies, came up to the group.

"It's so good to see all of you together," she simpered, "pretty soon there'll be none of you left single. Now it's Reggie and soon it'll be Pat and what are these rumors about you Cathy? I hear somebody is *very* interested."

Cathy eyes bulged and she let out a burp very audibly. The girls barely concealed their laughter. Whenever Cathy heard anything she thought was disagreeable, she made herself belch.

"Oh excuse me, pardon me. I didn't mean to do that. I guess I ate too many *pizzelles*. It must be the anise in them that makes me burp."

Mrs. Tomasino went on, oblivious to the giggles around her.

"Of course Celestina, this could have been your day if you showed any interest in Sal. Don't wait too long. The older you get, the less chances you have. Patsy, that was such a beautiful table your man sent you from Italy. So expensive looking."

Pat was surprised. Jimmy had sent her a table. One of his buddies dropped it off just the other day. How did Mrs. Tomasino find out?

"Mrs. Tomasino, I'll walk you to the car," volunteered Reggie. "Thank you so much for coming to the shower and thank you again for the tablecloth," and she escorted the old lady out.

"Mrs. Tomasino is incredible. How did she find out about the table Ricky sent? We just got it!" Pat said shaking her head.

Lu piped up. "I don't know how she gets her information. I swear to God, the night I got pregnant, Jimmy barely pulled himself out of me and *bam*! She knew I conceived."

"I think she's got radar. If there's a rumor around she zeroes in on it," Cathy stated. "I have no idea who is interested in me. I haven't dated anyone from the neighborhood in months. Couple of guys from work but that's all."

"Nope, I know she wire-tapped the whole neighborhood, houses, bedrooms, johns, the works and every night she reviews all the tapes in her basement. Don't believe me? Drive past her house at one or two in the morning and see if there isn't a light on in her cellar."

"And *how* is it *we* drive home so late?" queried Lu

"I've been working late a lot trying to put together a business plan. I gotta have one before I apply for a loan to start up my business. So there." Cele stuck out her tongue. Reggie joined the group.

"Reg, I'm so sorry about the remark Mrs. Tomasino made about Sal and me. I swear from the moment we were introduced, he did nothing but ask about you. I could have been bare-breasted and he wouldn't have looked at all."

"I know that, Cele."

Celestina was the one who introduced Reggie and Sal at Lu's wedding. Mr. R insisted that Sal meet and talk to Cele.

In her mind's eye, Cele saw the whole meeting again.

~ * ~

"Hi, I've been told to come on over and meet you. Reno is a cousin. I'm Sal Roccollo."

"Hello, I'm Cele Di Benedetti and I've been ordered to wait here until you showed up. Well, I guess we followed orders." They both laughed.

"Yeah, beautiful wedding. The Roccollos went all out. I have to say you bridesmaids and the bride are a bunch of terrific looking chicks. Each one of you."

"Thanks, we've been friends forever. We call ourselves *La Sorellanza,* the Sisterhood."

"Uh, the first girl who walked down the aisle, Jeez, she's a knockout and the second walked down and she's also cute. You all know each other long?'

"Oh yeah, like I said forever. Actually I'm the newest in the bunch. I met them in second grade when we moved here."

"Hmm, the first girl, what's her name?"

"Reggie," replied Cele with a smile, "Reggie Perrini. She's the sweetest one in our bunch. Lu was the Princess. Pat is the most serious as if any of us are serious. Cathy is the most fun."

"What about you?"

"I defy description, but Reggie is the group honey pot. She is genuinely sweet, kind of shy, nice to everyone." Cele watched as Sal melted into the ground.

"What else do you know about her? She date anyone?"

"Lots of guys come buzzing around but no, I don't think there's anyone special. Reggie's a little shy." Cele *was beginning to enjoy Sal's reaction to her every comment about her friend. "Let's see if I can remember a cute story about her.*

There was this one time in seventh or eighth grade when we convinced her to act as a lookout when we sneaked into the nuns' convent. There was one nun who bugged us all the time so we decided to get even. Reggie acted as lookout while Cathy, Lu and I got in the back door of the convent. We crawled up the back stairs to the nuns' bedrooms. We put a glass of water filled with tadpoles on her bedside stand. Reggie was too chicken to come with us but she was a good sport as a lookout. We laughed so much after, we peed. You want to meet her?"

With Celestina leading the way, the very happy Sal followed close behind.

"Reggie, this is Sal Roccollo, Mr. R's cousin. Sal Roccollo, this is Regina Perrini, friend of the bride. I just finished telling Sal the story of the time we put tadpoles in Sister Whats-her-name's bedroom and you were the lookout."

Reggie blushed. "Did you have to tell that story?"

"Oh there's more to it Sal. You want to hear the rest? Well, the next day when we got to school, Sister was on the warpath. We got a ten-dollar sermon about respect and how she was going to the police and have them check the glass for fingerprints and all. Poor Reggie really got scared and began to cry. Of course, Sister hones in on her and Cathy and I began to sweat it out thinking all the time Reggie will squeal on us. She didn't. She told Sister she just got the curse that morning and she was afraid she was leaking so Sister kind of looked at her in disgust and she left the room. That saved our asses."

Reggie was so embarrassed she turned as purple as the gown she was wearing. Celestina went on. "Anyway you'll be happy to know that Reggie doesn't have the curse today."

With that she walked away laughing.

"Is she always this outrageous?" asked Sal who was as purple as Reggie.

"No, today is a good day. She's been told to behave herself. Usually she's worse."

Thus began a romance that would soon become a wedding.

~ * ~

All brides were beautiful and Reggie was no exception. She oozed happiness from every pore. She was doubly joyful as Reno Roccollo offered Sal a position as a manager in one of his dry cleaning stores in Queens. This meant Reggie did not have to leave and move to Buffalo, which she was dreading. This was the cherry on top of her sundae of happiness.

"Hey Cele, come over here have a seat," Reno Roccollo called. "I've been wanting to talk with you but you seem so busy."

"I always have time for you, Mr. R. Actually I wanted to talk with you too but I was afraid it wouldn't seem proper." Cele lowered her eyes modestly.

"What's not proper about my daughter's friend wanting to talk with me? I'm flattered you should take me into your confidence."

"Mr. R, I'm going to start up a business. I'm finished with Fashion and Design School. Some teachers have told me I've got talent. I don't have the money to go into dress designing but I want to specialize in women's tops— blouses, you know, to start. I've got some good ideas and I think I could do it."

"Clothing is a tough business. Lots of competition out there. People with a lot of talent. What makes you think you're different?"

"I've got guts as well as talent. I'm willing to go out on a limb and I don't take *no* for an answer too easily."

Reno shook his head and smiled. "Good answer. You have a business plan? They're always looking for a business plan."

"I'm working on it. I need it before I apply for a loan."

"What about collateral? You got any?"

"Collateral? No, I don't have any assets. I got my body. Will a bank take that?"

" A bank, no, a banker, yes! Why don't you come see me at the office?"

"Mr. R., I didn't come here to ask for money. The best I can hope for is maybe getting a mentor like you. You know, to sort of guide me along. No one in my family knows anything about running a business. My father is opposed to this completely. I can't even talk with him and when I talk to my professors I get the usual textbook answers. I've got to really learn from someone who has business savvy. Like you!"

"I'm glad you came to talk with me. I can do that. I bet you'll make it, Cele, and I only bet on winners. You've got guts and a body. I'll find out about the talent later on." Reno gave her a long hard look and left the table.

Celestina was trembling inside. Did she just imagine what took place? Was it possible? Reno Roccollo would take her under his wing? She had been hoping for that for a long time and now she got her break. *Don't blow it* she said to herself, *this is your big chance.*

She sat there already planning what she would bring, what she would say, what she would wear. Her nerves got the better of her. She got up and went to the bar where she downed some Strega, a potent Italian liqueur. Cathy came up.

"What's up? You look like you've been hit with a thunderbolt. Are you alright?"

Cele did not respond.

"What's the matter with you, Celestina? Have you no shame?" It was Mrs. Tomasino. "I saw you talking with Reno Roccollo, the father of your friend."

Cele whirled around to face the old lady. "What the hell are you talking about Mrs. Tomasino?"

"Easy, Cele!"

"No! What were you insinuating? We were talking about business as if it's any of yours."

"Business? What kind of business should a young girl be thinking of? Just making her husband happy and having lots of nice, fat babies. That's the only business for a young girl."

"Yeah, well, that's not my idea of business."

Cathy moved behind her friend. "Back off, Cele. This is not the time or place."

"No, I'm tired of her sticking her nose into everyone's life."

"Don't make a fuss," Cathy whispered. "If you say one more word I swear I'll find Pig Man Torino and let it be known you've got the hots for him and can't wait for him to stick his pole into you. Don't spoil Reggie's day."

That threat mollified Celestina and she backed down and apologized. Mrs. Tomasino scuttled away puzzled by the girls' behavior today. Business indeed!

"What's gotten into you? She's a harmless old lady whose joy in life is to go around and be part of people's lives. She's probably lonesome as hell. Now what was that all about, your conversation with Mr. R. if I may ask? You look all hot and bothered."

Cele calmed down. "I asked him if he could help... you know give me advice about the business and he said

'Yes.' Cathy, this may be my big break, my chance to get started. I knew if I worked hard enough something would open up. I had thought about it a lot but never had the nerve to ask him. Jesus, when he said to come up to see him at his office I thought my heart would stop. Do you know what that means? That means—"

Their conversation was interrupted. Ricky Campione walked in and greeted the girls.

"Shh! This is a surprise for Pat. She doesn't know I'm here."

"When did you get back? Are you out of the service now?"

"As of July 3, 1960, I am Ricky Campione, civilian. Where's Pat?"

"She was talking with the Ciancis over there," Cathy pointed across the ballroom.

"You girls look great, really gorgeous!"

"Wait 'til you see Pat. She's beautiful!"

Ricky waved and was off. He got halfway across the ballroom floor before Pat spotted him. She let out a scream and ran to him, jumping into his arms. He picked her up and twirled her around, accompanied by cheers and whistles and applause from the wedding guests.

"Five will get you ten there's going to be two wedding nights tonight," Cathy giggled.

"No, I won't take that bet. I know one will happen but how will we verify the other?"

Then both girls stopped and called out together, "Mrs. Tomasino!"

Four

Queens, 1961

Cathy Ferrara got off at her subway stop and walked up the stairs to the street. She would wait for the bus that would take her the last six blocks to her house. It was a blustery, rainy night as a Nor'easter made its way down New England to New York City and out to Queens. She watched as gusts of wind blew papers, shook awnings, rattled street signs and shredded the few remaining campaign posters from last year's presidential election.

Arriving at home she found her father and mother sitting at the dining room table. It was strangely quiet. The usual TV was not on and Carol, her younger sister, was not blaring her radio.

"Hi, I'm home. Something smells good."

"Hi, kid."

"Cathy, I made some tortellini in brodo for supper. I'll get you some." Her mother hurried off to the kitchen.

"Great choice, chicken soup on a night like this. Where's Carol?"

"Off working on a school project."

"You let her out on this kind of night? Boy, I should have been born second. I can see who the family favorite is."

Her mother blinked back tears and carried the soup to the table. "Joe, you want coffee?"

Cathy sat down at the table aware of the tension. Her parents watched her eat in silence.

"You guys mind telling me what's the matter? Mom looks like she's ready to break down any second."

Her father cleared his throat. "Cat, we got troubles, uh, I got troubles. I've had a few business deals go bad on me and I owe some people some money. I gotta pay up."

"Business deals? What kind of business deals? How much do you owe?"

Her father jumped down her throat. "Look, I don't have to tell you anything. What I do is my own damn business."

Cathy put her spoon down and looked over at her Mother. Sylvia was wiping her eyes not quite keeping up with the tears. "Tell her Joe, you've got to tell her."

"I owe some money to Carmine Torino. He wants it now."

"So what-what do we do? Do we have to move from here? Can you get a loan from the bank? I got about six or seven hundred bucks in the credit union that I was saving for a car. I guess you can have it."

"That's not enough. I owe more."

Cathy took a deep breath. "What do you want to do?"

"I need a favor from you, a big favor and you gotta do it. I need a little time to put some things together, then I can pay him off."

"And the favor is what?"

"Carmine Torino says his son kind of likes you. He wants to go out with you. If you go out on a date, that'll give me some leeway. I can pay it off, Cathy, I know I can but you have to help me."

Somewhere in her brain a bomb went off and Cathy reeled backward. For a few seconds she could not believe what her father said. The telephone rang and her mother went to answer it. She put her hand over the speaker. "It's him," she mouthed.

Cathy shook her head too numb to speak. She heard her mother say that Cathy was taking a bath before dinner and to call back please.

"Let me get this straight. You want me to go out on a date with Pigman Torino so you can pay back his father. Are you crazy? Do you realize what you are asking me to do?"

"Yes! Yes, I do! I'm asking you as a father to help me out. This is payback time, Cathy. For all I have given you, a roof over your head, clothes on your back, the food in your mouth, now when I need something, you better return some of that with respect. I'm your father, for Chrissake."

"Parents are supposed to provide their kids with food and shelter and with all due respect, parents don't go around pawning their kids off like collateral on a debt."

Joe Ferrara saw this argument was not going his way. He stood up and thundered at his daughter. "You're going to go out with him and you're going to behave yourself and that's all I want to hear from you. Do you understand me?" With that, he left the room.

Cathy turned to her mother. "Mom, *please* don't make me do this. You talk to him. Tell him this isn't Sicily. Fathers don't go around pimping their daughters and that's what he's doing. He wants respect! This is not the way to get it."

"Cathy," she sobbed, "I've tried to talk with him today. He's afraid of what will happen if he doesn't pay. I'm scared too. One date, Cathy. Just one date. After that Dad will tell Carmine it just wouldn't work out. Maybe we can think of something by that time."

Tears and wails took over at that point and she could talk no more.

Cathy covered her face with her hands. *A date with Nicky Torino. Hell on earth!* Just looking at him repulsed her and to spend a whole evening with him would cause her to vomit. That's it! She could always make herself burp at will now she would make herself vomit at will if she had to.

The phone rang again. Cathy answered it. It was Nicky Torino. She found herself numbly saying, "Yeah Saturday is fine. Six-thirty? OK. Sounds fine. See you then."

Going into the living room she said to her Mother, "OK, tell Dad I agreed for one date. Don't ever ask me to do this again."

~ * ~

Saturday was the longest day ever. Cathy had to go, like everyone else, to weekly confession at church, which was always a chore for her. She hated to go and would skip it at every opportunity telling her mother a fib about her whereabouts. The girls used to do that all the time. One of them would walk in, see who was in line in front of the confessionals, then report it to the rest. After that they would take off for someplace, usually to watch and be watched by the neighborhood boys. Today for some reason she sought comfort in the church.

"Please help," she whispered in the side chapel. "I don't want to do this, just *please* make it easy. I'll do anything You ask in return."

Coming out, she recognized a nun, from her school days, who had been working on altar arrangements. There was another nun with her.

"How are you today, Miss Ferrara?"

"Fine, Sister, thank you and you?"

"I'm always glad to see our graduates remembering their reception of the Sacraments. I'm glad to see you haven't forgotten either."

"Oh no, Sister. You taught us well."

Sister beamed at that compliment. "This is Sister Mary Estelle," she said introducing the other nun. "Sister will be joining our teaching staff now. We've gotten so many students we have to split up our classrooms. This is Cathy Ferrara, she was one of our star athletes."

"Hi, how do you do," Sister Estelle put out her hand. "What did you play?"

"Softball and basketball."

"I did too."

Cathy was surprised. This new nun was young and smiling. Nuns aren't supposed to be young. They are supposed to be old and crotchety and never smile.

"Well it was nice to meet you Sister and good to see you again, Sister."

She left the chapel but not until she whispered one more prayer for that night.

That evening Cathy dressed with a little more than normal care. She would leave nothing to chance. Instead of her usual garter belt and stockings, she borrowed her mother's panty girdle and taking her bra she squeezed the bra snaps extra tight. There was no way that anything was going to be loose.

Nicky showed up promptly at six-thirty. She shot one final look at her parents before she left. Nicky took her first to see his folks. Cathy finally got to meet *the* Carmine Torino after all she had heard about him. He was the reputed head of the local mob. Ask anyone in the neighborhood about him and most people would look toward heaven and cross themselves. He was a short squat man like Nicky but while Nicky looked like Porky Pig, Carmine had a mean look about him even though he sounded jovial as he greeted Cathy.

"Heh, heh, heh, you kids have a good time," he snickered. Then handing Nicky the car keys he said, "Here take the Caddy but be careful. Don't stain the seats with anything." Then he and Nicky snickered again at their private joke.

Dinner turned out to be an extra large pizza at one of Carmine's joints. Nicky ate eleven out of the twelve slices while Cathy barely ate one. The entire time guys came over and talked with Nicky and teased with off-color remarks. Cathy prayed again this time for strength *not* to throw up. The only part of the evening that was sort of fun was when Nicky took Cathy dancing. He was surprisingly agile and had a good sense of rhythm. Actually he danced well.

Finally the dreaded evening came to an end.

"Thanks a lot Nick," Cathy said at the door. She fished for a compliment. "You really dance pretty well."

"Hey, we gonna kiss at the doorway?" he said already puckering up.

"Uh, No! You know first date and all that. It's not proper. I wouldn't want to give the wrong impression."

"Heh, heh, you don't know what impression I got of you."

"Well thanks again and good night." Before Nicky knew what happened Cathy got in the house and locked the front door behind her. Her father was up watching wrestling.

"There, I hope you're satisfied," she said. "I hope you can get the money and pay him back. I've done my duty." Then she went upstairs.

A few days later when Cathy emerged from the subway station there was Nicky leaning against his car waiting for her. She did her best to ignore him but he physically blocked her path to the bus stop.

"Hey didn't you hear me yelling to you, you want a ride?"

'That's okay, Nicky, really you don't have to go out of your way. The bus is fine."

"Naw, come on. I told your folks I would pick you up. It's OK with them."

"You asked my folks? Why didn't you ask me first?"

"Hey, it don't matter. Let's go to dinner."

"Nicky, thanks but I'm sure my Mom has something already and truthfully I don't feel like pizza tonight."

Nicky was not going to take no for an answer. "I'll take you to this place called Via Veneto. It's got good food. Get in!"

They drove in silence until the restaurant. Cathy deliberately kept the conversation to one-syllable words silently fuming about her parents' agreeing to this.

After dinner instead of going back on the parkway, Nicky headed off to a deserted strip by the shoreline. Cathy, totally unprepared for this, began whispering to herself, *"Please help, please help."*

"I figure we gotta talk about a few things," said Nicky, shifting in his seat trying to get his girth comfortable.

"There's really nothing to talk about Nicky. I've been at work today and I'm a little tired. I'd like to get home. I have a few things to do. We're planning a baby shower for Lu and I need to make some calls, you know, invite people, stuff like that.

"Yeah, heh, heh, it didn't take Jimmy long to knock up Lu. Reggie and Sal are probably banging up a storm too. We gonna have the same luck?"

"I don't think so."

Nicky chuckled to himself and, without warning, reached over and grabbed Cathy by the arm and hoisted himself on top of her.

"Get off, get the heck off me," Cathy pushed with all her might. "Get *off* of me!"

Nicky looked puzzled by her lack of enthusiasm. "What's the matter with ya? You're supposed to like this."

"*Like* this? Says who!"

"Hey, we got this understanding so you better start puttin' out a little. You know you gotta start giving me a little encouragement... a little affection."

"What the hell are you talking about? I don't have to give you anything. One date and dinner doesn't entitle you to any encouragement. Put that thought out of your head. Now take me home or drop me off at a bus stop. I'll get home from there."

"Hey now, wait a minute. I'm a pretty easy goin' guy but I gettin' a little pissed off with your attitude. I'm tryin' to be nice and pleasant and there you are gettin' on your high horse. Come on, baby, don't make me mad. All I want is a little pettin'. I know when to stop." With that he grabbed Cathy under the chin and squeezed her lower jaw so that her mouth was forced open. Then he put his tongue in and with his mouth made loud sucking noises like someone slurping a raw oyster. Cathy was ready to vomit and managed to clamp down on his lips. That made Nicky pull back in surprise and pain.

He squeezed her right breast until she cried out and taking her left hand put it on top of his already hard penis.

"You like to play rough. Geez, you're a regular tiger. Alright!" Nicky was genuinely pleased with Cathy's response.

"Get off of me, asshole. Touch me one more time and I'll kick you right in the balls." Cathy screamed.

Nicky stopped and looked at the near hysterical Cathy. "What the fuck is going on? What are you, some fucking prick tease? You better knock it off cause I'm telling you I'm not going to take this crap from you much longer. Now you start behaving like you're supposed to and start showing me some respect. It better not be like this when we're married, I'll tell you that. I'll beat the shit out of you if you give me trouble like this."

"Married! You expect me to marry *you*! Now who's crazy? I wouldn't marry you for a million bucks."

"Oh yeah, well you'd better talk to your old man about that because arrangements have been made"

"My old man? What's he got to do with this? What arrangements?"

"He owes my father a hell of a lot of dough and my father makes a deal with him. Your old man says is okay for us to get married and my father will *forget* about the money. You didn't know that? Jesus, he said it was okay with you. He said you were kind of keen on the idea."

Cathy was so shocked she couldn't respond. Thousands of thoughts swirled through her mind. *Her father! He sold her!* He had sold her body to pay off his debts to Carmine Torino.

"God, oh God, no!"

"Jesus, I'm sorry it came as a surprise to you. I thought you knew when you went out on Saturday. I thought you wanted it. Well, no matter, a deal is a deal. It's done!"

"I can't marry you, Nicky. I don't care what the deal is. I'm not marrying you!"

"Why the fuck not?"

"Because... because... I'm going to become a nun!"

Nicky Torino's jaw and dick went slack at the same time. "A nun! You're gonna be a fucking nun!"

"You got it wrong Nicky, nuns don't fuck! I think it's time to take me home."

Nicky sat back behind the wheel too shocked to say anything. He smoothed his hair with both hands. *Jesus, a nun! Cathy was going to be a nun!* He almost did it with a nun! He got a hard on with a nun! Quickly, before heaven could react and send down a thunderbolt, he made the Sign of the Cross and started up the car.

On her part, Cathy was stunned also. *Where did that come from?* How could she say that?

A nun! She didn't want to be a nun for God's sake!

They rode home in silence.

"How much does my father owe?" she asked as Nicky pulled up in front of the house.

"I don't know—twelve, maybe thirteen thousand."

Cathy gasped, that much money! How could her father have so much debt? What kind of business deal was it that went wrong? Then suddenly it dawned on her what had happen. She knew how he got into so much trouble. The same problem—again!

Cathy got out of the car and without a word went into the house.

~ * ~

The phone rang at Cathy's desk. She picked it up. It was Lu.

"Cathy, it's me, Lu. Hee-hee-hee-hee!"

Lu started to speak then burst out in hee-hees and ha-has that lasted for three minutes. Cathy already knew what she was going to say.

"Oh God! I've got to stop laughing. My mother heard from Francine Tomasino this morning that you were going to be a nun. Christ, I laughed so hard I think I dilated some this morning. Cathy, 'The Fox' Ferrara, a nun, of what order? Sisters of the Screaming Orgasm? Oh Geez, I'm laughing so hard I gotta pee again. I'll call you back."

Cathy hung up. Work was impossible. She had to talk with someone but whom?

Finally she dialed a number and left a message. A little after three thirty, the return call came.

"Sister Estelle, this is Cathy Ferrara. We met one Saturday at church and I need to talk with you."

Cathy got some answers. Feigning illness she took off work early and found herself in the rectory of the church she attended. She nervously paced the outer office, wondering what she was going to say.

Fr. Dominic invited her into his study.

"Cathy, the housekeeper said this was urgent. What can I do for you?" he asked leaning back into his chair.

"Father, I-I-I'm thinking of joining a convent and I need some advice from you."

Father Dominic sat straight up and for a minute was speechless. "Wow. Uh, Cathy, this is a surprise. You of all people! I mean, uh, well this is quite a surprise."

"You've said that once already, Father. Why does this surprise you?"

"Well, I, uh, I..." he gestured with his hand not knowing how to respond.

"Don't you think I'm capable of becoming a nun? Are you judging me as unfit for some reason?"

"I'm sorry Cathy. I didn't mean it that way. It's just of all you girls, you didn't seem like the type. Pat maybe but not you!'

"What's a nun type like?"

Father Dominic became repentant. "Any type is fine as long as God has chosen you to carry on His work in the world. Heaven knows we need all the help we can get and I'll be happy to assist you in any way. I apologize for my momentary lapse. What order are you thinking of? One of our sisters?"

"You mean the Holy Joes?" That was the nickname for the Sisters of St. Joseph who had taught Cathy and the girls at grade school. "No, Father, I don't think so."

"Well there are lots of orders. You will find one that appeals to you and best suits your particular gifts."

"Order? Oh well, I haven't looked at any specific one at this time." Cathy was trying very hard not to lie in the rectory.

"Well, when you find the right place, I'll be honored to write a pastoral letter of recommendation for you. Just let me know." Standing up, he placed his hand on her forehead and blessed her.

Cathy walked out of the rectory and across to the church. It was already getting dark outside and the church was dim and quiet.

"What did I do?" she asked. "Where am I going to find an order that'll take me? Oh, God, please help again."

Walking out, she passed a book rack that held some Catholic magazines. She picked up one and bingo! She struck gold. In the back were pages of advertisements from various orders.

Little Sisters of the Poor, she read. *No, working with the poor is too depressing. Carmelite Sisters... cloistered order... heck no... they'd never let me out of my room. Sisters of Perpetual Adoration, oh, you gotta pray all day and night. Sisters of Loretto, hmm... motherhouse is in Kentucky... no, Kentucky is too hillbilly. Sisters of Charity, Leavenworth Kansas. There's a prison in Leavenworth! Daughters of Charity... oh the airplane sisters. They wear those big white hats with side wings, God no! I'd look ridiculous in that habit. Go to be something closer.* There was an order of nuns in Hawthorne, New York working with the terminally ill. *Oh crap. I throw up at the sight of blood.*

Then an ad caught her eye. *Korea, Hong Kong, the Philippines, Central and South America... hey that's not a bad deal... become a nun and see the world.* It was a missionary order at Maryknoll, New York. *This is it! I can be a missionary. Heck I took four years of Spanish with honors.* Looking around to see that no one was watching, she tore out the page and left the church.

Her parents were waiting for her when she got in.

"What the hell are you doing?" Joe Ferrara screamed at his daughter. "Since when are you going to be a nun? You never said anything at all. We found out about it from strangers. Carmine Torino called me. You made me look like an ass in front of him!"

"No! You made an ass of yourself long before that. You sold me to Carmine Torino to pay off your *business debts*. You've been gambling again. You owe him twelve or thirteen thousand dollars."

"Joe, how could you? You said it was only five grand. You lied! You lied to me again!" Cathy's mother covered her face with her hands to stifle her cries.

Joe turned on Cathy his face contorted with rage. "You little bitch. You know what they are going to do with me.

They're going to come after me. They're going to give me a kneecap job. I'll never walk again. Is that what you want? You want to see me on crutches?"

"Maybe it'll take you longer to get to your bookie. You were going to sell me like a slave. You were perfectly willing to have me marry Nicky Torino, to live my life in a hell. You know, if I thought for an instant this would make you stop betting on every dog and pony show, I might even have considered it. But you won't stop. You went through the money Nona and Poppa left us. You promised Mom no more that time. You swore you were through. My marrying Nicky wouldn't stop you. You'd just continue. What next? What will you sell next time when you get in debt or should I say whom? Carol is much prettier than I am. She's younger. Boy, I bet you could get twenty-five thousand for her and, why not Mom? She's a good-looking woman. I think if she got dressed up real fancy she could work Times Square, three hundred a night maybe. This is a sickness with you. You need help!"

Cathy was not expecting what happened next. Joe raised his hand and slammed her so hard it sent her falling backwards. "If I get killed, my death is on your hands, *Sister*," he snarled.

Cathy's mother ran to her and helped her to her feet.

"Cathy, he didn't mean it. I swear to God he didn't. He's just scared. We'll work something out. Just please don't leave. I need you here more than God does. Please tell him you'll forgive him. Forgive your Father. We'll sell this house, we'll move to something smaller in another neighborhood. You... you just can't be a nun!

Don't do this, Cathy, to yourself. You know in your heart you don't want to join the convent."

Cathy went to her room. She sat on her bed for a while. She could hear her parents arguing, then she heard the front door slam and the car drive away.

She reached for the phone and dialed a number. "Cele, I need your help."

Five

It was Cele who got Cathy and drove her to the studio apartment Cele was renting in the city. It was Cele who alternately handed Cathy a Kleenex or brandy, whichever she needed. It was Cele who called Cathy's work the next day with an excuse for Cathy's absence. It was Cele who got the girls together the next evening.

"Hi, Cathy," Reggie said as the girls walked in. Pat just hugged her and Lu did too, holding her for a while. "We're here for you. What can we do?"

"Nothing," Cathy replied numbly. "Cele is going to let me stay here for a while but I will need some things from the house. I don't want to go back just yet. I can't!"

"I'll get there tomorrow," said Lu. " Just give me a list and I'll pick it up. Your father won't give me any trouble and your Mom will help me. Cathy, I know it's too soon but what are you going to do?"

"Well, I am going to the convent."

"No, come on, Cathy, you're not going through with this plan. You? A nun!"

"I told Nicky I was going to be a nun. I told that to my parents. Now I have the obligation to make good on my word. If the Maryknoll Sisters or some other order will take me, I'll go. I don't want to be a nun but I've got to stay in a convent at least one year. That'll make it look respectable. Then I'll come out and say it wasn't meant to be. At least I'll give it a try. By that time maybe Nicky and his father will have forgotten everything and maybe my father will have paid off his debt or part of it at least. That's the only thing I can think of doing. That saves face for everyone."

Pat spoke up. "Cat, do you know anything about getting into a convent? You know they are going to ask you all kinds of embarrassing questions. You need letters of recommendation from everyone. They're going to ask you about... you know... if you've ever had *it*. What are you going to say? What if they ask for a doctor's certificate that you're a virgin?"

The girls all jumped on Pat.

"No, that's okay! I can tell them with a straight face that I am. Granted I've done my share of French kissing and maybe a little heavy petting, but that's it."

"Oh come, how about Frankie Bartolucci and let's not forget Dominic Di Lorenzo and that guy in senior year from City College. Are you saying you never went all the way? You told us you did! You even told us how and when!"

"I was bragging. I never did it. I swear!"

Reggie exclaimed, "This is crazy. You're willing to go and be in a convent for a year just so everyone can save face. Lu, you talk to her. Tell her she's nuts."

"No, I don't know. If she doesn't, it'll make everyone look like a chump. If what they say about Carmine Torino is true, you know all those stories, Cathy's got to do this. You think you can last a year? Can we last a year without you?"

"Sure I can do it."

"You know you're going to miss out on a lot. My baby by that time, then there's Pat's wedding and Cele's business. Are you sure?" Reggie asked hoping she could change Cathy's mind.

"Yeah, I'll be fine and when I get out, we'll all be together. *La Sorellanza,* the Sisterhood. Now tell me something happy. What about your wedding Pat?"

Pat smiled only to happy to tell of the plans she and Ricky had made.

"We're not going to have a big wedding. I mean after Lu's and Reggie's shindigs who can compete? I don't want my Mother to go through all that expense. Ricky agrees with me. But we are going to Italy for three weeks for a honeymoon," she announced joyfully.

This announcement brought groans from the girls.

"Lucky you!"

"I only got to Bermuda."

"Oh, Italy!"

"I only have one favor to ask of you guys. If I get in somewhere, will you come up with me? Will you be there?" Cathy pleaded.

"We swear!" all the girls responded in unison. It was time for another group hug.

~ * ~

Several months went by and in late summer of 1961, Cathy was accepted to the novitiate at the Maryknoll Convent. The girls all got into Lu's car for the trip up. They laughed and sang and joked all the way trying to keep Cathy's spirits up and their own. Cathy chain-smoked until the front gate. They drove up to the entrance. Cathy looked at the convent building and her courage began to give out.

"Who's got something to drink? I need a drink."

Lu reached under the seat and pulled out a slim silver flask and gave it to Cathy who guzzled down half of it. Then each girl took a swig.

"OK, this is it. I can do this for one year." Cathy wiped the sweat off her brow. "Oh shit, I smell like a brewery. Who's got perfume or cologne?"

Instantly a few vials were produced and Cathy opened her mouth and poured in some *White Shoulders* cologne which Reggie had offered. She rinsed her mouth then spit it out on the lawn.

"What are you doing?"

"Hey, it worked for Scarlet O'Hara and it'll work for me."

Each girl in turn hugged her and whispered words of encouragement. Cele was the last. Both had grown quite close over the past months.

"Bye, Celes-TINA. I love you. Thanks for everything. I owe you big time. Lu, kiss the baby and your folks and guys get laid tonight for me. OK? See you next year. *La Sorellanza.* The Sisterhood. *Sempre come sorelle.*"

With that she picked up her bag and went up the stairs.

The girls stood quietly and nobody said a word. Finally Pat spoke.

"You know she'll be out of there. They are going to take one whiff of her and throw her out. She'll be out tomorrow or no later than the end of the week. We won't have to wait a year."

"Well, if she is, she'll have to take the train back because I'll be busy. I can't pick her up." Lu said crying in spite of her tough sounding words. "You've been a good friend to her Cele, the best."

"You have, too. You and your father especially. Does she know... I mean... what your father did?"

"No, my father forbad me to say anything. He just paid off Joe Ferrara's debt to Carmine Torino and I guess Joe left town. My father was so angry when he found out. It's a wonder Joe is still alive, the bastard. Their house is up for sale. I saw the sign. My mother went over to talk with Sylvia a lot of times. So did your mothers. I don't know where she and Carol will be moving. She didn't say. I don't know if Cathy even went to say goodbye to her mother. Did she ever go that you know of, Cele?"

"No, not that I know of. She kind of really changed these last few months. You all saw it. Maybe she was just gearing up for nunhood, you know, kind of getting in the mood. I know she cried a lot, not in front of me, but there were always wads of Kleenex on the floor by the couch where she slept. She was going through a hell of her own."

They turned and took a last look at the convent door and left.

~ * ~

Pat and Ricky's wedding was a small affair, certainly not the cast of hundreds that were present at Lu and Reggie's weddings. Lu was Pat's only attendant and the bride, like all brides, looked radiant. Shortly after Ricky and Pat took off for a honeymoon in Italy. Rome in all its glory was their first stop. Ricky rented a small Vespa and they toured the sites from the back of a motor scooter. Sightseeing by day, passionate sex by night... the perfect honeymoon. One morning Pat awoke to some sweet nuzzling.

"Hey, doll face, how are you this morning?"

"Delicious, how about you?"

"Great except I had this dream last night. I dreamt that you started kissing me from the top down, working your way down my neck, shoulders, arms, back, chest, stomach, right thigh, knee, all the way down to my right toes. Then up the left side, then you stopped in the middle and I got a blowjob that practically curled my toes. Was that a dream or did that really happen?"

"Well, if you can't remember, I'll keep you guessing? Did she or didn't she?"

"Would you like to refresh my memory? Come here."

Pat snuggled in the crook of Ricky's arm and with her finger drew pictures on his chest.

"Hmm, what's that? It feels like our initials in a heart."

"Nope it's a map of Italy and I'm tracing the route to our next stop. Assisi tonight then Florence tomorrow."

"'Fraid not darling. We're going the opposite way to Naples."

"Naples!" Pat sat upright in bed. "I thought we were going north."

"Oh, there's nothing wrong with Naples. It's beautiful, right on the bay, close to Sorrento, Capri, all sorts of terrific places like Pompeii."

"I'm sure of that but why the change of plans on such short notice?"

"Business, darling!"

"Business! On our honeymoon!" Pat said in disbelief.

"Yeah. I have to renew my contacts in Naples. I've been gone almost a year and I need to reestablish them for my job back home."

"I don't see the connection between procurement in Naples and working for the supply company."

"Pat, it's like this. I work for Abbodanza Supplies but the business has to establish contacts here in case we have to import some things. I know people here from my work with the Navy and it'll simplify the process if and when we have to bring in imports"

"Ricky! Abbodanza Supplies deal with plumbing, pipes, stuff like that. What could you possibly need from Naples in the plumbing department?"

"Marble bath fixtures for one, pottery artifacts for decoration—that kind."

"And for this we have to change our honeymoon plans?"

"Yeah, Pat, we do. Listen they hired me at the company. They were very impressed with some of my ideas for expanding, very impressed that I knew some people here. Abbodanza Supplies is going to be big, really big! We're going beyond pipes and plumbing."

"This is really important to you!"

"To us, Pat, this is really important to us! I want to grow with the company. I want to hit it big for us. Listen Pat, I talked to your mother before you and I got married. She told me how it was for you and for her after your father died. Oh yeah, she said you always got stuff, the right school but she also said that while Reno Roccollo and his friends were generous with her and you, it was always like an afterthought. 'Lu got a bike, we got to get Pat one. The girls go to camp well we have to make sure Pat goes too.' She said you never got anything first. Well that's going to change, Babe. You're going to get everything first from now on and I'm going to work my tail off to see that you do."

Pat leaned over and kissed Ricky. "I have everything I want already. I have you."

"Yeah, well, there's going to be more. Lots more," he replied kissing her back.

They left for Naples that day and the next day Ricky spent the entire day with Pat giving her a quick cook's tour of his old haunts. The following day he left to renew his old connections and the next day also. By the third day Pat complained bitterly so Ricky arranged for a guide to accompany Pat to the local sites

"She's a good kid trying to improve her English. She has a car and she knows all the ins and outs. Give her a try."

So Pat did but finally by the fourth day she was thoroughly unhappy with the situation.

"Tomorrow we're supposed to see Capri. I'm not going to see it without you. Either you come or I'll find my way back to Rome and I go see Florence and Venice by myself. When you're finished with your business then I'll meet you in Rome for the return trip from our 'honeymoon'."

Ricky relented and took Pat for a romantic trip to Capri but upon returning to their hotel he got a message saying he needed to go on to Sicily for one day alone. Pat was furious.

"Why can't I go with you? What is all this urgency about? Don't tell me this is business. I want to know what kind. I have that right."

"Pat," Ricky answered her sternly, "this is business and I'm not about to discuss it. I am meeting with someone who is interested in establishing some contacts in the

States. I'll be gone overnight, then I promise I'll be as attentive a husband as there ever was. We'll go to Abruzzi where my grandfather came from and do the whole bit but I have to go. Now you can either sulk or accept the fact that there are some things I have to take care of. Your choice but it would be a shame to sit in your hotel room and not take advantage of this wonderful place. I'll be back, I promise."

He left and true to his word when Ricky came back he was doubly attentive as he showed her around his grandfather's childhood village. The villagers turned out in droves to fete the newlyweds and to celebrate the return of a grandson of a former resident who made good in America. The last night in Naples Ricky and Pat were invited to dinner by Signor Mosconi. He was the new foreign associate of Abbodanza Supply Company. Signor Mosconi did not speak English so Ricky acted as interpreter.

"Signora Campione, I regret having had to take your husband away from you especially at this time but this was very important for my company and his to establish our contacts. You were very patient with us much more so, I might add, than most wives. As a thank you, I should like to present you with a small token with the sincere hope that you will return here often and perhaps next time bring a baby."

He handed Pat an oblong box. She opened the box and her eyes widened with surprise. Inside was a heavy gold chain necklace.

"Uh, Signor Mosconi, this is too much. This is beautiful."

"Not nearly as beautiful as you. I'm glad it pleases you."

"Oh it does, believe me. Had I known this, you could have had Ricky the entire time."

Signor Mosconi, as well as Ricky, was pleased with her response.

"First class all the way." Ricky winked at her.

~ * ~

It was Easter Sunday, 1962. Cathy was in the convent's kitchen cleaning up after the noon meal. There was excitement in the air not only because of the joyous feast that was celebrated but also because families were permitted to visit. Cathy volunteered to remain in the kitchen to finish cleaning up, thus allowing other novices extra time to spend with their families. No one was coming to see her so it was a surprise when the Sister, who was in charge of opening the door for visitors, hurried in to tell Cathy to come to the reception area. There was Celestina waiting for her.

"Oh my God, Cele!" squealed Cathy. "I can't believe it. You're here! Oh jeez, you're better than a chocolate egg."

"Less fattening too. Of course, you don't look like you need to worry. God, don't they feed you guys?"

"It was Lent remember, except here they take it a little more seriously."

"Remember the year in high school we gave up sex for Lent, like we had any."

"Come on, let's go outside and tell me everything. I got only an hour so you'll have to talk fast."

"OK, news of the sisterhood. Reggie sends her love and is sorry she couldn't drive up with me because she's ready to drop any second now. *And* she said if it's a girl her name will be Anna after Sal's great grandmother and Mr. R's grandmother and Catherine after you!"

"Oh, God! How fabulous! What's next?"

"Pat has finished puking her guts out just in time to go back for another trip to Italy. Can you believe it? I think this is going to be a semi-annual thing with them. Lu sends kisses as do the Roccollos. I saw them in church today on my annual visit. Lu's baby is darling but he started to fuss so Lu spent most of Mass walking back and forth in the rear of the church. I offered to relieve her but the kid doesn't like me and howled some more. Get ready for this. After church Mrs. Tomasino comes up and says to Lu, 'You got your hands full. How are you going to manage with two?' You should have seen Lu's eyes. They bulged out to here. She says, 'How in hell does she know? I haven't even told my parents.' Just as I told you. Mrs. Tomasino has bugged the entire neighborhood."

"Oh, what great news! Lu and Pat and Reggie! Would you believe it, another generation of the sisterhood! And what about you, CelesTINA?"

"My business is going. Would you believe it? I rented this hole in the wall in lower Manhattan. Actually it's a garage complete with rats and I have three Puerto Rican women on my payroll and I have a couple of contracts, they're small but it's a start and I have a new business name. I am now Tina Benedict!"

"Tina! Tina Benedict! It's nice, really it is. Kind of classy. Definitely high fashion. I approve. So you got your loan. Remember how you worried about it?"

"Well I did get one but not from a bank. Reno, uh, Mr. R invested some money. He's kind of mentoring me. I'm going to make good. I have too, not only for myself but I have to pay back his loan."

"That's great. Anything else?"

"Let's see, the girls, my business—oh yeah, get ready for this. Word has it, uh, Mrs. Tomasino, that Carmine Torino is sending Nicky to Italy to find a wife. Nobody in the neighborhood would give him a tumble so he's got to import one from the old country. Can you believe that?"

"I feel kind of sorry for him and for whomever he brings back. Imagine being new to the country and being married to him. Poor girl! I'll say a prayer for her."

"Well, that means you can come out now even sooner than you expected. Your year will be up and you can get out. You know what I am going to do. I'm going to design five exact blouses for each of us and on the day you get out, we'll all drive up wearing our blouses and you can change into yours. The sisterhood will be together again."

"Sounds nice."

"What's the matter Cathy? You don't seem excited. Remember you said one year. Don't tell me you are changing your mind?"

"No, I haven't made up my mind when exactly."

"Oh good, for a split second you had me worried. I thought you looked like you were going to tell me you like it here. Don't do it Cathy, you've got too much life, too much spirit to waste it here in a convent. You could come and be my administrative assistant. What a team!"

Cathy smiled. "CelesTINA, how are you doing otherwise? Menwise, that is."

"Well I'm busy. I work during the day, design by night, take business classes on the weekends. Reno warns me that I'll burn out at this pace but I thrive on it. Hey! You want to smoke?" Without waiting for a reply Cele pulled out a cigarette, lit it, and gave it to Cathy who took one big drag and began choking.

"Jeez, what are you smoking?"

"Camels."

"These taste like camel dung!"

"Well you used to smoke them. I got two more things." Slipping her hand into her purse she pulled out a slim flask and handed it to Cathy. "Take a sip, it's *limoncello*. Reno, uh, Mr. R made a batch and he gave me some to celebrate my opening. *La Sorellanza*."

"*La Sorellanza, Sempre come sorelle*." Cathy took a small sip and handed it back to Cele. *The sisterhood. Always like sisters.*

"That's it? You drained the flask last year. Do you need my perfume again?"

Cathy laughed, "No, not right now but keep it handy. What's the other thing you had for me?"

"I have a letter from your Mom for you. She came by the house a little while ago. My mother gave her my phone number and she called. She's doing well. She has an apartment in Washington Heights. She got a job as a school secretary. Your sister is doing well. Your Mom sent me this letter last week, which is why I came up. She was afraid you wouldn't want to see her or speak to her. I think your father is in Florida somewhere at least that's what Reno said one time. Here it is."

Cathy took the letter and put it in her pocket. "I've been praying for this all year."

"Do you hate them?"

"*No*! My poor mother was as much a victim of his gambling as I was. I don't hate him. I don't care for him much. I still feel betrayed but hate? No!"

The convent bell began to ring.

"I have to go back. This was such a short visit. You are a gift to me Cele. I don't know how to thank you except by praying for you."

"Yeah, well pray that I make a go of it. Bye Cathy. I'll see you in what... another two months? Hey, do you need my perfume? I wear 'Joy' now."

"Wow! Classy dame Tina Benedict! I really have to go. Take care of yourself, please. You are so dear!"

"Remember two months!"

Cathy went back in to the convent and walked straight into the reception room, which looked on to the parking lot. She watched out the window as Cele got into her car.

"I don't think so, CelesTINA," she whispered, "I don't think I'll be coming out but be careful, my friend. You are playing with fire. Don't get hurt and don't hurt others."

Six

New York City, 1963

Cele heard the doorbell ringing. Smiling, she tied her bathrobe belt and went to press the buzzer to let him in. He knocked on the door and she opened it.

"Hi," she said in her best *come hither* voice.

"Hi, yourself doll face, but what's with the flannel bathrobe. Jesus, if I wanted the flannel robe I would have stayed at home."

She laughed as she gave him a long loving kiss. "Come on in. Sit down, make yourself at home. I have a surprise for you."

He walked over and took off his coat and laid it on the back of a chair. Loosening his necktie, he first took off his jacket, then his tie and threw them on the chair. She disappeared into the little kitchenette and returned a few minutes later holding a wine bottle and two glasses. The flannel bathrobe had been discarded and she was wearing a peek-a-boo Frederick's of Hollywood outfit in red with black lace trim. Her bikini panties had a split crotch for easy access.

"Is this better?" she asked teasingly.

"It's better all the time. Come here, Babe."

"Try this first," she said pouring the dark purple wine into a glass. As she poured the heavy fragrance of wine permeated the air.

He sniffed approvingly. "Hmm, it smells of oranges, maybe almonds." Taking a sip he rolled the liquid around in his mouth. "Where's this from?"

"Sicily. I looked around for a long time until I found this. You told me about Sicilian wine." She poured herself some and sipped it. At the couch, she sat down, straddling him. "It's powerful, seductive, full-bodied," and leaning over him, she coupled his face between her hands and kissed him on the mouth. Small nibbles on the lips, then with her tongue probing his mouth, going in deeper, their tongues dancing a ballet, pirouetting and leaping. He crushed her close to him with one arm, the other reaching under her flimsy top searching for her breasts. He began fingering her already hard nipples, kneading them so that she moaned both with pleasure and pain.

"Take this damn thing off. It's served its purpose. Now it's in the way."

She leaned back and took off the top, never taking her eyes from him. Her breasts were generous, firm, dark-nippled and the sight of them inflamed him. He crushed her to his chest kissing her mouth, chin, neck, shoulders, until he came to her breasts. He put his mouth on one and began sucking vigorously like a starving baby. She kissed the top of his head and pressed it tighter to her chest as if fearing he might leave. They stopped a while to catch their breath and leaning back she took a sip of the wine...

a big sip this time. Quickly she undid his belt and unzipped his fly. His penis was hard and ready for what came next. Slipping to her knees she put her mouth over the end and drew it further in her mouth. Some of the wine dribbled out and ran down. With an undulating motion, she used her tongue, tantalizing him sometimes gently and sometimes vigorously. He leaned back completely under her spell. His breaths came in gasps punctuated by an occasional moan of pleasure. His hips began to move in rhythm with her mouth. Faster and faster.

"Baby," he gasped. "Baby, I can't stop. Oh my God! Baby, Baby." He arched his back pulling away from her. A jet of milky white semen spurted from his throbbing member and onto to her chest and stomach. He groaned as he lay back, spent, his breath coming out in whooshes.

"Oh, Baby, I couldn't wait. I couldn't hold it in. God, what you do to me. I can't last more than two seconds with you."

She kissed his penis again licking both wine and semen from it. "Hmm, tasty." She smiled up at him, "but it's my turn now."

"You bet, I think it's this wine. It's like Sicily, strong, intoxicating me."

"Really? Prove it."

He didn't have to be asked twice. He pulled her up on the couch and tore off the split crotch panties. He draped one of her legs over the back of the couch and the other she rested on his shoulder. Two accent pillows were propped under her hips. Then he began to kiss her, starting by her ankle, then up her calf, to her knee, to the outer thigh. By the time he reached her inner thigh, she was moaning with pleasure. Then he parted her pubic hair and exposed her most private parts.

He kissed her again and again until she felt she would burst into flames. Damn him! He knew just what to do. He wouldn't stop until he knew he had possessed her. She covered her mouth to stifle the scream that was coming from the very core of her being. It came anyway. She cried out and held on tightly as if to drain the last ounce of him into her. They finally collapsed, not saying a word. Gradually a sweet relaxation overtook them, as they lay entwined.

"I don't have to ask how it was for you. I can see for myself. You love it as much as I do. That's what makes it so wonderful."

"Uh, hmm," she agreed softly, " it's great and so are you and it happens to both of us every time."

"I think about that. What am I going to do when I can't have you anymore? You know I never thought I would feel like this. Like a school kid with his first romance. I think of you during the day and boom, I get a hard on. I have wet dreams at night."

"I hope you wear PJ's. Up, I've got to get up and take care of myself now. I'll be back in a minute. Don't leave! I may want a second helping."

"Twenty years ago no problem. Now—it may take me a while. Go on. Do what you have to. Maybe if I rest?" He laughed.

He watched her as she left. He was getting in deeper than he had expected. It started two years ago when he ran into her in Las Vegas. She was there selling her line at a couple of off the strip hotels. He was there with some friends for a guys' weekend out.

They were in one of the hotels on the Strip when Louie Di Fonzo nudged Reno.

"Hey, doesn't that look like the Di Benedetti girl, you know Lu's friend?"

Reno looked up and caught sight of Celestina ambling along casually scanning the gambling tables.

"Cele, over here, Cele! Come here!"

Cele did a double take then broke out in a big smile and came over to the three men.

"Don't tell me my father sent the three of you to check up on me?" she said with a laugh.

"Yeah, as matter of fact he did, and he wants to know that you're in bed at a decent time. It's past your bedtime," Reno stated.

Cele greeted each of the men, then turned her attention to Reno.

"I'm here peddling my wares. Actually I did okay, you'd be proud of me. One small hotel said they would like to order a bunch of shirts with cards and dice all over them for their cocktail waitresses. I'm really psyched by that."

"Hey, Cele," said Mickey, "why is it a nice girl like you is here instead of being at home with your old man and a bunch of bambinos? Huh?"

"Because this nice girl has a whole bunch of girlfriends who are at home with their old men and their babies so that leaves me free."

"Modern women! Who can understand them?" said Mickey shaking his head.

Reno invited Cele over to a roulette table. "Pick a number, any number red or black. See if you are lucky."

"Okay, nineteen black."

Reno plunked down a ten-dollar chip. The wheel spun... nine red turned up.

There was a groan.

"I just lost ten bucks." Reno said. "You didn't bring me any luck."

"Well, what can I say? Maybe I'm lucky in love and not at roulette," Cele responded, looking Reno straight in the eye. "I better get back to my hotel before I lose all your money for you and you'll add it to my account."

Reno frowned. He didn't look pleased at that comment although Cele had said it in jest.

"Please go back and tell my father I'm being good and I'm getting to bed at a reasonable hour Las Vegas style. I have to make some more calls tomorrow and I'll be home on Sunday."

"Don't forget church on Sunday," said Mickey with a laugh.

"Sure thing Mr. Mickey. Save me a seat next to you. Good night everybody."

Cele turned to walk away and had gotten a few feet before she heard Reno call to her.

"Hey, little girl, is this your hotel?"

"No, I'm staying at an El Cheapo, a few blocks from here. It's not a bad walk and with so many people still out it's safe."

"No, wait up. Hey you guys, I'm going to see Cele home or at least get her a cab. No friend of my daughter's should be walking around at one in the morning. I don't care how modern a woman she is. I'll see you guys later."

"You know that's not necessary Reno. I can manage. Stay with your friends."

Reno just shook his head, took Cele by the arm and headed for the exit.

"Did I say something in there that upset you? I saw you clench your jaw after I made the comment of putting the ten bucks on my account."

"You noticed, huh?"

"I notice a lot about you."

"Really! Well, yeah! I know the guys thought it was funny and probably didn't think anything about it but no more comments like, uh, just in case someone should put two and two together. My loan is my business, our business and no one else's."

"Agreed!"

They slowly walked back to Cele's hotel. Reno very protectively walked Cele up to her room. "You're safe now," he said.

Without warning, Cele leaned against him and gave him a kiss, not like the father of a friend kiss, but one on the lips that promised more if he was interested.

"What are you doing, little girl?" Reno asked tenderly.

"That kiss was an invitation, an invitation to come in," Cele whispered in his ear.

"What are you asking?" Reno looked shocked at the implication.

"I'm asking you to come in. I'm asking you to make love to me like you want to, and like I want you to."

"You're playing with fire, Cele."

"Yes, I am."

She was honest with him, not coy, but direct. He was what she had wanted. She understood the rules and he would have to understand her rules also. He was reluctant; she was persistent. They became lovers that weekend. He tried to end it when he returned home but couldn't. Come hell or high water he had to have her as much as she wanted him.

Cele came out of the bathroom and stood looking at him quietly.

"You look so serious. For a guy who just got laid and laid well, you should be relaxing with your tongue hanging out. Instead you're sitting there frowning."

He paused for a minute trying to find the right way to say it.

"You know Cele, I keep thinking this isn't right for you. Jesus, you're young. You should have all the things a young woman should have. A husband, kids, the whole works."

"I know what I want, Reno. Yeah I'd like to have a kid but only if it were yours growing in my belly. That will never happen. I know that and so do you. I have what I want right now and that's you and I'm satisfied. If ever the time comes for either of us, we both know the rules. It's good-bye and no questions asked. Until then... *te voglio.*" *I love you.*

"And I also." He kissed her again tenderly pulling her down next to him on the couch. "What are you going to do tonight?" He snuggled to her neck.

"Books—try some new designs, take a hot bath, go to bed, maybe suck my thumb."

"You know I gotta get going now. I'll call you maybe tonight. If I whisper a few things into your ear, you won't need to suck your thumb."

They walked arm in arm to the door and lingered over another last embrace.

"Bye, Cele. I'll call you."

"*Ciao*, Reno." She playfully nibbled his ear and neck.

She closed the door after him. Yes, this was what she wanted. She was content.

Seven

June, 1968

There was a knock on the door. "Enter."

"Praise be Jesus Christ."

"Now and forever Amen," came the reply. "Come in, Sister Catherine. Please sit down."

"Is it time for another heart-to-heart, Mother?"

"Does that bother you?"

"No, actually I have found them to be rather insightful. I always come away with plenty of food for thought."

"Good, I'm glad to hear that. Well, are you pleased with your assignment?"

"Oh, yes! I'm delighted. I've been keeping my fingers and toes crossed hoping to get this spot. I enjoyed my time there before so it'll be like going home."

Mother Superior laughed. "You know Sister Catherine, you still amuse me after all these years. Every other sister who got her assignment said that she had been praying for it for a long time. You kept your fingers and toes crossed. I hope you can uncross them now because you'll need them in Patzcuaro at the mission."

"Glad to have amused you, Mother."

"Oh you have Cathy, believe me you have. I still remember the day you came. We sisters did not have much hope for you and, while betting of course is frowned upon, we did bet you wouldn't last a week, then a month, then a year. It shows how wrong we were or how much God wanted you."

"Well, I have to admit it did take me a while to settle in."

"Do you know you hold the record for the most times Grand Silence was broken by a postulant?"

Sister Catherine squirmed in her seat. "Uh, my mouth always did give me a lot of trouble. It still does but I am getting better."

The older nun went on with her reminiscences. "I remember Sister Marcella, God rest her soul, who was the wardrobe mistress when you entered. She claimed she had to air out your clothes for three days before she could put them away. They smelled like a saloon. And the gum chewing, where ever did you get it?"

"I saved it for as long as I could. I think I chewed each piece I had left about a hundred times. You'll be pleased to know I haven't chewed for a long time. May I ask you something? Why didn't I get thrown out?"

"Oh, my dear, we were ready many times but you had a very strong ally. Sister Joan! Whenever we decided to say *enough*, she always managed to convince us otherwise. One time I remember her saying that she had prayed about you for a long time. She too, had just about decided that perhaps the convent was not the best place. One night after she prayed at her hour in the chapel, she said she heard a voice. We kidded her about anyone named Joan who hears voices, you know like Joan of Arc. She claims the voice said, 'Foxy Ferrara, I like her.' Since there was no one else in the chapel she assumed it was a heavenly message. I'm glad we kept you, Cathy. You have spirit, spunk whatever you want to call it. You will be a wonderful nun."

"How did you know my nickname was 'Foxy'? Only my friends knew that."

"We have ways. Cathy, I do want to talk with you about what I believe is still a troubling matter. I have seen you struggle with this for a long time and now that you are going to be taking your final vows, shouldn't you resolve this issue?"

"I assume you are referring to my family situation."

"Yes, this business of your father. It's been a long time to hold onto a grudge. Shouldn't you forgive him? Put this behind you Cathy."

"Mother, I have prayed so often about this that I have water on the knees. I just can't get past my feelings of betrayal. I still ask myself the same question. How could he have used me that way? How could you sell off your child to pay a gambling debt? I don't hate him, really. I don't but I just can't say those words, 'I forgive you'. I know it's wrong. I've tried but the words stick in my throat like a fishbone."

"Imitate the way of Our Lord. He forgave."

"Yes, Mother, but with all due respect he wasn't betrayed by his father."

"No, but by a friend."

La Sorellanza (The Sisterhood)   Barbara Wilson Wright

"My friends have stuck by me. We call ourselves the Sisterhood, *la Sorellanza* in Italian. They are very special to me."

"I'm sure they are. I would ask that this become a special spiritual task for you. Pray that you be given the grace to forgive. If you pray for this often, it will be granted. No prayer goes unanswered you know that. Sometime before you die you should say that you forgive your father for his error in judgment."

"I will make that my special prayer, Mother."

~ * ~

"Okay, girls, line up for a group picture. Cathy, you get in the middle and we'll gather around for a group hug."

It was party time at Lu's house. She and her parents hosted a party for Sister Mary Catherine on the occasion of her taking her final vows as a nun. Cathy was leaving for Mexico as a missionary.

"So what exactly will you be doing at the mission/" asked Reggie.

"Teaching kids, training catechism teachers since we can't be everywhere, working at the clinic with the sick."

"*You* are going to work at a clinic, you who threw up on the basketball court when Bunny Lesinski got beamed on the head and was bleeding. I don't believe it."

"Hey I've gotten better. I still get queasy but I'm able to control it. I pray I won't throw up in front of everyone. It works."

"You know Cathy, you're beginning to sound like a nun," said Celestina.

"Hey, if it talks like a nun and dresses like a nun, it probably is a nun!"

"Well, can nuns hear gossip?" Lu asked, " Let me tell you about your old flame Nicky Torino. You know he married a girl from Italy. You should see him now. He's got three no-neck kids like himself and he is completely henpecked. He has to ask his wife for permission to fart. Oops, sorry. She wears the pants in that family. Reggie and I saw them at the Mt. Carmel bazaar last year. He was towing around the kids and everything else and she was barking orders. Reggie and I screamed with laughter and we said Cathy has to know about this. Can you believe it?"

"Where was I?" asked Pat.

"I think that was when you were in Italy just before Christmas. Speaking of which, when are you leaving again?"

"Too damn soon," Pat answered disgustedly. "I'm sick of going there."

"Pat how could you be sick of Italy? To go there is a dream of mine."

"Cathy, just for you, I'll tell Ricky you're going in my place with my blessing."

She walked out of the room.

"Jesus," Cele said, " she really doesn't want to go. Why in hell doesn't she say something? Hand me those glasses, Cathy, and I'll finish washing them."

"Well, CelesTINA, aren't you going to tell us any news. You're the only one I haven't heard any gossip about."

"Clean living doesn't breed gossip!"

"Ha!" Lu and Reggie laughed. "What about you and that slick looking designer Cameron Barlett? He designs all kinds of neat things out of leather, country type stuff. Their picture was in Harper's Bazaar magazine looking very cozy with glasses of champagne in their hands. Tell me, us, all about him."

"Is he the one who gave you that gorgeous bracelet Cele?" said Cathy examining the heavy gold chain around Cele's wrist. "Look, it even has a gold disk hanging from it with an inscription" Then she began to sing out, "You are my sunshine."

"No!" Cele stated emphatically. "It's not from him. We are strictly business."

"Oh come on Cele, that photo didn't look like business. You can tell us."

"It is strictly business. It's an arrangement we have. If ever there is an occasion that requires him to be someplace, he asks me to go along. That's it! Business!"

"If it's just business, why don't we see pictures of him with other girls."

"Yeah, why just you?" chimed in Reggie.

"Alright you want gossip, try this. He is a flaming fag—he's very homosexual. He doesn't do women. We are seen together. Both of us know it is strictly business. Besides he's involved with a dancer from one of the Broadway shows and he's trying to keep it quiet. So there!"

"You've got to be kidding! That hunk is—I mean... he's so damn good looking. He designs such neat clothes. I bought Sal a leather jacket last Christmas designed by him. Are you sure?" Reggie asked Cele not quite believing her.

"Trust me. In the fashion business, most of the guys are homos. Why do you think they know women's clothes? They know what women want. They have a fabulous sense of style. You think some ordinary Joe knows about fabric and line? Get real!"

"Oh God, what am I going to tell Sal? His favorite leather jacket was designed by one of *those*. God, he'll burn it."

Cele shot Reggie a look of complete disgust.

"Sunshine, if that bracelet isn't from him, then who?" Cathy asked smiling.

"Just a friend" Cele spoke quietly. "I'm going to see if there are any more glasses or plates in the other room."

The trio in the kitchen began to sing, "You are my Sunshine, my only Sunshine."

Cele walked out of the kitchen so fast that she crashed into Reno Roccollo who was coming in. She stepped on his foot.

"Sweet Jesus, woman, those high heels are lethal. I'm crippled for life."

"Sorry Mr. R. These are my Valentinos, a hundred fifty bucks at Saks." She made a face at Lu.

Reno lifted up his pant leg and showed off his shoe. "These are Sears, twenty nine-ninety five."

"Fashion disaster!" muttered Cele and left the room.

The girls laughed but it was Cathy who noticed a split second tender glance between Cele and Reno.

~ * ~

It was time to say good-bye. The celebration was over and the girls gathered together for tearful farewells.

"It's almost like the Sisterhood is breaking up with your going," Pat wailed. "It's like we'll never be together like we were."

"In our hearts we'll be together, Pat. Geography can't separate us. It may be a while before I can do it with you but you guys have to promise me to do our cheer when the four of you get together. Just pretend I am with you. Here we go."

The girls gathered round and began the cheer they had chanted since junior high school.

"Holy Smokey, Crimin Crokey,
Watch out world while we do the Hokey.
Shake those boobs, shake those booties,
In all the world no sweeter cuties."

Cathy began to shake her boobs and booties with gusto while the girls clapped and cheered. Jimmy jumped in and began dancing a mean Twist and Cathy joined in very enthusiastically.

"Way to go Cathy, you are one hot nun!" laughed Jimmy. "The swinging Sister Foxy Ferrara! You do that in church and the collection will go way up!"

Cathy put up her hands and signaled for a stop. "Guys, this display will cost me a couple of rosaries tonight but it was worth it. *La Sorellanza, Sempre come sorelle.* I love you all."

~ * ~

Cele drove Cathy back to the city. She was going to spend her last day with Cele.

"That was a great party. I loved being with everyone and seeing half the old neighborhood."

"They all came because they still don't believe you are a nun. They had to see for themselves."

"Oh cut it out, it's been seven years since I went in. They should have gotten used to the idea by this time."

Then Cathy turned serious. "Speaking of seven years Cele, there was no mistaking the look which passed between you and Mr. R. Cele, what are you doing? If I saw it today someone else will in the future. Think of what you are doing!"

"I am thinking of it Cathy, but I can't help it. I love him! Can you understand what it's like to love someone so completely, so much that you don't think of anything else but him?"

"Yes, as matter of fact I do!"

'I'm not talking about loving God, I'm talking about loving a man."

"It's the same thing. I love God as much and as passionately as you love Mr. R. Love is love, Cele. The only thing is... my loving God doesn't hurt anyone."

"Oh come on Cathy, enough of the nun talk. How can you equate the two kinds of love? I love Reno. I want to be with him. I want to make love to him and have him screw my brains out in return. That's not exactly the same thing!"

"It is! I love God with my whole being. Just because I can't act on that love physically doesn't detract from it."

"What do you do—you know—like when you get the hots?"

"Are you asking me about my love life? It's okay! I'm a human being in spite of the fact that I dress in black and white. I'm not a penguin."

"Hey, remind me to tell you about the dwarf and nun joke. Alright, what do you do?"

"Well," Cathy took a deep breath, "When I get feelings, I pray, long and hard. If that doesn't do it, then I grab my sneakers and go for a very long hard run or play basketball, then a very long, cold shower. By that time I'm so pooped I don't even have the energy to entertain an impure thought as we used to say. There are times I must admit when I cry. It hurts. Don't you cry over this? What do you think is going to happen between you and Mr. R? What if Rosa finds out or Lu? Think of the hurt that will cause. Is it worth it?"

"Yes, I cry when we can't be together but I can't help myself. We are very careful. We are very private with this. We have some strict rules we stick to. I can't give him up Cathy and he can't stop himself either. We love each other that much!"

"Cele," Cathy whispered. "Be careful CelesTINA. Don't get hurt."

"I know what I'm doing."

Eight

The telephone rang and, wiping her hands, Lu answered it.

"Mr. Thianci, please," a child-like voice lisped.

"He's not here at the moment. Who's calling?"

"Uh, could you give him a message that he has an appointment at three-thirty this afternoon. Uh, thank you."

"Wait a minute, a three-thirty appointment? Today? Where are you calling from?"

There was no response. Lu only heard the dial tone. Jimmy has an appointment today, three-thirty this afternoon. It was Saturday. His business was closed for the weekend.

She walked out the sliding back door to the yard and saw Jimmy deeply involved in a conversation with the next-door neighbor.

"Jimmy!" She yelled a bit louder than usual. Jimmy looked in her direction and without acknowledging her continued to talk. Eventually he came in.

"What was that all about?"

"You had a phone call. Some Lolita type called for a 'Mr. THIanci'." Lu continued to imitate the voice. "You have an appointment at three-thirty today. This is Saturday for God's sakes. Since when do you have *appointments* on Saturday?"

Jimmy was silent for a second. "I made one for today. Do you mind?"

"Yeah, what kind and where? Who's it with?"

"Jesus, is this twenty questions or something? Do I have to tell you everything?"

"Yeah, you do as matter of fact. I'm your wife in case you have forgotten. I have a right to know especially since Miss Baby Doll called?"

"What in hell do you think I'm doing? I made an appointment to look at a new car. I want to check out a sports car."

"A new car? We've got two perfectly good ones. Isn't that enough?"

"Just want to see a sports car, just check it out, something fun to drive. Is that a crime?"

"And Miss Teeny Bopper is going to show you the car. What kind?"

"Porsche!"

"A *Porsche*!"

"What the hell is wrong with you, Lu? Since when did you turn into a nagging wife? When have I ever given you any doubts? Huh? Answer me! I make an appointment to see a car and now you make it sound like I'm blowing you off. What, you don't trust me? Trust! You've heard of it.

T-R-U-S-T! I'm going up to shower, then I'm off with Miss Tits. Grow up, Lu! You don't believe me, then follow me!"

After a while Jimmy came down freshly shaved and showered. He still had those boyish good looks that turned Lu on years ago and still did. Without saying a word he left.

Lu fumed, fussed and nervously paced the kitchen. Finally she could no longer stand it. She grabbed a telephone directory and flipped through the pages. Carefully she studied the ads and finally decided on Island Imports, a car dealership selling Porsches.

She dialed the number not quite knowing what she was going to say.

"Good Afternoon, Island Imports. How may I direct your call?" A crisp British-accented voice responded. This was the current rage among many businesses. A British-accented receptionist was thought to add a touch of class.

"Hi, this is Mrs. Cianci. I received a call earlier this afternoon for my husband regarding an appointment to check out a Porsche. Do you know who called?"

"I'm sorry, Madame. I did not place any call for you. Do you have a name?"

"No! That's what I'm trying to find out. The person did not leave a name. It sounded like a young girl's voice."

"I'm sorry, Madame. I cannot help you. We have a staff of over twenty salesmen and they share the secretarial pool. While I did not place your call, it's quite possible for any number of other staff to have done so. I would need a name to whom I could direct your call."

"Thanks a lot!" Lu banged down the receiver. She lit a cigarette. After a while she calmed down. Yes, it was true that Jimmy really had never given her any cause for suspicion. Maybe he was looking at a Porsche. Once they had talked about his ideal sports car and it was a Porsche. They really didn't need it but they could afford it. The business Reno had set Jimmy up in was doing well and they were financially comfortable. She began to feel foolish, then contrite. Getting up she began bustling around the kitchen.

~ * ~

Jimmy drove his car around the back of the car lot. A second later a mini-skirted, wafer thin, platform-shoed, long-haired blonde walked out of the building and opened the car door.

"Get in," hissed Jimmy. "Shut the door." and with tires squealing, drove out of the lot.

"Hi, Jimmy," said the girl in a babyish voice. "I'm glad you could come."

"Don't ever, ever, call me at home again. Do you understand? I don't ever want to get a message from you there because if I do, I'm going to boot your ass right out. And if I do that, you're going to be out on the street, butt naked without all those cute things I get for you," he said. He grabbed the girl by the wrist, "Like this, watch!"

"But Jimmy, you called me first. I couldn't get you at your business. There was no answer and I knew you were waiting. I had to call you at home." The girl began to weep.

"I don't give a shit! Don't call me at home! Got that?"

The girl continued to weep, wiping her tears with the back of her hand. Jimmy peeled down the parkway and finally turned off. He drove the car to a deserted street back of some warehouses. Long Island was getting so built up all the good parking places he knew of in his youth were gone. He shut the engine off and looked at the girl.

"All right! Stop the bawling."

"I'm sorry, Jimmy, but you did call me first," she sniveled. " I'm sorry, I won't do that again."

"Okay, okay. Dry your eyes and come show me how sorry you are."

The girl smiled at him and obediently and gratefully got down on her knees. She looked up at him and undid his belt and unzipped his fly. She was very sorry.

~ * ~

Lu heard the car drive into the garage. She waited for Jimmy in the kitchen.

"Well, where is it?" she asked. Her voice was soft.

Jimmy shook his head. "Nah! It's not for me. It's too low. Besides with the war in 'Nam and everything, I should support American stuff. I think I'll look at a Thunderbird or Corvette. What smells so good?"

"I made some gnocchi for you. My father's off tonight playing cards somewhere and my mother's home alone so

I sent the kids there. I thought we'd spend some time quietly. Do you want some wine?"

"Yeah why don't you get a Barolo?"

Lu hurried off to get the wine. Jimmy went into the living room. There was Frank Sinatra singing on the stereo, candles were lit, the smell of his favorite Italian dinner permeated the house and it was obvious his wife was contrite for her earlier behavior. She was planning to make amends. Jimmy sat down, kicked off his shoes and loosened his tie. Not bad, in fact it was a pretty good day. He had the blowjob of the year, he was going to have a good meal, and his wife was definitely in the mood. He quietly prayed he could get it up again.

Nine

1971

"Hey babe, come on, get happy." Ricky nuzzled Pat kissing her on the neck. Pat just shifted in her seat.

"How much longer before we land?" she asked in a very detached tone of voice.

"Oh about another hour and a half. Come on Pat, for my sake, can't you act happy? I mean, Jesus, we're on our way to Italy."

"Hip, hip hooray! We're always on our way to Italy. You know there are a dozen other countries in Western Europe. Why don't we just once go someplace else? How about England? France? Andorra, for God's sakes!"

"I told you why. We go to Italy to do business. The company wants you to go with me. They pay for everything and still you complain. God, the first time you were so damn happy. You couldn't wait. Now I need a team of horses to drag you here. Your mother, my mother are taking care of the boys. We got time to be together and you're acting like this is torture for you. What the hell is wrong?"

"Nothing I just don't like these trips. You go, you do business, I stay alone, I see the sights again alone and at the end we have a dinner with Mr. Mosconi and his latest whore and I get another gold necklace or bracelet. I've got enough of them to start my own shop."

"Forget it!" Ricky said disheartened.

They arrived in Naples, went to the usual hotel, Ricky made his usual telephone calls and the next day he made his usual business visits. Pat shopped, toured a museum, sat in the hotel bar, sat in the piazza completely without interest. Inside she was seething. She felt like cement was being poured into her, turning her into a hardened, solid block. When Ricky got home that evening she exploded.

"I'm leaving Ricky. I want to be home with the boys. I want to see their games. I can't stay here any longer."

"You don't have to. Tomorrow you can leave for Paris and I will join you in two days. We'll be there for the weekend and we'll leave for home. How does that sound?"

Pat looked at him in disbelief. "Oh my God, are you serious? Paris? France?"

"Yup, you can be there tomorrow night and get an early start on shopping. Save the tours for me when I get there."

Pat threw her arms around Ricky and kissed him a dozen times. " Oh my God, this is so great! I can't believe it! After all this time... Paris! Thank you, thank you! We will have such a good time together."

"OK, here's the drill. You will fly there tomorrow via Marseilles. Mr. Mosconi has some parts he needs to have delivered to a company there. These are samples parts, a very small package, not heavy. He's hoping to get approval to manufacture them here. It's small parts for a hydrofoil. He needs to get them there by tomorrow so he can compete in the bidding. It would be a great favor for him, if you can deliver the box. Someone will meet you at the plane, then take you around Marseilles and bring you back in time for a late afternoon flight to Paris. The Ritz Hotel has a suite for you and I'll be there the following day."

"You're joking?"

"No sweetheart, Paris awaits you—us."

The next morning Pat left for France. She arrived at the Marseilles airport and looked around. There was no one holding up a sign for her, no one to meet her. She stood around for a half-hour. Finally a man in a black trench coat approached. He nervously looked around, then coming up to her asked in broken English if she had something for him from Signor Mosconi.

Pat nodded and turned over a small package the size of a box of candy. The man immediately slipped it under his coat and turned away quickly.

"Excuse me, aren't you supposed to show me around Marseilles?"

The man didn't respond. Instead he ran for the nearest exit leaving Pat dumbfounded.

She waited at the airport until five that afternoon for a flight to Paris. When Ricky arrived the next evening she flew into a rage.

"What the hell is going on? Don't give me that crap about not talking about business. What was in that box Ricky? It sure as hell wasn't small electronic parts, that's for damn sure."

She recounted what had happened at the airport. "Was I being used?"

"No! Babe, please give me credit for having more sense than that. If I thought for one second you would be compromised in any way, you know I would never do this to you."

Ricky swore up and down a hundred times that he had no knowledge of what was in the box. He believed Signor Mosconi and assured Pat that everything was completely legitimate. He promised Pat he would look into the matter as soon as he got home.

Pat for her part informed Ricky that she would never travel to Naples again. Ever!

~ * ~

Reggie rolled over in bed. She raised herself on one elbow and looked at the clock radio. The time was 1:17 AM. Sal was not in bed. In fact, his side of the bed was not even slept on. She got up and went out of the bedroom and headed down the stairs to the living room. The TV was on with no sound and Sal was on the couch.

"Honey, it's one o'clock. What's the matter? Can't you sleep again?" Reggie asked sleepily. She sat down next to Sal and nuzzled him. "Come on, I can get you some warm milk or something else to relax you."

"Hmm... I'll pass on the warm milk but what do you have in mind for the something else?"

"A cup of tea?" Reggie giggled as she snuggled closer. "You've been working late three times in the past week. You *are* working, aren't you or are you tired from another reason?"

"No way honey, not me, not old square straight arrow. I'm not a Jimmy."

Reggie sat up eyes wide open in surprise. "Jimmy? Are you serious? Oh, does Lu know?"

"Hey don't go spreading tales. Especially not to Lu. I should have kept my mouth shut. It's probably not true. Jimmy just likes to shoot his mouth off. That's why he's such a good used car salesman. You never know when or if he's telling the truth. He likes to brag."

"That still doesn't explain why you work late so many times?"

"Well I just want to keep on top of the things at the stores and sometimes it's easier to work when there aren't so damn many interruptions all the time. No phones, no employees going in and out, no problems. It's quiet and I can check things out."

Sal seemed serious when he spoke. Reggie noticed that about him lately. Sal, who was on the quiet side, seemed even more introspective lately.

"Would you answer me just one question?"

"Sure if you'll answer me one. Go ahead."

"Is the business in any kind of financial trouble or in any trouble at all?"

Sal paused for a moment, then said, "No!"

"If there was any trouble would you tell me about it?"

"That's two questions. I only agreed to answer one."

"Don't joke with me, Sal."

"Honey," Sal's voice was serious, "the business is booming and yes, I would tell you. My question, I don't want tea or hot milk but I could use you to help me relax. Are you interested?" He smiled at her.

"Always!" whispered Reggie. I'm always interested in you."

~ * ~

Pat was already sitting in a booth when Reggie arrived. Sliding in she leaned over and blew Pat a kiss.

"Hi, how ya doing? How's everyone?"

"Good, thanks. How's everything going with you?" asked Reggie.

"OK! This is not much of a reunion. Two out of five." Pat shrugged her shoulders. "Lu is vacationing in Florida. Somehow she got Jimmy to take her for a second honeymoon. Between you and me I think they need one if you catch my drift."

"Yes I do, Sal said something about it the other night. He said Jimmy just likes to shoot his mouth off. I hope it's not true for Lu's sake."

"I heard his mouth is not all that he's shooting off, anyway, Cele called from Vegas. Listen to this, she got a contract to design some tops for a Vegas show at one of the big hotels. They're doing a number with the Beach Boys and she had to design some cover-ups. Then the girls whip them off and do their dance in bikinis at the beach. How about that?" Pausing for a minute Pat asked her friend, "Are you okay?"

"Yeah," replied Reggie, "I just miss getting together. We used to talk all the time about everything and now it seems we're going our separate ways. We're so busy with our lives. I feel it's been like this since Cathy left. If we break up, it's her fault! She was the one who kept us going."

"Speaking of Cathy, I got a letter from her last week," said Pat.

Reggie's face brightened, "I did too. She said that was letter writing night and she was going to hit all of us at the same time. Did she write you about the twins? Isn't that a hoot? Cathy delivering twins! I hope she didn't throw up all over them. You know Cathy and blood never did mix." Reggie chuckled.

"No she didn't. She mentioned in my letter that she will be moving soon to a province in southern Mexico called Chiapas. It's supposed to be jungle. Can you picture Cathy wearing her nun's veil and a sarong swinging from tree to tree yelling 'Hey Tarzan, me Cathy!' It's hard to believe that she's been a nun for three years already and away all that time. I hope she gets a furlough or whatever they call it before her next assignment. She did sound happy about it but I wish she would come back. One thing about Cathy, she always could put a new perspective on any problem we had but she made her choice and I guess she's happy."

"Well I'm glad she is."

The waiter came to take their order. "Can I start you off with some drinks?"

"Sure thing," said Pat. "I'll have a Stinger!"

"A Stinger?"

The waiter looked surprised. It was eleven thirty in the morning.

"Yes, it's brandy and Crème de Menthe."

Reggie just ordered a coke. "Last of the big-time party girls."

Pat scrutinized her friend. "What's up, Reggie? You look like I feel."

Reggie shook her head. "Did you ever feel something is getting out of control and you don't know what it is."

"Sure, that's the story of my life these days. Out of control!"

Reggie continued, "I can't even describe what I'm trying to say."

"Are you and Sal having problems?"

"Good God, no! Nothing like that but it's Sal I'm worried about. Pat, there are nights he doesn't sleep very much. I hear him getting up and when I ask him what's up he just tells me he's restless or hungry or something. I can't get him to talk about it."

"Reggie, is he ill? Has he been to a doctor lately?"

Shaking her head, Reggie hesitated, then continued, "It's got something to do with the business or some kind of business. Whatever it is, it's eating him up and I can't stand watching him being devoured!"

Pat put her hand out comforting Reggie. "Has he talked with anyone? Mr. R. perhaps? I mean after all he is Sal's cousin and I know he would help him out. Do you think the business is going belly up?"

"No, according to the books the money is fine, almost too good. There must be a lot of dirty people in Queens. The dry cleaning stores Sal manages are doing a booming business. Pat, I just have the feeling there's something not quite kosher. There is something else behind this dry cleaning business. Sal knows something but what?"

The waiter returned with the drinks.

"The sisterhood, *la Sorellanza, Sempre come sorelle* even if it's just the two of us."

The women clinked glasses and Reggie watched in disbelief as Pat drained hers.

Ten

Mexico, 1972

The mission in Patzcuaro was large. It consisted of a school, a small clinic, and orphanage. There were several missionary sisters who worked there as well as lay people who offered their services. With so many ministries, there was always plenty to do. Cathy had been here for a few years and soon she would be transferred to another assignment even more arduous than this. She would be going to the state of Chiapas in southern Mexico. It was one of the poorest as well as remotest areas and her training in Patzcuaro was a good preparation of what was to come. She was going to miss this place and would gladly have stayed longer but as her superior told her, she was needed in a place where her hardy constitution would be tested to its limits. Cathy relished a challenge and readily agreed to go. She had a month more here, then she would leave. Her students were very sad and even wrote to the motherhouse in New York begging that Cathy be permitted to stay longer. When her superior showed her the letter, Cathy was surprised.

"You know I didn't put them up to it. It's true I could happily stay here. I think they just want me because their basketball team needs a coach."

"You know that's not true. You have, since you came here, won their hearts. It will be sad for them."

"Well, I'll tell them that you can teach basketball as well as I can. They'll be happy."

"At my age, you've got to be kidding! I would like you to begin the separation process gradually. I'd like you to work less at the school and more at the clinic. I know perfectly well that you and blood don't get along but you will need some medical skills in Chiapas. They have so little there. We have received word that a medical team is coming down for a few weeks of *pro bono* work. This would be a good time to learn just a few things like simple suturing, perhaps setting a broken bone—what's the matter you look sick!"

"Sister, I can't stick a needle into someone."

"I was told you did a great job when you assisted at the delivery of those twins."

"Yes, but I didn't sew them together."

The superior laughed. "It's mind over matter, Cathy. You'll get used to it."

"It's not my mind, Sister, it's my stomach but having taken a vow of obedience, I will follow orders, *mon general.*" Cathy saluted.

"Good, I think you'll like this. Finish this week at school, then report on Monday. Tell the kids you'll see them and when you do you'll play basketball with them. It'll lessen their sadness."

Cathy reported to the clinic on Monday. The staff there was very excited because the medical team had just arrived bringing medical expertise and much needed supplies.

She went outside to help with the unloading, then it was time to meet the newcomers. The head of the clinic gave a flowery speech of welcome and the teams broke up to begin their assigned tasks. Cathy's assignment was to follow and work with a certain Julian Dobek. He was an ex-army corpsman and he would teach her a few skills.

"Excuse me, I'm looking for a Mr. Dobek."

"He's the tall guy with the glasses over there setting up. Hey Joe, you got company."

Cathy bounced over and introduced herself. A tall thin blond-haired sunburned man stood up.

"Hi, can I help you?"

"I hope so, I'm Cathy Ferrara, uh, Sister Catherine Ferrara and I've been assigned to work with you for a while."

"You're a nun? Jeez, you don't look like one!"

"What's that supposed to mean? What does a nun look like?"

"Not like you. Nuns are, you know, nun-like."

"Oh that's deep!"

He laughed, "Uh, I guess that didn't come off very well. I'm sorry. I'm Joe," he offered her his hand. He had a firm grip.

"Uh, nice to meet you but I was told to report to a Julian—"

"That's me but I hate that name. Who would name their kid Julian, except my parents? I go by Joe. If I offended you Sister, I apologize, I—"

"I just want to know why you think I don't look like a nun."

"Well, you don't look like the ones I had in Chicago. You got a bounce to your step and you smile."

"A bounce? Like a kangaroo?"

"I hope we didn't get started on the wrong foot."

"No!" Cathy said with a smile, secretly pleased he noticed she bounced.

"If you help me set up and put some of this away, we can talk and work and get acquainted at the same time. I need to know what you know about patient work and what skills you will need for the future."

"First skill I will need is to learn how not to throw up or pass out at the sight of blood."

Joe wiped his forehead with his hand. He looked at Cathy smiling up at him.

"You're kidding. For a minute you had me worried there."

"Nooo, I'm not," said Cathy shaking her head.

"Well lady, uh, Sister, get ready to work hard."

She was ready!

~ * ~

Joe was patient and a good teacher. He began with simple skills like giving immunizations. Cathy practiced giving injections to an orange the first day.

"This orange will be disease free for the rest of its natural life," she happily reported to Joe.

The next day, however, she had to begin giving real people real shots. The first dozen patients were hard. The children cried and Cathy cried even harder.

"I don't think I can do this," she said.

"That's okay, then don't," Joe replied, "Let them die of whooping cough or typhoid instead."

Cathy was better and by the end of the day she was quite proud of her effort.

Suturing was next. Once again a hapless orange found itself under Cathy's trembling hand. Joe demonstrated each type of suture and Cathy followed his example. Silently she cursed herself for not paying attention in Sister Leona's sewing class that she had to take for one semester in high school. The following day Joe came in with a pig's foot.

Cathy practiced all day while Joe aided the doctor in surgery. By the end of the day Cathy was exhausted and the pig's foot smelled very ripe. Daily, she reported her progress to her fellow nuns with great hilarity. That was the evening's entertainment.

"Tomorrow I think you are ready to assist me," Joe announced. Cathy's stomach already did a flip-flop.

"I-I... don't think I'm anywhere near ready. Couldn't I practice a little longer?"

"No, sorry. This is our fifth day here and we have four more days left. Then we pack up and it's back to Chicago for the team. I have to teach you as much as I can in the remaining time."

Cathy looked sad but recovered quickly. "This past week has flown by. I wish you could stay longer. It's been good working with you... you're terrific!

"Well, thank you. I didn't think nuns could notice terrific guys."

Cathy blushed a beet red. "Well... uh... I meant that in a professional sense."

"Sure you did, Sister Catherine," and he laughed.

Surgery began early in the morning before the clinic became an oven. The doctor removed a tumor from a man's forearm and asked Joe to close up for him. Joe got his equipment ready and asked Cathy to assist him. Two minutes into the procedure Cathy began to turn a sage green. In five minutes, she was hyperventilating and a minute after that the ceiling was coming down on her. Without missing a stitch Joe braced her back with his knee to keep her from falling over.

"Cathy!" He spoke sharply to her. "Cathy, get a grip on yourself. Take some deep breaths and look at the opposite wall. You are not going to faint because if you do, I won't be able to support you with my knee any longer and you'll land on your butt. Now take a deep breath!"

Cathy ran out of the room. Ten minutes later Joe found her slumped against the wall in the courtyard. Her red eyes gave her away.

"Hey, come on, Cathy, don't poop out on me now." He sat down next to her and put his arm around her shoulders. " We all get queasy every once in a while. I still do and you'd think I would have gotten used to it in Viet Nam. I saw everything there but sometimes it just hits you. The trick is to just get back in there and try again. You can do it. I have faith in you." He nudged with her with his knee.

She tried to reply but a new onslaught of tears came instead. Joe let her cry then helped her to her feet. "We are going to try it again, and again, and again and—"

Cathy hit him with her fist then followed him back into the clinic.

The next day found Cathy in the surgery room. The surgeon had to re-set a broken limb. He was almost finished when he looked at Cathy and said, "Sister, I need to cut this suture. Will you please help?"

"You want me to cut a suture here?" Cathy asked incredulously.

"Yes, please quickly so I can go on to the next patient. Cut it right here"

Cathy took the scissors in her trembling hand. She took a deep breath and snipped the suture where the Doctor had indicated. Instantly the surgical team broke out in cheers.

"Yeah!! Cathy, go for it. Good job!" Everyone was laughing. Cathy looked up. Joe winked at her. "Atta girl," he mouthed.

~ * ~

It was Sunday evening. The team, as a surprise for the children, brought with them some Disney movies. They borrowed an old projector and set up an outdoor theater. All the children sat in the orphanage courtyard for the entertainment. When Cathy sat down, instantly a half dozen children gathered around each claiming their share of her.

Joe smiled when he saw her. "Mother Hubbard!" he teased. Cathy smiled back. She was getting to like his smiles, his teasing, and his kindness with the patients and the kids. She found she could hardly wait for morning to come and when daily Mass was over she ran immediately to the clinic. The staff dubbed her "The early bird." Two more days left and the team would depart. Joe, too.

"This has been such a blessing for us Joe, to have you all down here. It's going to be very quiet without you and everyone will miss you guys."

"It's been a pleasure, a real pleasure and the team says they feel blessed that they were able to come and help. I understand they do that once a year. They go to different places and help out. Doc's been to Haiti a couple of times. When I become a doctor, that'll be something I will do also. You get so much out of it."

"Where will you go to medical school?"

"I don't know. Wherever I'm accepted. Why?"

"Because I'll pray for you. What school do you want to get in to? Harvard? Yale? Georgetown? If I pray, I may as well get specific."

"Whoa Cathy, I'm just a poor old Polak kid, nothing fancy for me. Just pray I get in some place. I've taken my MCAT and I should know the results pretty soon. Any place is fine. Right now after I leave here, I'm headed for some time off in Cancun. I'm meeting some buddies for a week of dissolute living, then it's back to the old grindstone for me. I plan on putting myself through med school so this will be a last blow out for me. I heard through the grapevine that you're being reassigned also."

"Yes, I have about three weeks left here, then I go on to Chiapas. That's why they wanted me to learn what I could just in case."

"You've done well Cathy. You should be proud of yourself, that is if nuns are allowed to be proud. The team really likes you and they said they would be more than happy to work with you again. That's a real compliment!"

Cathy thought for a moment. "Joe, if I don't get a chance to see you I just want you to know how very lucky I am to have you as a mentor, cheerleader, confidence builder. You are so gifted and you are willing to share yourself well... it's been a pleasure and a blessing. God bless you and enjoy the debauchery. You've earned it!"

"How about coming with me? Somehow I get the feeling, you might have been good at debauchery yourself. In your past life of course!"

"Julian Joseph! Behave yourself! Besides, I left my nun-like bikini in New York so I can't go. Thanks for the invite." Cathy laughed and excused herself.

The last night the team organized a farewell fiesta for the clinic workers. Cathy was invited and was given permission to attend. There was food, laughter, songs and dancing as well as good-byes and promises to keep in touch. Joe walked Cathy back to the mission, which was next to the orphanage. He held her hand as they walked along the darkened street. At last they reached the gate.

"Is it permissible to hug a nun?"

"Yes, hugs are good for everyone, even nuns."

Joe hugged Cathy. He held her in his arms and kissed her lightly by the ear. An involuntary moan escaped from her. Joe kissed her again on the forehead, and gently on the cheek and finally tenderly cupping her chin with his hand, he kissed her on the mouth.

Cathy trembled. Never in her past life, years ago, did she feel anything as remotely delicate as this. She felt herself relaxing in his arms and even responding to his kisses. Then, reality set in.

"Excuse me, I have to be going in," she said. "Good bye Joe, God bless you."

She swiftly ran inside the building.

~ * ~

"*Hermana,* you have some mail here for you," said the clinic secretary. She handed Cathy a postcard. It was a picture of a sunset at the beach. On the back was written a message from Joe.

"I sincerely, honestly, wholeheartedly wish you were here."

J

Cathy's heart stopped. She read and reread the card a dozen times tracing her finger over his words. Could it be he read her feelings? That last evening lingered in her mind. She checked the date. It was mailed five days ago and Joe would back in Chicago in a day.

She took a deep breath. "Where were you ten years ago? I wish to God I had known you then. Life might have been so different."

~ * ~

"Sister Cathy! Please go over to the clinic after evening prayers. Someone needs you. A messenger just came up."

Cathy left the chapel and walked down to the clinic. The lights were on and she went in.

"Hi Cathy!"

Cathy's mouth fell open. She could not speak for a minute.

"You're back! I thought you'd be in Chicago."

"Yeah, so did I! That was the plan. Ten days down here, a week in Cancun, having fun in the sun. So what happens? I meet a nun for God's sake and I fall in love with her. A nun! I can't believe it! I go to Cancun and all I do is mope around wishing to God I was back with her in a dusty, dirty town. That's what you've done to me Cathy. I'm back here and all I want is to be with you. I want you to come back with me to Chicago. I want you there when I go to med school. I want you there when I'm finished. I want you there when we get a house and I want you there when we have kids. I want you Cathy. After all these years I feel like I have found my other half, my soul mate."

Cathy backed away her eyes filled with tears. "I... I... I have thought about you all the time. When I got your card a few days ago, I couldn't believe it... that you somehow read my heart. I didn't know I was being that obvious."

"You were! It was like you had a neon sign over your head that read 'Cathy likes Joe.' Then you'll come with me?"

"I can't just leave right away. I have to finish my term here. I have only a week and a half longer before I go."

"Okay! I can understand that. Maybe when I get back I can start looking for a place for us to live. It won't be fancy because money's tight but we can manage. When you come, it'll be all ready. All I need is you with me. I know med school will be tough, time will be precious but with you—" He bent over and kissed her. Last time his kisses were gentle, now they were demanding, passionate and Cathy's response was equal to his. She could feel herself melting in his arms and she could feel his maleness hardening.

Then the evening bells rang. Cathy stepped back from his embrace.

"Joe, I have to go now."

"Okay, I leave tomorrow at seven for Mexico City, then I fly home. If you can't come with me right away, at least come to the station and see me off. As soon as you can, join me in Chicago and let the rest of our life begin."

He kissed her on the nose, on the forehead and very tenderly on the lips.

Cathy walked back to the mission on a cloud. "Joe wants me! Joe *wants* me! But wait, this is insanity... I'm a nun! I can't walk out on my vows. But, some of my former classmates had left. The world didn't end!"

She slipped into the chapel, grateful for the darkness. One light flickered on the altar.

"Oh God, is it wrong to love him? I promised you my life but isn't life with Joe a reflection of Your goodness?" She thought about Joe, med school, a home, lots of Polish Italian babies. Then she saw faces, sad faces waiting for someone to come but nobody did. She thought of a Polish mother-in-law teaching her the intricacies of Polish cooking, she thought of family gatherings. She thought of sad faces waiting for someone to come.

~ * ~

The next morning Joe was at the station early. He paced up and down waiting for Cathy to show up. He knew she just couldn't walk away from the mission today but he knew she would be in Chicago as soon as she could. He would wait for her.

A clinic worker ran up, waving a letter. He ran all the way from the clinic he said. Joe took the letter but did not open it. Looking at it made him afraid of what it might say. The train was coming. He could hear the whistle as it approached the town. Briefly he thought of running off the platform. Then he tore open the letter.

Joe,

I loved you from the first time I saw you. You said I bounced and that's probably true. That was my heart doing a flip-flop. I would have loved spending the rest of my days with you, seeing you through med school, having beautiful brown and blue eyed babies with you, living with you and loving you. But I cannot! I made a promise to God and I can't break it, not even for you! Be Happy. Do well and know that I will think of you always.

Cathy

Eleven

January, 1974

The telephone rang at the Roccollo home. It was nine fifteen at night.

"I wonder who that is?" asked Rosa. "I hope it's not one of the kids who's sick. Junior said the baby had a runny nose."

"Answer the phone Rosa, then you won't have to play the guessing game."

Rosa got up and went into the kitchen.

"Hello!" After a minute she asked, "Who is this? Reggie? Reggie, stop crying. I can't understand you. Just a minute, I'll get Reno."

She called to her husband and he came out to the kitchen. Putting her hand over the receiver she whispered, " It's Reggie, she's crying something about Sal. Here you talk."

"Hey Reggie, what's the matter?"

"Reno, it's Sal. He's not home yet and it's past nine. He went to Jersey around noon and said he would be back before supper and he hasn't returned."

"Reggie, calm down. He probably got stuck in traffic, or had a breakdown with the truck or stopped in to visit with some *paisans* and forgot about the time. Don't worry." Reno tried to reassure Reggie.

"Reno, he always calls me. He told me he would be home. I tried all three of the stores about seven. There was no answer at any of them. I called some of the people at home. They hadn't heard anything from him." She started weeping again.

"OK Reggie, tell you I'm going to do. I'll call around. I'll see if I can get someone from the warehouse and find out what time he came and when he left. In the meantime, get off the phone in case he calls and when he does, tell him tomorrow I kick his ass for making you cry. Now don't worry. I'll call you."

Reno hung up the phone. "That Reggie worries too much."

"No, replied Rosa, "you don't know what it's like sitting around worried sick waiting for someone to come home or to call. You have no idea!"

Reno looked with surprise at his wife. The normally docile, bland Rosa spoke fiercely.

"Yeah well I gotta make some calls," Reno answered uncomfortably.

~ * ~

Lu sat in bed watching Johnny Carson. Jimmy was sound asleep. The phone startled her and awoke Jimmy. "Jesus at this time. Get it will you? I'm trying to sleep."

"Lu, I need a favor." It was her father.

"I need you to get dressed and go over to Reggie's house and stay with her. We can't seem to locate Sal. I'll send your mother over. She'll get the kids off to school. Get Jimmy's ass out of bed. I need him here."

Lu conveyed the message to Jimmy. Even he looked concerned and got out of bed in a hurry. When Reno Roccollo asked for something, it was done immediately.

Lu found a weeping Reggie when she arrived. Reggie repeated her story again and again to Lu.

"I know you think I'm over reacting but I'm not Lu. He has never in the twelve years we've been married forgotten to call if he's late. I'm the one who forgets."

"Okay, Reggie, think about it, if he was involved in an accident, there would have been a call. He had his wallet with him, ID, driver's license. He had a business truck with the dry cleaning store name on it. You would have been notified by the Jersey police or a hospital. No one from there has called." Lu was trying to rationalize reasons for Sal's absence and alleviate Reggie's fears. She was not succeeding.

"What if he got sick or passed out? What if he's slumped somewhere in the truck and needs help? What if the truck rolled over and he's in a ditch?"

"What if he stopped to eat, met up with someone he knows and right now is hoisting a few beers and forgot the time. Huh?"

"He would *call*!"

"Alright, has he been sick at all, you know, like high blood pressure or sugar diabetes, something that would cause him to pass out?"

"No!"

Lu was at her wits' end trying to calm Reggie. She suggested they make plans for the next day. The kids should go to school. Her mother could take them and this would leave Reggie free to drive to Jersey in the morning. About one in the morning, Reno and Jimmy came over. Jimmy looked solemn for a change. He was going to drive over to Jersey and look around the warehouse section to see if he could find the truck. He kissed Reggie and assured her he would call immediately. It was a long sleepless night. In the morning, Reggie managed to rally for her two kids. She sent them off to school without telling them about their missing father. Reno returned shortly thereafter with a police officer.

"This is Pat Sullivan," he said, introducing a big, blustery looking cop. "He's Irish but don't hold that against him. He's a good cop. He's here to help."

The police officer briefed Reggie on what he was going to do. He asked Reggie's help in getting a recent picture, description of clothing, anything else he could use for identification. He explained he would contact some guys he personally knew and ask for their help and he would be in touch. Jimmy came back looking exhausted and reported he could find nothing. No one at the warehouse had seen Sal arrive. Lu called her doctor and got a sedative prescribed for Reggie, then called Pat for assistance.

The day dragged on as more people came over with offers of help. With each phone call, each visitor, Reggie was becoming more distraught. Why, she railed, why wasn't someone doing more to find him? The parish priest was called to console her. That sent Reggie over the edge. She now knew something bad had happened. She was faced with telling the children, when they came home from school, that their father was missing and she called her in-laws in Buffalo. They would fly down immediately. Later two detectives came from the Missing Persons Unit. They asked Reggie all kinds of questions. Was Sal in any trouble? Were they having marital problems? Was it possible that Sal had a girlfriend on the side? Were there any financial difficulties? Did he ever leave home before? Was he suicidal? By the time they left, Reggie was on the verge of collapse.

There was no sleep in the house again that night.

Cele drove up the next morning and was admitted immediately.

"Hi Reggie, how are you holding up?" she asked hugging her friend. Reggie could barely speak. Lu and Pat just shook their heads.

"Cele, please tell me again how it was when Sal first asked about me at Lu's wedding." Reggie pleaded with her.

"Well, Mr. R told me to wait and he would find me someone at Lu's wedding. He even hinted he could fix it so I would catch the bouquet if I wanted. Sal came and one of the first questions he asked me was who was the first girl who walked down the aisle. God, that seems so long ago, doesn't it?" She continued her story and that gave Reggie some comfort. "A lot of things happened at your wedding, Lu. Pat met Ricky, Reggie met Sal, Cathy met Nicky Torino. Two out three isn't bad."

"Cele, it's a good thing you didn't marry Sal, " said Pat. "This could have been you here today." Cele and Lu looked in astonishment at Pat. She was sitting numbly in a chair in Reggie's bedroom.

"No chance of that Pat. Cathy and I decided that night that marriage was not for us. Neither of us slept on the pieces of wedding cake. I didn't want frosting in my hair and somehow Cathy knew marriage was not for her."

"God, I wish Cathy were here right now," Reggie said tearfully. "She could pray so Sal would come home. God would listen to her." Reggie broke down for the hundredth time. Pat got up and left the room.

"Lu, you look like hell. I'll stay here with Reggie and so will Pat. You go home and take a nice hot bath. Your mother told me you've been here for two nights. Go on, you've got bags under your eyes that hang down to your chin."

"Thanks a lot, I needed to hear that from you but I will go. I need a break," she whispered, "from Pat more than anything." She shook her head.

Pat returned a minute later carrying a half snifter of brandy that she offered to Reggie.

"I don't think Reggie should have that, Pat," Lu said shaking her head. "She took another Valium about an hour ago and she doesn't need to be zonked out anymore than she is."

"Oh well," said Pat. " I hate to waste this and I can't pour it back." With that she tossed down the brandy in front of her flabbergasted friends.

Cele and Lu were stupefied!

"Okay, Lu, why don't you slip out now and get cleaned up? I'll stay and Reggie and I will talk or whatever. Pat, you look tired too, dear. Why don't you head for home?"

Lu said her good-byes, hugged Reggie and left.

"Reggie, what can I do for you? What can I get you?" Cele asked solicitously.

"Cele, is there any way you can get in touch with Cathy? I would feel better if I could talk with her. You know more than any of the others how I miss her. Lu's always busy, Pat's going off someplace, you've got your business. I have only my family, Sal, the kids and the memories of how we were all together. That's all I ever wanted. Just family and friends," Reggie said plaintively.

"We had good times didn't we? God, we were together so much. It's like we were sewn at the seams to each other and I think I resented anyone who tried to join us. There was just no room for anyone else. We were perfect. Pat the smarty, Lu the princess, you the sweetie, Cathy the clown and me the drama queen."

The girls began to reminisce. Reggie seemed less anxious and Pat relaxed a little. The past was easier and happier to talk about than the present.

About a half-hour later Lu reappeared very pallid.

"Reggie, some policemen are here to talk with you again. Let's go down, all of us together."

Cele and Pat looked at Lu. They guessed what the news would be.

Two uniformed policemen were in the den. They asked Reggie to sit down. One of them cleared his throat. "Mrs. Roccollo, it is my sad duty to tell you we have found a body matching your husband's description and—"

That was as far as he got. From Reggie there came an agonizing scream like that of a wounded animal struggling for life. Her cry reverberated throughout the house and into the back yard where some family members were talking. She clutched at the policeman's lapel hoping if she hung on he would tell her it was a mistake.

Cele held her up and with Lu's help managed to get her to the sofa. Pat sank down to the floor covering her head and ears trying to block out the cries. Sal was dead! Her Ricky could be next. Her screams joined Reggie's.

~ * ~

Family and friends gathered at the house following the funeral. Small clusters of people talking quietly and reverently about the deceased. Children ran in and out of the house ignoring admonitions to behave themselves. Reggie was in the bedroom lying down for a bit before coming downstairs. Lu and Pat were there, maintaining their vigil. Somewhere in the house a phone rang and a minute later Cele came running up stairs.

"Reggie, honey, quick pick up the phone. It's Cathy!"

Reggie swung her legs off the bed and picked up the phone.

"Cathy! Cathy, is that you? Oh God, Cathy, I wish you were here. I needed you so much. Cathy, please, I'm begging you pray to God. He'll listen to you. *Please*, ask him to send Sal back to me. I'll be so good. Cathy ask Him. Tell Him I'll do anything, anything at all if He would just send Sal back."

"Oh Reggie, I wish I were back there too. I would hold you and kiss away your tears but you know I can't pray for that. Sal is with God and he's at peace but I can pray for you and I will. Everyday I will pray that you are given the strength to carrying on your life as Sal would expect you to do. He would expect you to take care of the kids and yourself and he will be there watching over you just as he did in life. I believe that. Love doesn't die Reggie, it lives in you."

"How am I going to live without him, Cathy? How will I manage?"

"He will be there, Reggie. In the stillness of the night, in the activities of the day, he will be there for you. Listen for him in your heart. Sometimes it'll be very hard, very lonely, but you can count on him and God. Together they won't let you down. How are the kids? How's my Anna Catherine?"

"She made a picture of heaven with Sal there and—" Reggie could say no more. She handed over the phone to Lu.

"Hey, Cathy, wish you were here. How are you?"

"The question is how are you, Lu? Cele told me you've been living over at Reggie's for the past week. Take care of yourself. You're going to have to be twice as strong for a while. Are you all there? Is Pat there also?"

Lu handed the phone over to Pat.

"Hello, Shister Cathy. God we wish you were here. I mish you so much."

Lu and Cele looked at each other. Pat was weaving unsteadily as she talked. Her speech was as unsteady as she was. Finally Cele whispered to her. "Pat, Cathy's paying for this call, let's keep it short. You can write her."

"Cathy, we love you and we'll take care of Reggie," Pat said and she handed the phone back to Cele.

"Cele, thanks for letting me know and arranging this call." Then raising her voice she yelled into the phone for all to hear. "I love you guys, I pray all the time for you my sisters. *La Sorellanza.*"

"Sempre come sorelle," came the reply from the girls.

"How did you manage this, Cele?"

"You asked me, Reggie. I was able to get in touch with the motherhouse and they told me exactly where Cathy is. There are no phones close by so I sent a telegram and she was able to get to a town and we connected. You know I would have gone down there myself and brought her back for you. Like Cathy said, the sisterhood forever. Group hug, we all need one."

The girls got together and hugged each other holding on for support. Reggie held Lu tightly.

"I could not have managed without you, Lu. God you've been so good, so patient with me all this last week. Pat, Cele, thanks. It's not going to be easy but you guys will help me won't you?" Reggie dissolved in tears again.

~ * ~

The day was drawing to a close. The mourners were departing. Cele and Lu were cleaning up the kitchen for the tenth time. There was so much food that Cele decided to put some in the garage. Walking in she witnessed a row between Pat and Ricky.

"God's sakes, stop it Pat! What the hell's the matter with you? Get hold of yourself. You're making an ass out of yourself in front of all these people. All this talk about me being next and the business I'm involved in. We don't discuss business with anyone. Keep your mouth shut and keep away from drinking the goddamn booze. I'm sick of it! You're a fucking embarrassment to me and at a time like this you should be thinking of Reggie, not yourself!"

"I am thinking of Reggie," shouted Pat. "I'm thinking of all the times she told me about Sal and how he was worried and bothered by something. Something wasn't right and he knew it. That's why he was killed. This was no robbery as they told Reggie. He was knocked off because he knew something. I know! And that is what's going to happen to you, too, if you continue working with those bums here and in Italy. You're going to wind up in the Pine Barrens, too."

"You dumb drunken bitch. You don't know what the hell you are talking about and you keep your mouth closed."

Pat was out of control. "No I won't. I know what you do. I know what they make you do from Italy. I know what you made me do in France. I won't stand by and let this happen to you."

She flung herself at Ricky. He raised his hand and Cele stepped in.

"Don't you dare hit her. Don't you dare hit my friend!"

"Cele, mind your own fucking business. She's drunk out of her mind. Crazy woman!"

"Ricky, you touch her and you'll be jerking yourself off with your teeth. I'll break both your arms, I swear to God. Leave her alone. She's scared just like the rest of us. Come on Pat, let's go for a walk. We haven't had a chance to talk together much these past few days." And with that, Cele led Pat down the driveway and down the street. They walked in silence for a long time.

Finally Pat spoke. "You know what I said is true. The time you were in Vegas last year, Reggie and I met for lunch. She talked with me a lot about what was happening to Sal. I thought it was just Reggie talking and worrying but now I know what she said must have been true. I don't think Sal was the victim of a robbery at all. He was set up because he knew something."

"Pat, in a way Ricky is right! You don't say anything especially to Reggie. She's got all she can handle at this time. It's horrible enough to lose your husband but to think that he was killed like that is too much. The world is a crazy place these days. It could have just been as the cops said, a robbery. You know what I'm saying?"

"Yeah, I guess I do," Pat replied numbly. "I guess I have had too much to drink lately. I was just trying to kill the pain."

"Can I ask you something? What did you mean when you said something about being made to do something in France?"

"Oh, two or three years ago, Ricky asked me to take something, a package, to Marseilles when I was on my way to Paris. He claimed it was small electronic parts for the manufacture of a hydrofoil that was designed by his business partner in Naples. I know better now. I knew it then except I couldn't believe it. Those were no parts I was carrying. I think it was drugs. Ricky denied it but that was the last time I went to Italy," Pat went on.

"He goes alone now. I'm scared Cele, scared of what may happen. I feel like my life is on a runaway train and no matter how hard I try to apply the brakes, I can't stop it."

Cele hugged her friend for a long time.

"My shoes were not made for walking. Let's head back. Pat, anytime you need me you know how to get in touch. We can do lunch, a sleepover, anything at all. Does Ricky get angry like this all the time?"

"No, he doesn't, really, I'm serious. I guess this time I pissed him off badly. I'll go and apologize. I guess it was the brandy talking."

Arm in arm the girls walked back to the house. Pat went in to collect her kids. A contrite Ricky appeared and called to Cele.

"Cele, you probably won't believe me but honest there's no way I would hurt Pat. You know that! It's just lately she's been irrational and this business with Sal just pushed her over the edge. I'm sorry you saw such an ugly side of us. I apologize for both our behaviors. I don't know what got into us. We really are not this way. You know how it is with married folks. We lash out at each other without meaning to."

"I guess that's why I'm not married. Just don't hurt her. Don't hurt Pat, she's like my sister."

Cele went into the house and like everyone else, said her good-byes. She promised Reggie she would check on her every few days, then she left. It was already dark when she stepped out. As she walked across the grass to her car she could hear voices. She recognized Reno's. There were two other men talking with him. One was Reggie's father and the other was Sal's dad.

"We are asking you for justice Reno. My daughter's husband, your cousin was killed. Those children have no father tonight. I want vengeance. I want you to find out who it was and we will take care of it. Blood calls for blood!"

"Vinnie, I swear, we'll find who did it and justice will be done. Just don't go crazy and start sticking your nose everywhere. What if you get killed? What good will it do for your family? Your wife and your daughter will have no man to look after them. I'll take care of it. After all, Sal was my blood also."

Cele slipped away quietly and got into her car. Her hands shook so badly she could scarcely fit the key into the ignition. Was it true what Pat said? Did Sal know too much about something? Was his death a planned murder?

Twelve

Lu got out of the cab and began to walk down Fifth Avenue. There was so much traffic tied up that it was easier to walk. However even above the noise she heard someone calling her name.

"Lu! Wait up."

"Pa? What are you doing here? What are you doing in the city?"

"Business! I'm here on business. And what are you doing here? Why aren't you home washing or cleaning or taking care of the kids? Huh?"

"Because I have an automatic washer, a cleaning lady and the kids are in school, and Jimmy gave me a gift certificate from Tiffany's. That's why I'm here!"

"A gift certificate! Jesus I pay him too much."

"Hey Pa, come on with me. Let's go. Come with me to Tiffany's. Come on!"

"Get outta here. What do I want to go there for?"

"Oh, come on, you can buy me something, too."

Lu threaded her arm through her father's and pulled him toward the store. As they approached the door, she tugged at her skirt.

"That skirt's too short on you."

"Pa, this is 1975 not 1795. We are on Fifth Ave in New York and if you look around everyone is wearing mini-skirts. This is not Sicily."

"Jesus, bare asses hanging out. Some of these women need two mini-skirts to cover themselves up. Don't let my granddaughter wear anything like that. It's bad enough her mother dresses like some loose woman."

"Caroline already does wear minis, Pa. Now come on. Don't embarrass me in Tiffany's."

They walked in and were immediately greeted by a salesman well trained in the art of pandering to clients. Lu told him what she was interested in and he led the way. They passed by a display case featuring a glittering diamond necklace that beckoned all to come and admire.

"Oh my God, would you look at that! Have you ever seen anything that gorgeous?"

"Is Madame interested? I'd be happy to show it to you?"

"I'm sure you would! That'd be a hell of a commission." commented Reno.

"Pa!" hissed Lu. Then smiling at the salesman she inquired about the price.

"Forty-six thousand!"

"Forget it, Lu. I love you but not that much. Besides where would you wear it? To the supermarket? To church? To pick up the kids?"

Lu tried to maintain her composure. With her elbow she poked Reno in the ribs. "This is Tiffany's, Pa," she muttered under her breath. "Why don't you look around, Pa?" She said with clenched teeth.

Reno walked away. *"Pezzonovante."* Snooty old money. They walk around here with noses up in the air, like their shit is crushed fruit. He probably had more money stashed away than they did. Lu went about her business. After she made her purchase she went looking for her father. She found him staring at a beautiful hand blown bowl. It was on a lit pedestal. She watched him as his eyes caressed the *objet d'art*.

"Now that's what I call beautyful" he murmured.

"An excellent choice. This is Murano glass," offered the salesman.

"I'm Italian, I know about Murano glass."

"Of course, and obviously, sir, you are appreciative of the incredible craftsmanship, the artistry that went into the making of this piece. Please notice how the sides of the bowl are shaped like flames leaping out of a fire."

"Yeah, a bowl of fire."

"Exactly, sir, that is the title of this piece, 'A Bowl of Fire'. If you look at it carefully you will see that the artist begins each flame with a spark. You can see the yellow at the bottom, then allow your eyes to travel up and you will see that spark ignite and gleam then glow like a flame. In its own way this is as much a work of art as a David perhaps."

Reno said nothing but before walking away he looked back at the piece one more time.

"Why don't you get that for Ma?"

"Naw, she'd use it to serve fruit cocktail."

"Pa, you are incorrigible!"

"That good, huh!"

~ * ~

The cab pulled as close to the curb as possible. The traffic around the theater was heavy as many taxis vied for a spot to discharge their passengers. Lu, Pat and Reggie got out. Almost at once there was a scream of recognition and Cele ran to them.

"I'm so glad you guys got here. This will be great."

There were hugs all around with an extra big one for Reggie. It took a lot of convincing but finally after being nagged about getting out, Reggie agreed to come into the city and see a play. This was girls' afternoon out and Cele had gotten tickets for "A Chorus Line" although she had seen it several times herself. They all went in and found their seats.

"What have you got planned for us?"

"Theater, dinner at a neat Moroccan place where you sit on the floor, eat couscous with your hands and they even throw in some belly dancing lessons if you wish and if you're up to it, you've got to come and see my new place. Upper East Side, no less. I predict in ten years from now a penthouse on Park Ave."

"You really are making it aren't you!" said Pat. "Your hard work is paying off. I'm so proud of you!"

"Yup. Do you want my autograph now?"

"No, not really. You forget, somewhere in all those pictures at the house buried in boxes are some, which could be used for blackmail purposes. Like this is the real Tina Benedict. Who has the picture of us stuffing our bras with cotton balls?"

"Oh I do," said Reggie. "I was looking through some stuff and I came across it about a month ago. I showed

Anna Catherine the picture. I thought it was hilarious. Her reaction, 'how dumb'."

"Caroline thinks we're a bunch of dinosaurs. Only you, Cele, are the cool one!" said Lu.

"That girl is smart!"

The play was excellent, full of high jinks and the restaurant was hysterical. Pat found a plastic spoon in her purse and was auctioning it off to anyone who did not want to eat with her fingers.

The belly dancing lessons were taken with so much exuberance that the rest of the patrons applauded enthusiastically and demanded "Encore." Even Reggie. who often burst into tears at other social events, participated wholeheartedly.

"Oh, God! I needed this," she said as the women waited for the elevator in Cele's new apartment building. "This was so much fun! Only thing to make it better would have been Cathy's presence. Can you see her belly dancing in her habit, shaking her coif and whipple, throwing her white collar to the audience?"

"She would have done it too," said Lu, "but in her last letter she said she doesn't wear her habit any more. She dresses in street clothes except for her head covering and her crucifix. She said with all the changes this was the best to get rid of those hot habits that just got in the way."

Cele led the women proudly into her new apartment. Of course it was tastefully decorated and she delighted showing them her view of Central Park, which could be seen if they stuck their heads out of her front window. Each room was inspected and admired. In the bedroom, which was large by apartment standards she had a simple

Japanese styled bed and in the corner was a tall lit pedestal with an *object d'art*. It was "The Bowl of Fire."

Lu was dumbfounded. That was the piece she had seen at Tiffany's. Here it was in Cele's house!

"Where did you get that piece from? I saw it at Tiffany's. It's gorgeous!"

"Yes it is. It's my favorite," Cele replied simply, then escorted the girls out of the room.

"When did you buy it?" Lu curiously asked.

"I didn't, it was a gift."

"That's some gift!" Pat stated. "Someone must like you an awful lot."

Cele attempted to change the subject. "Drinks anyone? Cokes, mineral water? I have some champagne."

Lu was determined not to change the subject. "You know my father and I were at Tiffany's together. I bought earrings with Jimmy's gift certificate. My father couldn't get enough of that piece. He kept looking at it. I thought he was going to buy it for a minute."

"Really! Hey are you sure you don't want anything? How about if I show you my latest designs? I have some preliminary sketches here at the house. Do you want to see what you'll be wearing next season? Hair is supposed to be short and layered like a gypsy look and so peasant blouses will be in."

Lu warily looked at Cele who was getting increasingly nervous. She asked again about the bowl subtly this time. "Is the bowl a gift from someone special? You haven't mentioned anything lately about who you are seeing. When you get close-mouthed, that means it could be getting serious?"

"No! No chance of that! Now do you want to see the sketches?"

The girls followed her in the den where they spent some time giving their opinions. Cele seemed distracted and not as light-hearted as she had been earlier in the day. In fact when the girls decided it was time to go, she seemed relieved.

On the way home the girls discussed Cele.

"I can't figure out why she doesn't get married. Her business is damn successful. What more does she have prove to herself? We got to start looking around. There's got to be a Cele type somewhere. I know she's not celibate. She's told me when she gets the urge she gives in. Do you think she's involved with a married man? I always thought she was too smart for that," Pat stated.

"Oh I hope she does find someone. She's got such a good heart. She's been a blessing," Reggie said. "One time she took Anna to a fashion shoot with some models. Anna was thrilled. I was so glad because it was the first time after Sal... after everything and Anna was really happy. Cathy said in one of her letters that Cele sends her money for the missions all the time. She's real generous."

Lu said nothing. She wasn't listening. She was still stunned by the appearance of the bowl in Cele's house. How did she get it or rather *who* gave it to her?

~ * ~

The next day was a Sunday and as was the practice after church Lu and her family went to her parents' home. Rosa asked about the girls' trip into the city as she had the children over for supper.

"Fine Ma, we had a good time, especially Reggie. She had a blast and it was good to see her enjoying herself. She didn't cry once. Cele's apartment is nice and of course it's perfectly decorated as you would expect. Hey, Pa! Remember that glass piece that we saw in Tiffany's? Guess who has it? It's sitting in Cele's bedroom!"

"Really? Business must be good!" That was all Reno said. He got up and left the room. Lu had a strange feeling come over her, one she couldn't shake. There was something. Cele seemed very tense when questioned about the bowl. Why for God's sake? Her father too seemed touchy.

~ * ~

Monday morning Lu left for the city as soon as she got the kids off for school. She took a cab and was in Tiffany's by eleven. She sought out the salesman who had waited on her not long ago.

"I was in here a while ago. You sold me some earrings. My father came with me. You showed him a piece of glasswork that looked like flames. Do you remember it?"

"Oh yes of course, it was sold. Beautiful work."

"Yeah it was lovely. Uh, was there only one of those or do you have more. I'd like to buy one."

"No that was a one of a kind, however, we have contracted with the artist to show a few more of his pieces. If you like Madame, I can notify you when some more arrive."

"No, I want to know who bought that piece."

"I'm sorry. You must know Tiffany's does not give out that information. Our sales are confidential."

"I know that Tiffany's doesn't but what about you?" Without waiting for a reply she peeled a roll of money out of her pocket. One twenty-dollar bill, followed by another and another and still another. The salesman looked blankly at her. She pulled off two more. "That's all I have except for cab fare."

Very discreetly the salesman took the money and slipped it into his pocket. "One moment please, Madame." He left and came back shortly. "It was sold in February, on the twentieth. It was a cash transaction and it was delivered to a Miss Di Benedetti."

"Who was the buyer?"

" A Mr. Rocco."

Lu walked out of Tiffany's in a daze. Her father... Mr. Rocco!

~ * ~

Tina Benedict Inc. as the sign stated on the doorway, was frantically busy. Phones were ringing, the noise from the sewing room was deafening, cutters were busy, staff was running around with samples, clients were inspecting merchandise, and in the midst of all this was Cele like an orchestra director, conducting the entire score effortlessly. Lu walked up to the receptionist who had two phones to her ears and was simultaneously speaking into both. She mouthed the words, "Just a minute please". Lu did not wait but walked right into the storm.

"Hey lady, wait a minute," yelled the receptionist. "Do you have an appointment? You just can't go walking in!"

"Watch me!" answered Lu. Looking around, she asked directions for Cele's office. The receptionist hung up both phones and came from behind her desk.

Lu spotted Cele, with her mouthful of pins, working around a model. She paused for a moment to take a critical look.

Lu went straight toward her. "You fucking whore!"

Cele paled momentarily, then regained her composure quickly. The model stepped back hoping to get out of the way. The receptionist ran up. "Sorry Tina, she just walked in, didn't stop even though I called to her. I'm sorry!"

"That's all right. Would you excuse us for a minute? Why don't you take a break? I'll catch up with you in a bit. Rhonda, hold my calls!"

With that she escorted Lu to her office, closed the door and pulled down the blinds that covered the window. Outside the door the staff looked at each other in bewilderment and alarm at this intrusion by an obviously angry woman.

Cele looked at Lu. "It's not necessary to make a scene in front of the staff." She knew why Lu was here.

"Not make a scene? You're damn lucky I was in control of myself because I feel like yelling to everyone here, telling them about their bitch of a boss! You Goddamn son of a bitch whore! You're sleeping with my father! I was with him at Tiffany's. I saw him looking at that piece. I even told him to get it for my mother. He gets it for you! I can't believe it! My father, my very own father and *you*! With all the guys out there, why do you have to fuck my father? Can't you find someone for yourself? I can't get over it. We were friends! We grew up together! You were at my house all the time. My mother opened her arms and her house to you and this is the way you repay her kindness by sleeping with her husband!

You *snake*! You... cock sucking whore! My God, you were my friend!"

Cele was restrained saying nothing while Lu vented her anger. "You betrayed me! You betrayed my mother! *Why*? Answer me, God damn it, WHY?"

"Because I love him."

"You *love* him? You love him so you two-timed us, you deceived us! You call this love? What kind of tricks did you use to lure him in bed, you witch? What did you promise him? A blowjob every time, kinky, lurid sex?"

"It's not like that, not like that at all."

"Oh really and just what did you hope to gain with this? Did you think he was going to leave my mother and go off with you because if so, you are so very mistaken. My father loves my mother! He will never, *never* leave her and go off with you! Get that through your head!"

"I know that," Cele said softly, "I knew that right from the start. We would never, nor could we, have a future together. I accepted that! That was one of the conditions he insisted upon when we began."

"When you began? How long have been sleeping— seeing him?"

"Twelve, thirteen years!"

Lu was not prepared for that. She stumbled backwards, hitting her leg on a table.

"All that time, twelve, thirteen years! I've been married fourteen years."

"I know. I fell in love with him at your wedding. That's when I decided there was no other man for me. He was what I wanted. Lu, I'm sorry you found out and I'm sorry you are angry. I love him! Plain and simple, I love him!

He's a wonderful man. He's smart, funny, sensitive. He's a very, I guess you could say, complicated man yet his life is very compartmentalized. His family, his business, me— we all have a certain part in his life yet none of us interfere with the other. Business is business; he doesn't let it mix with his family. I am who I am but yet I don't interfere with his family and you and your mother and brother would never come into his business. This is the way he conducts his life."

"I know how my father conducts his life. I don't need you to tell me."

"Do you really know your father, I mean, do you understand him? Do you know his likes, his dreams? Do you know he likes the ballet? We go every year. The first time he saw it he said it was like watching a fairy tale. If you touched one of them they would break."

"My father at the ballet? This same man who was thrown out of Ebbets Field because he threatened to put a contract out on an umpire for making a bad call? This man *likes* ballet?"

"Yes he likes jazz too. He says it sings to his soul. He made pottery one time at a friend's house. This is your father! Reno Roccollo!"

Lu could not believe what Cele was saying. Suddenly her father was becoming a stranger to her. She walked away in disbelief, then spinning around, she lashed out one more time at Cele.

"I don't ever want to see you again, Ever! If you ever come around, I'll kill you. I'll scratch out your eyes. I'll create a scene like you have never seen before, got that?"

"No you won't! I won't allow you to. If perchance we do run into each other we will be civil. I will ask you about your kids and you will ask me about my business, that's all! I will not let you embarrass your father. You got that! Furthermore you will say nothing to your mother. She does not know. Your father has never said anything disrespectful about her. In his way, he loves her and you will not hurt her!"

"No, you have done that already. I won't hurt her any further. But as for my father—that's a different story. You damn fucking whore of a bitch."

"Just remember one thing, I wasn't alone in that bed."

Lu opened her mouth to say something but changing her mind, she walked out of the door slamming it behind her.

~ * ~

Reno Roccollo started toward the elevator then went back outside. He stopped by a flower vendor and got a bouquet of long-stemmed dark red roses. He went back to the apartment building. He whistled quietly down the corridor and rang the doorbell.

"Hi, doll face," he said as Cele opened the door.

"Hi, yourself. Come in."

"What? You going someplace? You're all dressed up in a suit. Look what I got. I like red roses!"

"R-Reno, remember when we first got together and the rules we made. Rule number ten—whenever either of us felt it was no longer good, we would say good-bye and there would be no questions asked. Just good-bye! This is it. Good-bye!"

Reno studied Cele's face for a minute. "Is there someone else?"

"No questions, Reno. That was the rule!"

He nodded. "Enjoy the roses" and with that he turned and walked out the door.

Cele closed the door behind him. The composure she had just a minute ago vanished and slumping against the door, she sobbed as though her heart would break.

Reno walked down the hallway to the elevator. He pressed the bell and waited. Then he turned abruptly and walked back to the apartment. He was almost ready to press the doorbell when he paused. He could hear Cele crying inside. There was no one else. He knew the reason. Someone had found out about them. He went back to the elevator. The car was there and he got in. The door closed, he hit the Lobby button and when the car reached the ground level, he got out and left. He never returned.

Thirteen

November, 1975

Pat sat in the car outside her boys' school. It was dismissal and she was glad she made it in time. She had been late the past few days and the kids were complaining. She honked the horn as she saw them coming out. The boys, Anthony and John, plus two of their friends piled into the car. First thing they did was turn on the radio loudly.

"Can't you make it softer? It's blowing me right out of this seat!"

"Nope," said Anthony, her eldest, "The Monkeys can only be heard loud."

Pat rubbed the side of her head. She was feeling fuzzy when she first got into the car and now the feeling was worse. It was like moving on eggshells.

"Mom! Look out! There's a delivery truck right behind us and you cut him off. Jeepers!"

Pat looked in the rear view mirror. The driver behind her was giving her the finger, in fact, all five of them.

"Sorry, didn't see you, mister," she muttered.

The car in front of her was going very slowly. She kept braking to avoid getting too close. The kids were jolted back and forth.

"Mom are you okay?" Anthony asked. He was sitting in the front seat.

"Yeah, sort of. Where do your friends live and I'll drop them off."

"They're coming to my house. We're going to kick back and do homework."

Why is that car going so slowly? She stepped on the accelerator to pass. It was a two lane residential road and she pulled into the opposite lane. Screams from the kids alerted her to the danger. There was a station wagon coming straight at them the driver frantically beeping the horn. Pat could do nothing else except head straight for the sidewalk. Up over the curb the car went, then came to a screeching halt. Pat leaned her head on the steering wheel. The eggshells were breaking in her mind. Minutes later a police car pulled up behind them and the officer came up to her.

"Step out of the car, please, ma'am? Did you see what you were doing? Jeez, lady, you got a car full of kids. What were you thinking? You kids okay in there? May I have your license please?"

Pat swayed as she fumbled for her purse and pulled out her wallet.

"Have you been drinking, lady?"

"No, no I haven't. I'm not feeling too well. I had to pick up the kids at school."

"Leave my mother alone," John said coming to the defense of his mother. "Can't you see she is sick."

The officer looked at Pat. "Lady, if you're that sick, you have no business picking kids up from school. You should have asked someone else. You're damn lucky you didn't hurt them or yourself. How much farther do you have to go?"

"Just a block and a half more—Dalton St."

"All right. Tell you what I am going to do. I'm going to follow you straight home very slowly. You're lucky I'm not giving you a ticket."

Pat drove to the house with the police car right behind her. The kids got out and ran to help her out of the car and into the house.

"Get your mother to bed," admonished the cop.

~ * ~

Pat could feel someone stirring in the bedroom. She moaned softly as she turned over.

"What the hell happened today? The kids called saying you were in an accident. I came right home. The car's okay except the front end may need alignment. What happened to you? Are you drinking again?" Ricky stood by the bed. He did not look happy.

"Whatever happened to 'Hello, How are you'?'" Pat said. Her mouth felt like it was stuffed with cotton.

"Answer me, have you been drinking?"

"No! I told the cop that and I'm telling you. I have not had anything to drink."

"Well then, what the hell is it? "

"A lot you care."

"Don't start on me again. Don't start with that crap! God, do I have to get a babysitter for you? Someone to keep tabs on you during the day? You could have killed those kids—ours as well as the other two. What am I going to say to the parents? I'm sure those kids went home and said you were probably drunk."

"I'm *not*! I told you that already. I just wasn't feeling well. I shouldn't have gone to pick up the kids but I didn't want them to wait out there."

"Why not? They've waited out there two times this week already. You're going to see a doctor or a shrink. I've had enough of this. You are going to get straightened out before you kill someone. God help you if you hurt the kids!"

"I won't hurt the kids ever. I promise. I'll be okay. I'll get up now and fix supper."

"Don't bother, it's seven o'clock. We've having pizza, again!"

Pat lay back in bed. "Fine," she murmured.

~ * ~

Lu was watching TV when the doorbell rang. Answering it, she was surprised to see Ricky Campione standing there. He did not look happy.

"Hey, what's up? Come on in."

Ricky walked into the living room and slumped down in a chair.

"Lu, I need you. I need help with Pat." He proceeded to tell her of the events of the day. "She says she doesn't drink any more. She's stoned out of her head instead. God! When I think she could have killed those kids, my blood runs cold. What is she doing to herself?"

"I don't know Ricky, I saw her at the Nunzio funeral last week. She looked awful. I've never seen her like this. This isn't Pat! She needs to see a doctor and we've got to get her there. Can I ask how's it going with you? You don't look so great yourself. Come on, want something to drink?"

Ricky shook his head. "I just want things to be OK. I don't want to worry about the house or the kids or anything when I'm at work, which is where I should be. I've got a mountain of work and yet I fly home to take care of things there. I'm needed in both places it seems. He sighed heavily. "Where's your old man?"

"Working supposedly. At least that's what he says."

Their conversation was interrupted by Caroline who walked in. "Hi, Uncle Ricky."

"Hey, Carolina! *Nothing could be finer than to be with Carolina in the morning,"* Ricky sang out.

"Oh yuck, how uncool! My name is CaroLINE!"

"Oh yeah, not cool. I hear that a hundred times from my two. Dad, you're so not with it. Dad you're a dinosaur. When did we become uncool Lu? I remember us being pretty hot stuff. When did we cool off?"

"We haven't," laughed Lu. "I'm still pretty hot stuff even if *nobody* else thinks so and you Uncle Ricky were always hot!"

Caroline made a face and left the room. Lu walked Ricky to the door. "I'll check with Pat and I'll get Reggie to help. We'll do something. Maybe we can get to the bottom of this. Don't worry. We'll take care of her. See you."

"Thanks, Lu. Jimmy's a lucky guy and you're right. You're still pretty hot!"

"Yeah, sure!"

~ * ~

A couple of days later Pat and Lu got together. They were going to Reggie's house. Reggie called them and said she was ready to tackle the closet where she had stored all of Sal's stuff. It was a cold blustery day and Reggie was feeling as cold as the weather.

"Hi guys," she said as she opened the door for them.

"Hi yourself. I brought some extra boxes from Ma's house. She always has a supply."

"And I brought apple squares from the bakery," chimed in Pat. "Let's eat before we tackle this."

"Thanks a lot. I really appreciate it and I think I'm ready to do this. How about a group hug before we start." The three girls hugged together.

"These group hugs are getting smaller," said Pat. "Anyone hear from Cele?"

Lu said nothing. Reggie mentioned she got a phone call from Cele who was checking up on her. "She's been great. I hear from her definitely once a week sometimes more and I appreciate it considering how busy she is."

The girls sat down to tea and dessert, then went down to the basement. Reggie took a deep breath before she opened the closet door. "I don't know what we'll find in here. Dora at work just stuffed things in boxes from his office." She reached up and lovingly touched a leather jacket. "This was his favorite jacket. You know the one designed by that Barlett guy that Cele claimed was a homo. Sal just laughed when I told him." Reggie started to puddle up. "Stop me, do not let me do this or I won't get through."

The girls sat down and began to sift through the stuff. Most of it was office notes, desk stuff, some clothes Sal had kept at the office just in case. In about an hour they were done.

"You did real good, honey," said Lu. "You handled this well. Is it getting easier?"

"Not really, you just learn to live with it. It's hard to believe it's almost a year. It's hard to believe I made it. It was like Cathy said on the phone at the funeral. I do feel like Sal is with me some of the time. I can feel him guiding me whenever I have a problem. Does that sound crazy?"

"No! It sounds beautiful and I believe you," Pat said wistfully.

~ * ~

Lu drove Pat home. She pulled into the driveway and stopped the car.

"I'd ask you to come in for a minute Lu but I'm beat," Pat said, "I think I'll nap for a while. Thanks for the lift." Pat fumbled with the door.

"Can we talk for a bit before you go in. This won't take long, then you can nap." Lu looked serious. "Pat, what are you doing to yourself? You're looking so thin these days, so worn out. Are you sick and not telling anyone? Are you seeing a doctor?"

"Oh for Christsake—don't you start with me! Ricky's on my back all the time. He's even got my Mother in on it and now you too! 'Go see a doctor, go see a shrink.' I'm sick of it! There's nothing wrong with me. I'm *fine*!" Pat replied emphatically.

"Then why do you look so haggard? You're skin and bones and you—"

"What, are you jealous?"

"No, damn it! I'm worried about you and so is your family!"

"What? Did Ricky ask you to talk with me?"

"And what if he did? So what? He loves you. I do too and it hurts me to see you like this."

"See me like what?" Pat asked defiantly. "Go ahead tell me. I can take it."

"Alright, I see you as a budding alcoholic, maybe even a junkie. There, I told you the truth. I know it hurts but that's what I see happening to you."

"I can't believe it! I can't believe you would actually say those words to me. Whatever happened to friendship, Lu?"

"Friends tell each other the truth even though it hurts."

"Yeah? Well maybe someone ought to tell *you* a few truths about things in your life."

Pat managed to open the door and got out slamming the door behind her. She walked straight in to the house without looking back.

~ * ~

"I'm coming, just a minute," yelled Reggie. She opened the door to find two men standing on the doorstep. They looked familiar but she couldn't place where she had seen them.

"Mrs. Roccollo, I don't know if you remember us from last year. I'm Agent Dan Fogerty and this is—"

"Robert Burns. Bob Burns. We came to see you last year shortly after your husband's passing."

"Oh yes, I remember, I think. Everything was pretty fuzzy last year at this time. What do you want?"

"Could we come in?" Agent Fogerty produced his badge and showed it to Reggie.

"FBI?"

"Yes, ma'am."

Reggie invited them in and sat down in the living room.

"How are you doing, Mrs. Roccollo?"

"It's been a very hard year but I have managed with the help of family and my friends."

"Good, glad to hear it. Mrs. Roccollo, getting down to business, last year we were here because we wanted to talk with you concerning your husband's uh... death."

"Yes I sort of remember that. You said you were investigating it. What have you found out? I never could understand why the FBI was interested. It was a robbery that went wrong, at least that's what the Jersey police said. Have you found out anything different?"

"Nothing we can share with you at this time."

"What I still can't understand is how someone can be killed here in the United States and the investigations have shown nothing. No killers caught—nothing! I mean this isn't Russia where people disappear off the streets. How can your investigation and the cops find *nothing?* I don't understand. The only thing I can think of is you must not be very good investigators."

"We can understand your frustrations, Mrs. Roccollo, really we do but what we want to know is if you have found anything among your husband's personal things that might give us some clues. Did he leave any papers? Notes?"

"Wait a minute! If this was a robbery, why are you looking for any papers? What kind of clues?"

Bob Burns shot his partner a look of disapproval. Fogerty had said a little too much.

"I want to know. I have that right!"

"I'm not at liberty to say anything right now."

"You're not at liberty to say anything but you want to know if Sal left any clues? That does not make sense."

Dan Fogerty chose his words carefully. "All right, Mrs. Roccollo, this is what I can tell you. Right from the start, we had a feeling that something was not right, I mean the circumstances of your husband's death. A truck taken in broad daylight, no witnesses, wallet taken but not other valuables like the watch and the expensive-looking ring he was wearing, and no fingerprints found in the truck. It was wiped clean. That just didn't add up. That plus the fact that some people reported Sal, your husband, was not happy with work. We found that out from some of the people we interviewed at his office. The day he left, he was heard to say something about getting to the 'bottom of this once and for all.' Do you have any clue what that could have been? That's what we need to know."

Reggie was stupefied. She could only numbly sit there. It took a minute for everything the agent told her to sink in.

"Then it wasn't a robbery," she murmured. "He was right."

"I beg your pardon, did you say something?"

"No! What kind of clues are you looking for?"

"Papers. Notes. Letters."

"No, just the other day my friends and I went through his office boxes. There was nothing out of the ordinary. Office junk, that's all."

"Well if you ever find anything at all let us know. I gave you my card last year but here is another." Then he got up and went to the end table where there was a picture of the family. He returned to Reggie. "Mrs. Roccollo, I don't want you to say one word to anyone about our visit here, do you understand? Not one word. Swear to me on the picture of your family, you will say absolutely nothing at all to anyone. I'm half Italian. We used to swear on our ancestors a lot at home so I know how important that is. Now swear!"

Reggie touched the picture and nodded still very much in shock.

"Hello? Anybody in here?" called a voice from the kitchen.

"It's my mother!"

Fogerty put up his hand.

"Yeah, Mom, we're in here."

Mrs. Perrini, along with Mrs. Tomasino, walked into the living room.

"I had to take Francine to the doctor's and she insisted on coming to see you, Reggie. I didn't know you had company."

"How do you do? I'm Dan Smith from US Insurance. My partner, Bob Jones."

"Don't try to sell me any insurance," said Mrs. Tomasino. "I don't plan on living much longer so I don't need any."

"Well, perhaps you want to leave something for your family?"

"My family is worthless. They pay no attention to me. I have to rely on the kindness of my friend, Mrs. Perrini here, to take me to the doctor."

Turning to Reggie she said gruffly, "And you should be careful Reggie, these insurance men can't be trusted. It's a racket selling you more insurance than you need."

"Actually it's a college fund for Anna Catherine," said Bob Burns. "Pretty soon she'll be in college before you know it and the time for saving is now while she's thirteen."

Reggie couldn't believe it. How did they know her daughter's name and age? Of course—they were the FBI!

"Thank you we'll be going. Let us know when you want to start that policy Mrs. Roccollo and Mrs. Tomasino, let us know if you change your mind."

"Like I said, I'm not living forever. I don't need one."

The agents walked to the door. "Remember not a word, not even to your mother."

Reggie walked back in. "I'll make coffee Mom, we can visit in the kitchen."

Mrs. Tomasino picked up the agent's card from the table. Reggie quickly took it from her hand.

"I was just looking. Maybe I should buy some insurance from them and tell my family. Then if they think they're gonna get some money, they'll be nicer to me."

Fourteen

January, 1976

"Hi, Cele."

"How did you know it was me?"

"You usually call this time of night."

"How are you doing, Reg? I'm sorry I missed the memorial Mass for Sal. Did you get my flowers and the stuff for the kids?"

"Oh, Cele, I don't know how you do it. The kids loved your gifts and your letters to them. Thanks a lot for caring. I did pretty well. Actually, I did very well. At the memorial service in Buffalo, I was the one who held up my in-laws. I don't know where I got the strength."

"What are you doing tonight?"

"I'm putting Sal's clothes out for the Goodwill people to collect tomorrow. I'm ready to do this. Pat and Lu were here to help me with some of the stuff a couple of weeks ago. Tomorrow it goes."

"Are you saving some for the kids?"

"Oh yeah—Sal's watches and gold chain and other jewelry but the clothes have to go. They will be so out of style by the time Sal Jr. is ready for them. Better some poor person makes use of them than getting moth-eaten in the closet."

"You know you're starting to sound like Cathy. I think you should save one or two things for the kids. You never know."

"Maybe you're right. That jacket by the designer you used to go with may still be in style. I'll go rescue that."

"Bye, Reggie. Love to the kids."

Reggie went down to the basement and pulled open one of the boxes. The leather jacket was folded on top. She pulled it up and hugged it tightly to her just as Sal hugged her the Christmas morning she had given it to him. *"Stop,"* she told herself and with that she went to hang it back up in the closet. She felt something in the chest pocket. It was some pens and a pencil Sal had left in it. She walked over to his now unoccupied desk, opened the top drawer, threw in the pens inside and tried to close the drawer. It was jammed. She pulled it forward and jiggled it but the drawer remained stuck.

"Damn it!" she muttered as she went to the workshop area of the basement to get a flashlight and screwdriver. Getting down on her knees, she flashed the light in the drawer and saw the offending pencil poking up. It was stuck on the top of the drawer. She shoved in the screwdriver and managed to push the pencil down. She heard the top of the pencil break and finally, the drawer was free. She shined the light in to see what had jammed the pencil and there taped to the top of the drawer toward the back was a small memo pad. They used to keep several of those around when the kids were little for them to draw on.

She pulled off the tape and opened the pad. There was writing in Sal's small scrawled penmanship. She went upstairs, sat down on the couch and began to read, her eyes widening with each turning page. My God! Sal was keeping a journal. There were entries going back two years with references to events prior to that.

Something's fishy, it's been so damn hot nobody is bringing in dry cleaning, Spring Blvd. Store did $50 worth of business in one day. Receipts read over a grand this week. No way!

Sal was detailing business transactions with notations that this was fishy or that was suspicious.

Esther called said there was a delivery of chemicals. Not dry cleaning stuff. Checked on it. It was ammonium chloride...what the hell is that used for? Company said it was an error—not sure.

I don't trust that Garofalo accountant. He can't add straight. 1+1 doesn't make 6. I wonder are there two sets of books. One that I don't see. R doesn't seem too concerned. He said he'll talk with them. Jesus, what's going on?

Three hours later she finished it. The last entry was a week prior to his death.

Another ten cases of ammonium chloride. These were supposed to go to Abbodanza Sup. I got to talk with Ricky. I know what that junk is used for and I'm sick about it. If I report it, what the hell will happen to me and Reg and the kids? I got to do something.

Reggie's blood ran cold. Sal was right all this time when he said something was wrong. Everything became so clear. He was on to something, something horrible and apparently this knowledge was why he was killed.

"Sal, please tell me what to do with this. Do I go to Reno and show him? Do I call those guys who were here a couple of weeks ago? My God, Darling, how could you have lived with this knowledge? Why didn't you share it with me? We could have done something about this and you would still have been here with me and the kids."

Reggie rocked back and forth while millions of thoughts ran through her head. Standing up quickly before her resolve gave way, she went to the kitchen and looked on the bulletin board for the card the agent gave her. It wasn't there. She looked in the general junk drawer in the kitchen. It wasn't there either. *Think,* she said to herself. Then she remembered taking it away from Mrs. Tomasino and putting it up on top of the china cabinet in the dining room. It was there. She picked it up.

"Sal," she said quietly, "I'll finish this business for you darling." She dialed the number on the card and left a message. "I think I found what you want."

~ * ~

Reggie was ready when Lu came to pick her up a few days later. They were going out for lunch.

"Is Pat going to meet us."

"No," Lu shook her head, "you and I have to do some talking about Pat. We've got to get her some help. I'm really worried about her. She looks like a zombie most of the time. Ricky is worried. I think we have an addict on our hands."

They pulled into their favorite spot for luncheon, unaware of the car following them.

Two men walked in and sat at a table not far from Lu and Reggie. The girls talked mostly about Pat and what they could do to help her.

"I tried to talk with her, Reg, but all I got was denial and anger. She was pissed off at me when I brought the subject up. Poor Ricky, if she's as belligerent with him all the time as she was with me, I feel sorry for him. He seems at his wit's end. Maybe you can talk with her. Maybe you're better at this than I am. You always did talk sweetly to everyone but..."

"You know Pat and I talked a lot. There is something going on with Ricky that is bothering her. I understand what she's going through because I felt the same way with Sal. You all considered me a worrywart but I was right, you know. Sal was concerned about something at work. Promise me you won't say a word to anyone. Swear it! I found a booklet Sal was keeping. I still can't make sense of it. I turned it over to the FBI."

"You did *what*?"

"I turned this pad over to the FBI. Two agents have been coming to my house. Lu, they think Sal's death was no robbery. He was murdered for something he knew."

Lu slumped back into her seat completely speechless. Finally she spoke,

"I don't believe it! After a year, the FBI comes to tell you this. Where the hell were they when Sal died? Why did it take them so long to come to this conclusion? Why haven't they arrested someone if they know so much? Reggie, please be careful. Don't trust outsiders. Talk with someone, my father, he will give you good advice. How do you know who these people really were? You can get badges and ID's anywhere. Oh God, Reggie, what have you done? I hope you haven't put yourself or the kids in danger. Don't trust outsiders, especially the damn government. They've got rats, who squeal, all over the place. Let's go to my father. If there is anyone who knows what to do, it's him!"

"Lu, I can't! I can't talk to anyone about this. I haven't even told my parents. Nobody knows. I hope I did the right thing for Sal's sake. I'm begging you, don't say a word. I only told you because I trust you and I had to tell someone. You are my closest friend and we are family. I have to get to the bottom of this. Promise me!"

Lu shook her head. "I still think you are making a mistake, Reggie, talking with outsiders. A real big mistake!"

"Well, we'll see."

The women left the restaurant and a few minutes the two men left also.

~ * ~

It was eight fifteen that evening. Lu walked into her parents' home. Her father was in his usual chair in the den. He looked concerned as he saw his daughter come in.

"What's the matter, Sunshine?"

"Pa, I really have to talk with you. It's important."

"Your mother is taking a bath. Now tell me what's the matter, Honey? Jimmy not treating you right?"

Lu shook her head. "It 's Reggie Pa, I think she got herself in real trouble. Somebody is after her who claims to be from the FBI," Lu whispered.

Reno Roccollo got up and shut the door.

Fifteen

Lu could hear the phone ringing as she pulled into the garage and shut off the car engine. "I hear you," she yelled. "Keep ringing." She ran into the kitchen and picked up the phone. All she could hear was hysterical screaming on the other end.

"Ma! Ma! What's the matter? I can't understand you. What's the matter? Ma, stop crying now! What is it?"

It took Rosa a few seconds to compose herself, which she was not fully able to do but between sobs and supplications to heaven she managed to spit out the words, "Your father's been arrested."

"Jesus, Ma, when?"

"This afternoon. They called me from the office. They came and got him and took him away in handcuffs. It's going to be on TV tonight."

Reeling from the news, Lu struggled to pull herself together. She took a few deep breaths and was surprised when calmness permeated her body and mind.

"Ma, listen to me, listen to me please. I am coming right over now. Do not answer the phone or the door. Go into your bedroom and stay there. I'll call the Ciancis and tell them to pick up the kids and keep them at their house. I'll be right there. Remember, no phone calls to anyone!"

Lu's first thoughts were of her children. She called her in-laws and made arrangements for them to pick up the kids from school and shield them as much as possible from the news. Then Lu jumped into her car and drove to her parents' house. There, chaos awaited her. There were press cars and reporters parked outside the house. A policeman was standing there directing traffic. Lu by-passed him and drove up the driveway.

"Hey lady! Are you family?"

Lu did not respond. Stepping out of her car she made a beeline for the back door. She could hear cameras clicking and reporters yelling questions at her. A particularly aggressive reporter started to follow her cutting across the lawn. Lu turned around. A flashbulb went off in her face and Lu went berserk.

"Get the hell off this property, you bastard! Get off!"

Another flash went off. That was like waving a red flag in front of her. Lu lunged at the reporter catching him broadside. He did not see her coming and when she barreled into him, he tumbled to one side and his very expensive camera fell to the other. It landed on the sidewalk with a crash.

"Goddamnit, what the hell are you doing? That's a thousand dollar camera."

"Oh really, well it looks like a thousand dollar piece of junk right now. Get off this property!" Looking at the policeman she yelled, "Aren't you going to do anything? This fucking reporter is trespassing. Arrest him!"

The policeman ran up to prevent a shoving match between Lu and the angry reporter.

"You heard the woman. She's right. The street and sidewalk are public domain. You're on the grass, which is private property. Get off."

"That bitch just broke my camera. You saw her! She shoved me and knocked the damn camera out of my hand. A thousand bucks. I'm suing your ass lady."

"Go ahead, *Sue*! That's after you get out of jail for trespassing and harassment. I want this man arrested now and that goes for the rest of those bastards out in front. They step on one blade of grass and that's it for them. If you won't do anything then I'll call someone who'll do something about it."

"Who are you going to get? One of your father's hit men? Mafia broad!" the reporter sneered.

"Okay, buddy, get off or I'm going to arrest you. Now just leave." The cop directed the man off the grass and down the driveway. Lu could hear the man complaining to the others about his broken camera. The back door was locked but she had a key and let herself in. Her mother had done exactly what Lu told her. She was sitting in her bedroom. The hysterical crying had given way to numbness.

"Okay, Ma, let's call Aunt Maryanne in Brooklyn. Stay with her because you'll get no rest here. Who is Pa's attorney? Has anyone called you from the police station? Has Pa called?" Lu was surprised by her own calm, cool-headed behavior.

"No one has called. They said from the office, the cops just walked in with a warrant and put him in handcuffs and walked out with him. They said there were TV reporters and everything. It's going to be on the news tonight."

Lu began making a series of phone calls. Of course, Jimmy was not to be found. Their other grandparents had picked up her kids. Aunt Maryanne was not happy but agreed that her sister should stay with her and she learned that the Angelini brothers were already notified and they would represent Reno. A backyard neighbor offered his services to drive Rosa and they managed to sneak out the back way without alerting the reporters. Lu was left alone in the house and she sat in the darkening room, afraid of putting on the lights. At five thirty, she turned on the TV and sure enough, one of the local TV stories was about, "Local businessman arrested for alleged Mafia ties."

Lu's heart sank as she watched her father being escorted out by police. There was pandemonium all around but Reno looked calm. Before getting into the police car he stopped to make a statement. "I am disgusted by this persecution. Just because I am a businessman and my name ends in a vowel, right away I am accused of being in the Mafia. I am appalled by this discrimination toward Italians. I have always been a good citizen. I work and I pay taxes. This is an affront to all Italian Americans."

Some reporters yelled questions to him but he ignored them and got into the car.

"You tell them Pa! You tell those bastards. You show them!"

~ * ~

The Angelini brothers were lawyers. They were twins. Victor Angelo and Angelo Victor Angelini were long time associates. They were smart and clever. Maybe because they were twins, they seem to have twice the brainpower. What one didn't think of, the other did. They assured Lu the next day that they would do everything to get Reno out on bail. In the meantime just sit tight and stay calm. Those were their instructions. How could she stay calm with her father in jail and her mother sick with worry and her husband nowhere around for support?

Later that evening, when she did see Jimmy he was very unsympathetic and downright insensitive to her situation.

"Look Lu, I can't be connected with him right now. It's bad for business. It'll give me a bad rep. I'm going to play it cool. I don't want the kids to be hurt either. It's not their fault Reno got mixed up with something. I want them to stay with my folks and I don't want them to be known as Reno Roccollo's grandkids. I want them out of the picture. I don't want to see them on the front page like you." Jimmy was referring to the picture of Lu in a tussle with the reporter at her folks' house. The caption under the picture read, "Mobster's Daughter Defends Dad".

A few days later Reno Roccollo made his first court appearance. He was charged with racketeering, laundering drug money and other assorted crimes. His petition for bail was denied. He was going to spend time in jail before his trial.

Lu was devastated. Around her parents' neighborhood, the atmosphere was changing. Some changes were subtle like the way local merchants treated her when she came to shop. Gone were the smiles and jokes. Some were hostile like a few ladies who turned their backs when they came into church. Some were cruel like the teasing her brother's kids got at school because of their last name.

Lu felt an increasing sense of isolation. She tried to get in touch with Reggie. There was no answer for days not even at her parents. Pat was out of it. Her speech was so slurred it was difficult to understand her over the phone. A call to Ricky confirmed her fears. Pat was sinking into a world of uppers and downers followed by vodka chasers. Ricky was sympathetic but it was obvious he had more than he could handle. Even worse was the insistence of her father that no one from the family was to come and see him in jail. Rosa was beginning to get migraines from the stress. Junior, her brother, was under pressure from his wife to distance himself for their kids' sake. Lu was feeling as isolated as a leper.

One day a few weeks after her father's arrest she got a letter. There was no return address and her address was typed. She opened the letter. It was from Reggie. It read:

Lu,

You betrayed me! How could you do that to me and the kids? We were family, Lu. You were the only person I told about the notebook and the FBI. Not even my parents knew. I just had to tell someone and I trusted you. You swore, you promised me you would not tell and you did. You almost got us killed. A few days after we had lunch I was driving with the kids. We came to a stoplight and two guys jumped out of the car in front of us with guns. One came on my side and the other pointed a gun at Anna's head. You know what they said? "This is what happens to rats who squeal." They were going to kill us Lu. The only thing that saved us was the fact that while I didn't know it then, the FBI was following us to act as protection. They shot at the guys, wounding one. They got us to a safe place and hid us. Now the kids and I have to go into hiding. Life will never be the same for us. God forgive you Lu because I never will.

Lu fell to her knees. She was shattered. She read and re-read the letter. *No, it was not possible.* She did not betray Reggie. Reggie was her friend, her sister, she was family! Her cousin Sal was married to her. She would never, ever, do anything to hurt Reggie. There was a mistake. Somebody else set Reggie up not her. She only told her father because she was worried. Reggie was so sweet, so naïve; she was being misdirected by the FBI. Her father had said he would take care of it. He would do anything to help Reggie. Oh God, please don't let Reggie misunderstand. This was not a betrayal. She just didn't want Reggie to be deceived.

~ * ~

Reno came to the visitors' room at the jail. He was expecting a visit from his lawyers but Lu was sitting there instead. She looked at him coming in dressed in the bright orange prison garb, hands handcuffed behind him. He frowned as he saw her.

"Lu, I didn't want you to come. I didn't want you to see me like this. I told the Angelinis this."

"They had nothing to do with this. They didn't know I was coming. I'm your daughter for God's sake. It's my right to be here."

Reno nodded. The handcuffs were removed and the guard stepped back to a spot by the door.

"It's good to see you even though I'm not happy about you being here. This is no place for you. You shouldn't have to see this. How are the kids?"

"Fine, Pa. They're doing okay. They ask about you. Caroline wrote you this letter and Jimmy said to tell you his team is in second place in the basketball league."

"How's your mother?"

"Good days and not so good. She has a new doctor who's treating her migraines. They are getting better actually. She hasn't had a bad one in almost a week. The medication is working although it makes her like a zombie. She lost about ten pounds and she looks good."

Reno nodded. "Junior?"

"He's having a hard time. Teresa left with the kids to stay with her family for a while. He's working hard, going to school and he's worried about Ma and you."

"He's a good kid," said Reno. "And what about that husband of yours? Is he treating you right?"

Lu nodded but didn't say anything. He father had enough troubles without her telling him about the rat that Jimmy was turning out to be. She fumbled in her purse to get Caroline's letter. She tried to stuff it in between the wire barrier. The guard came immediately and ordered Lu to stop.

"Jesus, it's just a letter from my granddaughter. What, I can't have it?"

"That's okay Pa, I'll read it to you."

It was a newsy letter from a teenager who talked about friends and school and a boy she liked. Reno seemed to relax as he listened.

"She is my sunshine just like you," he said proudly.

"Don't call me that Pa. You gave that name to someone else. Cele!"

"So it was you who found out. I wondered about that."

"This isn't the time or place to speak about it, Pa. I just couldn't believe it. Why?

Reno was silent for a minute. "I loved her."

"What about Ma? Don't you love her?"

"Your mother is a good woman. I respect her for sticking it out and it wasn't easy for her. As for loving her... let's say we both did the best we could under the circumstances."

"What circumstances, if I may ask?"

"Well," Reno spoke hesitantly, "we had to get married. No, nothing like that. Uh, Rosa was not pregnant. No! It was a deal for both families. She was an obedient daughter and she listened to her father. Look that's all I'm going to say. I need you to listen real carefully."

Reno leaned closer to the wire barrier and spoke in a low voice checking the guard every few minutes.

"The bastards have frozen my assets—all of them. I can't get a dime of my own money. The Angelinis have to get paid. They're not exactly doing this for free. Make sure your Mother is not at home. I don't want her to know and you don't say anything especially to that rat of a husband. I know what he's been doing!"

Lu's eyes widened with surprise. She thought she had hidden Jimmy's extra marital activities from everyone.

"I guess we were both hiding surprises in our lives."

"Never mind that, just listen. Go into the basement in the furnace room. Behind the furnace on the floor is a small door. I told your Mother it was where the pipes are located. Open it and get a small, gray strongbox. Give the whole thing to the Angelinis. Your mother is set—the house is hers, it always has been and she will get about two grand a month for expenses. Will you do that? I may have to ask you again to help me get my money so I can pay my bills."

Lu nodded her consent.

"Pa, I have to ask you something. Did you have anything to do with Reggie? You know she was almost killed. She thinks I was the one who betrayed her by telling you." Lu was crying. "I only did it because I was afraid for her... that she was being taken advantage of. Please tell me you didn't tell anybody." Lu looked up at her father with pleading eyes but a stranger looked back at her.

Sixteen

Washington DC, 1976

The door buzzer rang softly. Reggie and her children looked at each other apprehensively.

"I'll get it. You kids stay here," Reggie said as she got up from the couch and walked to the front door. The buzzer rang again. She pressed the button on the intercom.

"Who is it?" she asked timidly.

"Snug as a bug," came the reply. She breathed a sigh of relief. That was the code that was used by the agents in New York when she and the kids were brought to a safe house following their attempted murder over six weeks ago. Still, every time the doorbell rang or a knock came at the door, her stomach knotted up. She wondered if she would ever get used to it—get used to this feeling of fear for herself and her kids.

"Hi, Mrs. Roccollo," said Agent Burns. With him was another man. "How are you doing today? Did you get any rest last night?"

"Yes and no!"

"Well, that's normal considering all that you have been through. How are the kids?"

"Still shell-shocked and getting very restless about their confinement. I like family togetherness but six weeks of not going out anywhere is too much. We both need a break from each other."

"Mom?" Sal Jr. peeked out of the den and around the corner to the hallway. "Are you okay?"

"Sure honey, it's Agent Bob and—"

"Sorry, this charmer is Fred Goertz," Bob Burns said introducing a slightly built, balding man. "He's been assigned to you and he's one of the best."

There were how do-you-do's and Fred playfully punched Sal Jr. in the shoulder. "How's it going, kiddo?"

"Alright I guess. This is a better place than the one in New York. At least this has a yard and everything. Mom won't let us go out though."

"Don't worry, I'll square it with your Mom," Fred winked. "Where's your sister?"

Sal pointed to the den.

"I'll meet her in a minute. I need to talk with your Mom first, then I'll be in with you and give you the whole scoop."

Reggie went in the living room and sat down. "May I get you anything?"

"Actually later I'd like some coffee. I hope you found everything to your liking. We stocked this place for you before your arrival yesterday. If there's anything you want or need, let me know." Fred Goertz smiled.

"I'll have to be returning to New York," said Bob Burns. "My assignment was to get you safely here which

I'm happy to say I did and now Fred will take over. He'll be your guardian angel for about a month or longer if that is what it takes. As I said he's one of the best and I know whatever he does, he will always keep your safety and that of the kids, as his top priority. I have confidence in him and I know you will too once you get to know him. I'm going in to talk to the kids, then I have to beat it. So I turn you over to Fred." Bob got up and went to the den.

"Okay, now then Mrs. Roccollo, I'm going to start with you first, then we'll talk with the kids together. Whatever, and I mean this sincerely, *whatever* you need, you let me know immediately. If I can do it, if it's not too extreme, consider it done."

Reggie nodded. There was something very earnest about Fred Goertz.

"I'd like to tell you a little about the program. This is the WPP, commonly known as the Witness Protection Program. It's not too old. We've been sort of in business officially since 1970. I know both Dan Fogerty and Bob told you a little. We protect those people who have helped the government bring criminals to justice by their testimony or in your case by bringing to light your husband's diary. We got enough evidence to break up a piece of the Mob. Even breaking off the tip of the iceberg helps but as you know an iceberg is two thirds bigger under the water. That was pretty darn gutsy of you."

"I did it for my husband," Reggie said tearfully. The tears fell down her face and she couldn't speak for a while. Fred just quietly waited until Reggie was composed.

When she was ready, he continued. "We, meaning the US Marshal Service, will assist you in getting new identities, relocate you, provide job training, employment until such a time when you are ready to become self-sufficient. Even after that, if the need arises, we will help you again."

"Are there lots of people like us? I mean, on the run?"

"Some yes, but none of them are as nice as you folks. You know we have the obligation to protect criminals as well so if there is a mobster or drug dealer who turns in evidence and is in danger because of it, we have to offer him protection also. Believe it or not, sometimes it takes a crook to catch a crook. Working with you is going to be a piece of cake compared to some of the cases I've been assigned to. I'll go over everything step by—"

That's as far as he got as Bob Burns stepped back into the room along with Anna Catherine and Sal Jr.

" I really got to get going. I'm out of here on a two o'clock flight so I guess this is good-bye for a while. Mrs. Roccollo, take care of yourself and the kids. You'll do great. You too, kids." He quickly exited the room and motioned to Fred to step out with him. A few minutes later Fred returned.

"Hi, Anna, I'm Fred. Your new "Uncle" Fred. How are you doing?"

"Yeah! Right! Fine! Just *fine!*" Anna turned angrily away and stormed into the den. She flopped on the sofa, blinking back tears.

"Anna! That's no way to talk."

Fred waved to Reggie and followed Anna into the den.

"I know you're angry about all of this but—"

"No! I *love* this! I *love* being dragged out of my house, I *love* being cooped up in an apartment for a month. I *love* not being in school. I *love* not having my things. I *love* not being able to call or talk with my friends. I just *love* all of this!"

Fred nodded his head. "I know that. It could be worse you know."

"Oh really? Just much worse can it be?" Anna asked sulking.

"Well, you could be dead along with your Mom and brother."

"I wish I were dead!! Death is better than living like this. I hate this. I hate you," she said turning to Reggie, "I hate you and I hate Daddy for doing this to all of us. Why couldn't he have just left everything alone? Why couldn't you have just burned that damn book?"

"That's enough!" Reggie spoke sharply. "I've had all I can take from you. You haven't made any attempt to be pleasant. I know how hard this is. I'm going through the same thing but I don't have the luxury of complaining all day long like you. You had better straighten up there girl or—"

Anna burst into tears and screamed. "You don't understand! You don't know what it's like. You have no idea what I'm feeling. I want to go *home!*" She slumped back on the couch. Fred sat down next to her.

"Anna, I do understand. I do understand what it's like to leave your home and everything behind. I know what it's like to be afraid and wonder what every new day will bring. Believe me, I understand some of your feelings."

Anna wiped her face with her hands. "Oh yeah, just how do you know?"

"My name is Fred Goertz, I'm German. I was born there and lived there until I was nine. My father was a Lutheran minister who spoke out against the Nazis. One day there was the knock on the door and they took him away right before my eyes. I never saw him again. Friends helped us to escape to Holland and from there we made it to Canada, then to Milwaukee where I lived for years. I do know what's it's like to leave everything and everyone behind. I remember as a kid being so lonesome for my home. Every night I would think about my room and think about my things that I left behind. I remembered exactly where each thing was that I wanted. I remembered each friend that I had—everything."

Anna and Sal looked at Fred sympathetically. Anna had stopped her crying.

"Did you ever go back? To see your house and things, I mean?"

"Yeah. I joined the Army and was sent overseas to Germany because I spoke the language. I did go back to my town. It wasn't the same. It had been bombed extensively. Not even the church was spared where my father had been pastor. My house was an empty lot. Three quarters of my neighbors were gone or dead. I saw one guy I knew from my class. He kind of remembered me."

"What about your Daddy?" Sal asked.

"Oh, he died in a concentration camp along with a couple of other ministers from our town and a few priests. Like your father, he was brave. He saw injustice and he spoke out against it. Your father saw some things that were bad and he spoke out about them too. Both were brave men. Your mother is brave also. It took a lot of courage to do what she did. She could have burned that book in the fireplace at your house and your life would have gone on the same. You would still be there in your own room with your own things. She, like your Dad, made the decision to do what was right—namely to stop the smuggling of drugs and punish those who were profiting from it. Your Dad paid for that with his life and you have to honor him by accepting what has happened and going on with your life. That's what's expected of you."

The kids were quiet for a minute. "Can we ever go back just to see like you did?"

"No, not for a very long time and that's what I'm going to talk with you about now. Your new lives. By the time you're finished here in Washington, you will no longer be the Roccollo family. You will have new names, new backgrounds—new everything."

"You mean my name won't be Sal anymore?" the young boy asked incredulously.

"Nope, and that's your first assignment for the day." He left the room and returned with his briefcase. He opened it and took out a small booklet, which he tore in half.

"Boys' names for you and girls' names for Anna. I want you to pick out a new first name for yourself, any one you like. You get to choose this time so take your time. Think about it. Next, I want you to pick out a new birthday. It can be the same year but a new month and day. Got that?"

He and Reggie left two astonished children.

"Thank you for what you said. That helped I think. I'm so sorry about this. I've had second thoughts so often and I have cursed myself, and even my husband for starting this. In fact I was angrier with him than I was with Reno and his bunch. I never realized what this would do to my family and truthfully I would never have done that if I had known then what I know now. I would have kept my mouth shut and I would have burned that Goddamn pad. I want you to know that."

Fred nodded. Then he began to tell Reggie about what the future would hold. She too would need a new name, new birthday. She and the kids would have a new background so they would have to learn a lot about the place where they supposedly came from. They would be tested many times to make sure they all had the same story and had all the same facts. They would be relocated in a new part of the country and Reggie would have to choose a career so she could earn a living. That was hard for her because she was what she always wanted to be a wife and a stay-at-home mother. That along with every other aspect of her life would have to change. Their training went on for over a month. Gradually they became comfortable with their new names and backgrounds and were ready for graduation to their new lives. One day just before they were ready to leave Fred came over with a huge moving box that he dragged into the garage.

"Open it," he said gleefully and stood back as the kids tore into the contents.

Anna squealed as she lifted up her old pink gingham coverlet that had been on her bed. Her Barbie doll collection was there as well as her assorted teddy bears. Sal grinned from ear to ear at his Little League trophies and MatchBox car collection. For Reggie there were two baby books and her wedding album.

"These will have to go in a safety deposit box," said Fred, "but at least you have them and you can look at them whenever you feel the need. The trophies were inspected for any identifying marks but they're clean. These are reminders of your past lives which will always be part of you. Nothing can erase the fact that you were once Reggie, Anna and Sal but there's a new life out there now for all of you. Make it a good one!"

There was a tearful group hug. "My other news is your Dad and Mom. Reggie, they will be joining you in a while. They will be in the Program also and you will be reunited with them in a couple of months or so."

"What about Noni and Grandpa Roccollo in Buffalo? Will they be with us too?"

Fred shook his head. "No, and for the time being, we discourage any attempts to contact them or any of your friends. You can keep in touch through secure mail-forwarding channels. You can let them know you are safe but you cannot receive calls from them or visit them. Those are the rules. We talked about that before."

"I have a friend. She's a nun, a missionary. Can I ever write to her? I need her support so badly."

"I will leave you with instructions to follow so you can hear from her via letters. I don't think nuns would be dangerous. Don't they take vows to be quiet or something?"

"Not Cathy, she's was anything but quiet. I know I'll never be in touch with any of my old friends. One in particular I don't ever want to see again but Cathy I would trust with my life. The two others, well I'll miss them because we were so close but I need to have Cathy."

"I understand. Well tomorrow is departure day and drum-roll please while I name your new residence in the state of—" Fred pointed his finger at Sal who pounded on the packing box. "North Dakota!"

There was silence as all three former Roccollos let the words sink in. They could not hide their disappointment.

"Gottcha!" Fred laughed. "Boy, you should see your faces! How about Florida instead?"

Shrieks of delight echoed in the garage of the safe house in Washington, DC.

"Yes! Florida!" Sal jumped up and down. Anna was happy. In fact she grinned broadly for the first time in months. Her eyes sparkled at the thought of a new life in Florida. Only Reggie was silent. Her eyes misted over as she turned to Fred.

"Florida—that's where I went with Sal on our honeymoon."

Seventeen

Reno Roccollo's trial began in October, 1976. The wait had been a terrible time for the family. The previous summer, holidays, and birthdays were particularly bad. No one wanted to celebrate but for the kids everyone agreed it was necessary. The tension between Jimmy and Lu was so thick it could be cut with a knife. Mrs. Roccollo's migraines kept her miserable and the fact that Reno refused to allow his family to visit him in jail dampened everyone's spirits. Even Pat, from whom Lu was hoping to get support, was not around. Her drinking and drug use was so bad that her family checked her into a hospital. Ricky took the boys to Florida for a vacation. Now what the family had been dreading all these months was about to begin.

Everyday Lu showed up at the courtroom and was escorted to a front row seat behind Reno. Lu was shocked when she saw him on the first day. He had aged in jail. While her mother lost some weight and looked good, Reno's weight loss made him look haggard. He had taken great pride in his appearance. He worked out at the local gym and for a man of fifty something years, he had always looked remarkably fit. Now his suit fit poorly. His once tanned face had acquired a jailhouse pallor. He nodded at Lu, winked and gave her a thumb's up sign. He mouthed the words, "Everything is going to be okay."

The judge came in and a court clerk read the indictment. The charges were incredible. Racketeering, money laundering, extortion, conspiracy to smuggle drugs, the list went on. The only thing not on it was stealing from church poor boxes. Reno entered a "Not Guilty" plea on all charges.

The prosecution led by a small, nervous, bespectacled man made the opening statement. He painted such a lurid picture of Reno that Lu wanted to jump up and scream for all to hear that those charges were ludicrous falsehoods. A prejudicial bureaucracy contrived them in order to squelch any initiative taken by an immigrant society. This Waspish establishment was suspicious of any outsiders making good and in order to win public opinion would throw around terms like Mafia and *Cosa Nostra* in an attempt to frighten the people. Her father was right when he called them *pezzonovante,* his derogatory term for the establishment. Lu's Italian blood was boiling and during a brief recess she confronted the Angelini brothers about it.

"Why don't you say something? You know that weasel is lying about my father. He's a politically ambitious Jew trying to become the next Attorney General. Well he's not going to besmirch my father's reputation just to get into office."

"Lu, get used to this or get out. You're going to hear a lot of crap from him. Bite your tongue. We're ready! Don't worry. Don't let your Dad see you getting upset. He needs to concentrate on what's going on without worrying about your reaction. We'll bring this sucker to his knees."

One of the Angelini twins patted her arm in reassurance.

They were good, Lu had to admit it. Their opening statement was passionate, fiery and touched on all the points Lu had made to them. This was a conspiracy to paint all Italian-American businessmen as corrupt *Cosa Nostra* members. Reno Roccollo was not Al Capone. He was a businessman, a family man, a good American and the government had better be able to prove all those charges or risk losing this case. Lu felt a little more relaxed after the argument and when court was recessed until the next day, she gave her father the thumb's up sign.

The days that followed were long and emotionally strenuous. Sometimes Lu felt buoyed by the proceedings and at times she wanted to strangle the prosecutor but she managed to control herself. If the prosecutor thought this was going to be a judicial cake walk he was mistaken but he had a few surprises up his sleeve and he began to pull them out one at a time.

One morning the prosecutor called out for a witness.

"The State calls Miss Celestina Benedict to the stand."

Lu's heart sank as Cele approached the stand. She was as dramatic looking as ever as she took her oath. She took her seat on the witness stand and surveyed the courtroom her eyes pausing for a second to look at Lu.

"What is your name?"

"Celestina Di Benedetti. My business is under Tina Benedict."

"Occupation?"

"I'm a dress designer and a businesswoman. I own Tina Benedict Designs."

"How long have you known the defendant?"

"Since I was in the second grade"

"What is your relationship with the defendant?"

"He is a family friend."

"Anything else?"

"Yes, Mr. Roccollo helped me start my business."

"Really? How?"

"He gave me my first loan when I began my shop."

"How kind of him but why didn't you go to a bank for a loan?" the prosecutor asked sarcastically.

"Because of the five banks I went to, none would grant me a loan."

"Why not?"

"Banks discriminate against women."

"Oh come now Miss Benedict, people get loans all the time. How do banks discriminate? It's illegal."

"Tell that to the banking industry."

"You were discriminated against?"

"Yes! One bank said my business plan was inadequate. The next bank said they don't loan money to women starting a business because it's too risky. Another said they would lend me half if I could get my father or husband to co-sign for the loan. Another banker said he'd consider it but I had no collateral and still another offered me a loan if I used my body as collateral. By the way, I later saw one of the bankers with his wife. She was wearing one of my designs."

"With all these people telling you 'No' why did you go to Mr. Roccollo?"

"Why not? He was a family friend. I showed him my business plan. He took a chance and backed me. It paid off. With some luck, a little inspiration, and a lot of perspiration I made it and within seven years I paid off the loan with interest."

"Very admirable. Tell me Miss Benedict, what did you use as collateral for this loan? Did he ask for anything?"

"What do you mean? Where is this question going?"

"I just want to know what you gave as collateral. After all, if Mr. Roccollo were a good businessman, he would ask for something. No?"

"No, my name was good enough. That and the desire I had to make it."

"Hmm, an astute businessman backs a virtual unknown girl in a business venture without asking for anything in return. You must have had one heck of a good business plan."

"I did!"

"Are you sure he didn't want anything."

"Like what?"

"Like an opportunity for money laundering. Using you, an ambitious young woman, he backs you financially, makes arrangements for safe delivery of your products, insuring no labor problems, easy availability of materials and as a payoff you return his investment by facilitating the free and easy transfer of money."

Both Angelini brothers jumped up with objections. Cele remained unfazed.

"No. I never laundered money for him. There was never, ever, any unscrupulous business dealing. It was a straightforward loan that was repaid. Period!"

Mr. Epstein, the prosecutor, pursed his lips together and thought carefully, for a second about his next line of questioning.

"Miss Benedict, I don't know much about the garment business. I do know that there are always strikes, union versus non-union. I do know there is a lot of money spent on security. Designs and products get stolen. Trucks with merchandise get hijacked. Did you ever experience these problems?"

"No, none of them."

"And why do you suppose that is?"

"I have no idea. I have always treated my workers fairly, even when I had just three women working for me. I used some innovative practices, like on-site child care and flex time. My workers have appreciated that and are loyal. As for trucking problems I have used the same firm since I began. I've been lucky."

"Are you sure luck has anything to do with it? Or are you being protected? Did you know Mr. Roccollo was allegedly with the Mafia? It was common knowledge around the neighborhood."

"I think you've been reading too many Mario Puzo novels. My family and I are Italians. We lived in a mixed neighborhood where there were many Italian-American families. We don't go around referring to people as Mafia, or Godfather."

"Do you deny knowing anything about the Mafia? Do you deny its existence?"

"Oh no, the Mafia did exist. It was a secret society pretty much like your Masons. It began in Sicily centuries ago to fight tyranny."

"Well, it certainly has come a long way from fighting tyrants."

One of the Angelini brothers stood up to protest.

"Your Honor, is there a point to this line of questioning? We do not deny that there was centuries ago such a society. What we are about right now is to prove that our client is not a member of this society and is innocent of the charges levied against him."

"I'm inclined to agree, unless there is some tie-in, would the Prosecutor continue with another line of questioning?" the judge replied.

"I will, Your Honor, but I am leading up to a tie-in. I submit that Mr. Roccollo used Miss Benedict here as either an unwitting participant in his money-laundering racket or she willingly allowed him as repayment for his loan."

There were loud calls of objections.

"Just a minute, Mr. Prosecutor," Celestina countered, "Aare you insinuating that I was amenable to any sort of illegal financial transactions or that because Mr. Roccollo backed me when I began my business, I repaid him by laundering money? Just because I am Italian-American and he is also, does not make me a partner in any crime, any plot by the Mafia to engage in illegal activities. I resent that. May I ask you a question? Did you attend New York University School of Law?"

"Yes I did, I am a graduate. What does that have to do with anything?"

"You graduated in 1947?"

"So what of it?"

"At that time there was a Professor Day teaching at the Law School. He was found to be a card-carrying member of the Communist Party, which advocated the violent overthrow of our government. He was there, you were a student there, so are you a Communist too?"

There was a ripple of laughter in the courtroom that did not please the judge. He banged his gavel. Mr. Epstein, the prosecutor, turned scarlet with anger. Storming to the judge's bench, he demanded that Celestina be declared a hostile witness.

"Order!" demanded the judge. "The jury will disregard that last remark and the witness is cautioned to refrain from making any inflammatory statements and stick only to answering the questions. And no, Councilor, I will not declare this witness as hostile. You began this line of questioning and the fact that she got the better of the argument does not make her hostile. Guilt by association will not work in this courtroom. Either prove she has engaged in criminal activities or get on with the questioning."

Mr. Epstein fired one more volley.

"Outside of an *innocent* business relationship with Mr. Roccollo, was there another one?"

"Yes, we shared a personal and private relationship."

"Were you lovers?"

"I already answered that question."

Mr. Epstein smugly smiled at the jury, then turning to his seat he stated, "I have no further questions."

An Angelini brother stood up. "Your Honor, I have one question to ask of the witness. Miss Benedict, did you ever hear the defendant, Mr. Roccollo, ask or suggest or imply that you launder money for him or his businesses or that you keep a second set of books to facilitate this activity?"

"No! Emphatically not! Never!" Cele responded looking at Reno.

"No further questions!"

Celestina stepped off the stand and walked out of the courtroom. As she passed by Reno she gave him a nod. The judge ordered a short recess.

Outside the courtroom there was a mob scene of reporters. Celestina was besieged by them asking questions and taking photos. One of the Angelinis came up and grabbed her by the arm pulled her into an adjoining conference room.

"You did great! You made him look like an asshole." Vic Angelini patted Cele on the back pleased with her performance on the stand.

"Maybe, but he did make some references which will make me look suspicious."

"Don't worry, he was fishing. He came up blank." Vic reassured Cele.

Celestina remained silent. After a few minutes she left the room and made her way to the elevator. The door opened and she got in only to find herself in the presence of Mr. Epstein.

"You were good, I'll grant you that," he said sardonically, " except this is an open and shut case. We've got him down cold and unless you change sides, you'll go down with him innocent or not."

"Is that a threat or a promise?"

"Neither. It's a fact. By the way, my wife wears your designs. She likes them."

"Great! What about your girlfriend?"

Epstein blushed. "Cute, real cute! He's going down. I hope you don't."

But he was right! Within a month of the trial one investor after another pulled out. Within three months, the contracts stopped coming in. The IRS took a very long close look at Cele's financial records. She personally went out, barnstorming buyers but the scandal kept many of them leery. Time after time she was rejected with the same old story. "Can't do it Tina, we have to be careful. We have a reputation to maintain." In less than a year, the business that Cele had founded and nurtured as carefully as a baby was bankrupt. Cele left town.

~ * ~

The Angelini brothers put up a good defense and the government's case was beginning to fray around the edges. Lu was very encouraged until one day toward the end, the prosecuting attorney came forth with one final witness, Vinnie Perinni, Reggie's dad. He came in and didn't even look at Reno. Lu's heart sank. Why? Why is Vinnie turning against her father? For God's sake they were *paisans*, friends, neighbors. She was not prepared for what came next.

The prosecutor began with questions about Sal Roccollo's death and it came out. Sal's death was no accident. It was a hit ordered by someone to silence him. The word was that Sal was going to talk about some illicit activities involving money laundering. His notebook detailed transactions that were out of the ordinary. While the dry cleaning business was thriving and he managed several stores, the money coming in was phenomenal. Thousands of dollars a month that could not be accounted for were being deposited in accounts under the business's name. The last part of the testimony was most damning. Vinnie broke down on the stand.

"I asked you for help, for justice to find the killers of my son-in-law. You told me you would take care of it and yet nothing happened. Six months went by, nothing. We asked again, your cousin and I pleaded for help and still nothing. Finally we went on our own. We went around to ask and that's when we found out you did nothing. You never made any inquiries. Nobody knew anything and you know why? Because you, *you* ordered the killing yourself! You were the one who ordered the spilling of Sal's blood. You made orphans of my grandchildren by killing their father. Still you weren't satisfied. You ordered a hit on my daughter, my Reggie driving with her kids, and these killers came out and were going to shoot her right in front of the children, then turn the guns on them. My Reggie, my grandchildren running for the rest of their lives as I will have to. Blood calls for blood. I wish you rot in hell. I spit on all the years of our friendship."

While pandemonium broke out in the chamber, Lu covered her face and ears with her hands. She stood up and screamed, "No! No! My father is innocent. He is not a murderer. He is not a criminal. He is a good man, a good father."

She broke down and was escorted out by Victor Angelini. She turned and looked at her father. He had his back to her. She called out his name. He never looked back and he never answered.

~ * ~

Lu sobbed on Victor's shoulder for what seemed like hours. He got her a cab for the trip home, then went back to work. The damage to their case was extensive and both brothers needed to put their heads together. They did succeed in part. The prosecution was never able to prove it was Reno who ordered the hit on Sal. They couldn't prove some of the money laundering charges. Loan sharking was dropped. What the government was able to do was get Reno on tax evasion, extortion and some of the minor charges.

~ * ~

The job of telling Rosa about Reno's sentence fell to Lu. She and her mother sat in the darkened den of the family home. Rosa never came to any of the court proceedings but she kept up with the events through the papers and the Angelini brothers.

"Say something Ma, please. Talk to me."

Rosa broke her silence and began. "I'm sorry you had to go through this alone, Lu. I wasn't much help and neither was your brother. Junior wanted to come but I told him no! You could get away with it because of your last name but they would pick on Junior because he's a Roccollo and that would make his life so hard. You know how he's trying to become a lawyer. His name would make it impossible. He'd always be remembered as Reno Roccollo's son. I couldn't come either. I tried a couple of times. I got dressed and went into the city alone one time but I couldn't do it. I couldn't see him sitting there. He probably didn't want me there anyway."

"Ma, please, you know that's not—"

"Yeah, it is Lu. He's a man full of pride. He wouldn't want me to see him that way. And besides, the day I was planning to come was the day Cele was there. I wouldn't want to see her and embarrass her."

"Embarrass *her*? You're worried about *her* feelings? After what she did to you and to us, the family? She's the last person I would worry about." Lu spoke emphatically.

"I knew about her. I knew for years."

Lu was dumbfounded by her mother's revelation.

"You knew? And you never said anything? Ma! Why didn't you do something?

"Like what?"

"Give Pa an ultimatum. Tell Cele she was never to come around to your house. Anything! You just didn't have to take this lying down you know!"

"I knew that but what good would it have done, huh? Besides I wasn't that upset. In fact I was a little relieved. I knew Reno would never divorce me. I got the assets like the house and money. What else would I have wanted?"

"How about your husband's love?"

"Lu, your father and I have been married almost thirty-eight years. But that doesn't mean we loved each other for thirty-eight years. I never told you but this was not the marriage I wanted. This was the marriage my father and Poppa Roccollo wanted. Reno wasn't thrilled either but this we had to do if his family and mine were to survive.

"What choice did I have? Reno didn't have a choice either. We made the best we could of it. Cele wasn't the first but I will say she was the one who lasted the longest. Maybe Reno did love her. I feel sorry for her because now she has nothing but trouble."

"Did you know what Pa was into? You know, being part of the Mob, that kind of stuff because I didn't. Listening to everything they said in court was like seeing our life in a new way. The Mafia for God sakes."

"Sure I knew, how could I not with my father and Poppa R. We all knew and I knew what I was getting into. My only fear was that something would happen to him and I'd be alone raising kids. Thank God that didn't happen. One condition I made when I got pregnant with both you kids was that *never* were you and your brother to know. Reno agreed and he kept that promise to me."

"How did you handle all of this alone? You could never tell anyone what—"

"Oh come on, all our friends knew. They were part of it, too. Vinnie Perrini, Frankie Damato. I wasn't alone. I had the company of other wives who were in the same boat. We helped each other just like my mother and her friends. We prayed together, we played together, we cried together. You know your Sisterhood. It's nothing new, Lu. I had one too."

"What are you going to do now, Ma? You want to come live with us?'

"Naw! I think I'm going to enjoy being free for a while."

"Free?"

Rosa shook her head indicating that the conversation was over.

Reno received a sentence of twenty years in a federal penitentiary. He refused to allow Lu or Rosa or the family to visit him in prison.

~ * ~

The day after the sentencing Lu, Caroline and Jimmy Jr. were at the table having supper. It was a very quiet meal as nobody felt much like talking. Rosa declined to join them saying she really preferred to be alone at this time. Lu heard the garage door go up and a few minutes later Jimmy Cianci walked in. He got a frozen look from Lu and a lukewarm reception from the kids.

"Well so much for hip, hip horray, Dad's home," he said sarcastically.

"Daddy, it's seven thirty, we've been waiting for you to come home. We started dinner without you," Caroline said looking sadly at her father.

"Sorry Buttercup, I got hung up at the office and I was late going to the gym for a workout. Hey, Jimmy, word has it that sign-up for Spring League is on Friday of this week. You and me got a date to sign you up. Yankees, Mets, look out for Sizzlin' Cianci!"

"Sign-ups were last Friday Dad. I already heard from my new coach. We start next week."

"Uh, sorry about that. Time flies when you're busy."

"Kids, leave the table. I wanna talk with your Dad alone for a few minutes. I'll do the dishes tonight Caroline. You and Jimmy will owe me tomorrow. Go on!"

"No! I haven't seen my kids all day. I'm their father. I'm entitled to their company when I get home from work."

"Kids, leave now! Please!" Lu's voice was stern.

Caroline and Jimmy looked at their mother and each other. Caroline nodded at her brother and both slid away from the table silently.

"Why the hell did you do that? I gotta a right to see them."

"Oh yeah, were the hell were you yesterday and today? You know what a traumatic time this has been for them. They loved Pa and they are taking this badly. Why the hell couldn't you be around and be supportive for them! Working out my ass! You were working out with your dick."

She stood up and went into the laundry room and returned to the kitchen table. She threw a small square package on the table.

"This was in the pocket of your gym shorts. I washed them today. Since when do you need a super-sized condom?"

"Since I started working out my pecker has grown a couple of inches and the ladies appreciate that I am careful."

"I bet the whores do!"

"You can call them what you want, at least they are *real* women not some pompous Mafia ex-princess. You heard me—ex-princess! What are you gonna do now that your old man is a jailbird? Huh? Who are you going to run to for protection? Boy, Reno's sentencing was a good example of how money talks. All the stuff that he was into and he gets twenty years. He'll be out in ten! He got less than what he deserved."

"You bastard! After all he did for you!"

"After all he did for *me*? What exactly did he do? He made me a 'manager' at his used car lot then he wouldn't let me manage my way out of a paper bag. *Everything,* everything I ever wanted to do, he would squash me down like a bug. I had lots of good ideas, things I wanted to do to make the business even better and he just tossed them out of the window. He made me feel like a worthless piece of shit!"

"Maybe he saw your true value!"

Jimmy raised his hand and was inches away from Lu's face when she screamed.

"Get the hell out of here! Get the hell out of this house now. This house that you've been living in so well was meant for me! This was his house for me because he knew you could never give me what I deserved. Take your stuff, your gym shorts, your super-sized condom, your black book and your clothes and get the fuck out of here. My father may be headed for prison but Reno Roccollo still has friends here that are loyal. If you ever touch me, all you'll get for the rest of your life are blow-jobs because you'll have no hands to put your dick in for a *workout* with your whores."

With that Lu walked out of the kitchen. The marriage was over!

Eighteen

1977

A cold, raw March wind blew down the concrete canyons of New York, chilling the people who scurried around its streets to the bone. Lu walked down Fifth Avenue and despite the spring outfits being featured in the store windows, there was nothing that warmed her heart. The trial had ended. Her ordeal, and her family's, was over and what passed for normalcy returned. The scandal was all but forgotten as her neighbors got on with their own lives.

Back to normal... how could that ever be? Her father was gone, her marriage was over, her friends—her support throughout her whole life—were gone also. Cathy was somewhere in Mexico, Pat was hospitalized after an almost fatal dose of downers and Drambuie, Cele was out of the picture, and Reggie had dropped off the face of the earth. She gazed unenthusiastically at the Lord and Taylor windows wondering what Caroline might consent to wear for Easter. She felt a tap on her shoulder and her frazzled nerves caused her to jump.

"Whoa! Easy there gal! I just touched you with my hand not a gun."

It was Ricky.

"Hi! Don't mind me. I'm just a little jumpy these days. How are you?" she said giving him a hug.

"Okay! The question is how are you doing?"

"I'm doing... I manage but then do I have a choice? One of us has to stay strong. You know there's a guy in mythology. I just saw his picture. He's holding the world on his shoulders. That's how I feel."

"Yeah, his name was Atlas and I know what you're saying all too well. I've been holding up my share of the world."

"Yes, I know. Why didn't you call me? I would have come right away."

"She didn't want you, Lu. She didn't want you to see her the way she was. It was pretty bad, Lu. There were pills and bottles of vodka all over the place and she still denied using the stuff. That last weekend was bad especially when the kids found her. Another couple of hours or so she would have been..." Ricky's eyes misted at the thought. "Hey, can I buy you a cup of coffee? Or maybe on this cold day an Irish coffee sounds good."

"Yeah, you know I'd like that. Then if we cry, we can blame it on the whiskey."

Ricky put his arm around Lu and walked down the street until they found a quiet spot for a drink.

"Seriously Lu, how are you? How's your Mom?"

Without meaning to, Lu began to weep. For a minute she couldn't say anything and they sat in silence until their drinks came. Lu took a big sip.

"This feels good, it's warming me. Ricky, I'm so lost, so alone. That's what bothers me more than anything is this feeling I'm alone in the world. I've lost my world; my father is in prison. He was transferred there two weeks ago. The Angelinis said not to see him right now. In fact, not for a long time, per his request. I don't know him any more."

Lu wiped her eyes. "How can a man be my father for all this time and I don't know him? They were talking about a stranger in that court. My father is a good man. You don't know how good he is. They never brought up anything like that. He supported an orphanage in Sicily for years. He sent money, lots of it, every Christmas. He loaned money to friends without expecting repayment. I know he donated money to the church. Salvation Army always got a contribution. You know he was the one who paid off Joe Ferrara's debt to Carmine Torino because he didn't want Cathy's dad to get hurt. To this day I bet she doesn't know that. He was a good man. Why? I have to know why he was treated like such a monster!" She drank some coffee and waited for Ricky's answer.

"I don't know what to say, Lu. To me, Reno Roccollo will always be a great guy. Maybe he was set up by somebody who had a vendetta against him. He was a powerful man and men like that have enemies. I don't know. Just keep thinking what a fine father he was and tell that to your kids over and over again. That's what I'm doing with the boys. I keep reminding them that Pat is a great person, that she loves them, she's a good mother and that once she gets better she'll be that way again. I can't destroy that image of her and you shouldn't either. How's Jimmy?"

"Ha! Ever hear the story of the rat deserting the ship? After all that my father did for him, setting him up in business after we got married. What were the Ciancis? Nothing, for God's sake! Jimmy's father was a produce manager at the A&P store. Jimmy got set-up in a used car business, my father got us the house. Jimmy never had it so good. So how does he repay all this? By walking out. Good riddance! He's got nothing now except Miss Tits. If he came crawling back on his belly, I wouldn't take him. He's been screwing me for years and I finally got wise."

"The kids?"

"They don't seem to care one way or another. My mother, however, is doing fine. Great in fact, like she has lost a weight around her neck. After the initial shock, she bounced back better than any of us. It was as though she was free. She's a changed woman. I've never seen her this peppy, this alive. It's like looking at a new person and I have to wonder was I that blind all these years? Did I not see my folks as human beings? Did I not see what was going on between them?" She changed the subject. "Where's Pat now?"

"She's in Connecticut. There's a place in Hartford where they treat people like her." Ricky could not bring himself to say "alcoholic" and "addict."

"I'm not supposed to go up to see her until she's ready. That's what the rulebook says. You want another Irish coffee?" he asked.

"Yeah, in fact I would. This is the first time in a while I feel warm inside. Mostly I've been cold like ice."

Ricky signaled the waitress for another round. "What have you heard from the rest of the Sisterhood?"

"I heard from Cathy. Do you know this trial even made the news in Mexico or wherever the hell she is? She wrote a real nice letter, really very nun-like about there's goodness in everyone and how we should remember the good stuff."

"And Cele, how's she taking this? I heard she did a heck of a number on that prosecutor. I wanted to come to court and show my support but I had to work and with Pat and everything. I would have liked to see her in action."

"Cele and I don't see each other any more."

"Oh it's because of your Dad. Well, I can understand that."

"What do you mean?"

"Lu, it was common knowledge. I suspect even your Mom knew. I'm surprised that Cele let it continue for so long. She seemed smarter than that. Maybe she was being used and didn't know how to stop or figured if she did stop her business would grind to a halt and you know how she felt about that business of hers."

More tears came. Running out of tissues, Lu wiped her eyes with her hands.

"I never talked with my father about it after I found out. I kept it a secret trying to protect my mother. Later on in jail I spoke of it just once to him. All he said was he loved her, Cele that is. That was the first realization I had that maybe I didn't know Reno Roccollo. My Mother knew! I guess I've walked around with blinders on all this time. Then when Vinnie Perrini got up on that stand and said that about my father... I couldn't take it."

Ricky picked up Lu's hand and kissed it. She held onto his hand. They sat and talked and comforted each other. It felt so good to talk with someone and share the pain. They reminisced of happier times, spoke of mutual concerns and laughed at the absurdity of life.

"How about dinner?" Ricky asked. "I'm tired of pizza, take-out, Chinese food. How about a nice dinner, a bottle of wine and I'll get you home sort of reasonably early"

~ * ~

The dinner was long and relaxing. Neither of them wanted the evening to end. Misery loves company!

The blustery winds gave way to a cold driving rain and they snuggled together in the taxi ride home.

"The kids are out. Caroline is spending an overnight at a slumber party and Jimmy is at a friend's. That's why I went into the city this afternoon. I knew I wouldn't have to hurry back. Would you stay? I don't want to be alone. I need..."

"Sure, why not."

Ricky poured each of them a brandy. The fireplace was lit and good old Elvis sang his heart out on the stereo. When Elvis sang *Are You Lonesome Tonight* Ricky and Lu slow-danced, cheek-to-cheek. A kiss at the end of the dance led to another and another.

"I have a favor to ask you," said Lu. "Don't think the worst of me but would you screw me in Jimmy Cianci's bed. That would be the best revenge I can think of."

"No! I want to screw you and have you return the favor but not with any shadows in bed with us."

"There won't be anything between us, believe me, not even a rubber."

Lu turned off the lights and led Ricky upstairs. They undressed each other slowly.

"I always heard you were one damn hot chick. Those stories are obviously true."

He unhooked her bra and slipped off her panties. Lu fell back on the bed and as Ricky bent over her she tugged at his shorts.

"Just as I suspected," she said kissing him.

"What was that?"

"That you were better than averagely endowed." She sat up and kissed and licked him all over. Their mutual pleasure drowned out the sound of the howling storm.

~ * ~

Pat took the train back to New York. She was doing so well with her treatments that the doctors had okayed a weekend trip home. She wanted to surprise her family. She arrived at home to joyous greetings from her sons and mother. Ricky, she was told, was in Italy for the week on his usual business trip but would return tomorrow.

"How happy he will be to see you looking so well," exclaimed both sons. It was good to be back and not see her home through a haze. She lovingly touched her pictures. She smoothed out the coverlet on her bed. She sniffed the bottle of aftershave on the bathroom counter. Pat went downstairs and happily took requests for dinner.

"You know what I really want," said her oldest son Anthony, "some of your tuna fish casserole."

"But you never liked it."

"I didn't but I missed having it like I missed not having you around."

"I want those cheese-stuffed hot dogs and the salad with all those different kinds of beans in it," chimed in John.

"I made them all those things," said her mother.

"Yeah but not like Mom. Moms do it best of all."

~ * ~

"Hello, Ciancis."

"Caroline? This is Aunt Pat. How are you?"

"Hey, Aunt Pat, Mrs. Tomasino told Grandma you were home. How are you?"

"I'm doing fine, really I am. Is your mom home? I really want to talk with her."

"No, she isn't. She's taking some time off. Mom needed a break. She's gone to Europe just to get away but she will be back sometime soon. I don't know exactly when but Grandma does."

Rosa came on the phone.

"Pat, oh my God, it's good to hear your voice. Come over sweetheart and we'll talk. Lu is coming back tomorrow. She'll be so glad to hear from you. She missed you."

"I've missed her too. I've missed talking to what's left of La Sorellanza. I've heard from Cathy and I've heard about Reggie. I'm sorry, Mrs. R."

"That's life for you. Come tomorrow night if you can. Surprise Lu."

"Well, maybe on Sunday, Ricky is off to Italy this week on a business trip. He'll be back and I want to spend time with him."

"Sure thing sweetheart, but we'll see you all right?"

~ * ~

Pat dressed with extra care. She tried on a dozen outfits trying to find the right one. She had lost so much weight that most of them hung on her. " First thing, I'm going to eat like there's no tomorrow she thought. No fettuccine Alfredo will be safe from me."

She took a cab out to Kennedy airport and went over to the Alitalia baggage pickup. Ricky would be arriving at the usual time. Perhaps they could stop for coffee before they got home to the boys. A few minutes alone was what she wanted. The passengers began arriving to claim their luggage. That's when she saw them. Laughing, Ricky and Lu walked with their bags. Ricky had his usual one small bag. Lu had three oversized bags. Both laughed more as

Ricky groaned his way lifting the bags for the customs inspector.

Pat was surprised but not as surprised as when she saw Lu reach up and kiss Ricky. It wasn't an old friend kiss. Ricky laughed and threw his arm around her and got a cart to haul the bags out through the door to the waiting area. Ricky pushed the cart through the throng of people with Lu right behind him. Pat stepped up and stood in their way. They blanched as they saw Pat.

"Hi!" exclaimed an obviously disconcerted Ricky, "When did you get in? Why didn't you let me know?"

"You were in Italy. I wanted to surprise you and obviously I did. Both of you."

"Pat, it's not what you think!" cried Lu.

"You don't know what I think. No explanation is needed."

With that she walked away and turning back she murmured, "*La Sorellanza*! Fuck it."

~ * ~

Two days later, Pat returned to Connecticut to the hospital where she had been treated. She was very proud of herself. She did not drink or take any pills to ease her pain from the past weekend. Her doctor nodded when she told him of the events that transpired and her reaction to them.

"That's a great sign Pat. You're obviously getting well when you can withstand a trauma like that without falling back to using your old crutches." He referred to her now acknowledged alcoholism and drug dependency. "You deserve a big, *Atta Girl*."

A few weeks later Pat checked herself out of the hospital and came back home. She was needed there by her family. The previous week, Ricky had been arrested and charged with conspiracy to smuggle drugs into the country. She had to be strong for her sons and she was.

"Tell me what happened," she asked when she got home and unpacked. The boys were off to school and her mother had been home taking care of them.

Clara Damato just shrugged. "I don't know all of it. One day last week Ricky goes to work. The next thing I know is I get a phone call from him. 'Call the Angelinis. I need them down here in jail and don't let the boys know. I'll get out as soon as I can on bail and for God sakes don't call Pat.' What could I do? I called the brothers, told the kids some fibs about Ricky and I didn't call you. Bail was set at two hundred and fifty grand. Where were we to come up with that kind of money? I don't have that much. The Campiones didn't either. We could have put the house up but he decided no. That's when I called you and told you. How are you doing Pat?"

"You know Mom, I always knew this would come to a bad end. I lived in dread for so long. Every time I tried to tell someone about my feelings, including you, all I got was put down. Ricky kept telling me I was crazy. He was too smart to get caught. He knew what he was doing. Mom, you didn't help much either". Pat looked at her mother "You just didn't believe me. When Sal was killed,

I just knew Ricky was going to come to no good. I prayed and prayed he wouldn't end up like Sal. Reggie was right and I was too." Pat sighed deeply.

Clara for her part said nothing for a long time. "What do you want me to say to you? Ricky never discussed business with me. He said back when you were going to get married that he was going to do everything he could to give you the good life. I was thrilled! God knows we weren't poor but it was a struggle no matter how generous Reno and the bunch was. That's why you didn't go to college. You were smart enough but I couldn't afford it. I never said anything because for the first time in your life you were living like I had hoped for you. You had a nice beautiful home and new cars and nice clothes and you went on trips. You had everything I couldn't give."

Pat wearily rubbed her eyes, then leaned over and hugged her Mother. She held her for a long time saying nothing.

"Mom, I had everything but peace of mind. I knew what Ricky was doing. Do you know he even got me to do something for him? When I found out, I never went on another trip with him to Italy. I shut my eyes and opened my mouth for booze and drugs instead. I should have spoken up more. I should have taken the boys and gone on my own. I should've told someone—you!"

"I'm not the one to tell anything to, Pat. I never said anything to you, never said anything about your father or how we lived. I kept my mouth shut too. Like mother, like daughter, I guess."

"Tell me what about my father?"

"Frankie didn't die in a car accident. He was working for the Mob just like everyone else. Just like Reno, Vinnie—the whole bunch. He was killed in a robbery. He was the getaway driver. He was shot. Died a few blocks away. Some of the guys managed to get out. To keep me quiet, the Mob paid for my expenses. They got the house and they paid some of the bills. Reno was generous, I'll say that for him. I never told you. You know *Omerta*, silence to the death."

Pat stood up and walked out of the room. She needed some space to absorb this news but deep down it didn't come as much as a shock. Maybe she had known the truth all along.

When the boys got home from school, all four of them—Pat, the two boys and Clara—sat down and mapped out a plan for their future.

"The first thing I promise you, I will never go back to doing what I have done and that was to drink and use drugs. The second thing I promise you is that I will always tell you the truth about our situation. I will tell you both good news and bad news and we will take it from there."

She stuck to her promise. As soon as it was possible Pat arranged to meet with Ricky in jail. She knew she couldn't face this alone so she called for help from Cele.

"Hi girlfriend." Cele hugged Pat. "God, it's good to see you. I'm surprised you want to see me. I am a leper you know."

"Hey, you know what I kept hearing in all those months of treatment? 'That which does not kill us makes us stronger.' We'll get through this. You and me. With the exception of Cathy I guess, that's all that's left of La Sorellanza. Have you heard anything about Reggie? Where she is? How she is doing?"

"No! It's like she fell off Jones Beach Pier and was swept away. I've called dozens of times. No answer. I wrote. I drove to her house. It was empty, dark, nothing. The Perrinis, the same thing... *niente, nothing, zip!* You know I heard about this program the Feds have where they take people away and give them a whole new identity, everything brand new and it's not just for Communist defectors either. Do you think she and the kids are in that?"

"I don't know."

"Okay, what can I do for you Pat?" Cele asked. "What's on the agenda?"

"Cele, can you come with me to the jail? I have to see Ricky and I need you to back me up."

"I think he'd rather see you alone!"

"No, I don't expect you to go in with me but could you just wait outside and be there when I come out? Can you take that much time off from the business?"

"Sure thing, hon—there is one thing I have plenty of right now and that is time on my hands."

"Your business is not going well? You were raking in the bucks. I remember a penthouse on Park Ave."

"Things change. That was then, this is now!" Cele looked away, blinking back tears. "It's been five months since the trial. I've lost most of my contracts and all of my backers. I've let people go left and right and I'm back to where I was ten years ago... or worse."

"You got taken in on this too huh?" Pat asked sympathetically.

"When do you want to go and I'll be there."

It was obvious to Pat that Cele did not want to talk about it.

Pat, with Cele as backup, saw Ricky at the jail. They sat opposite each other in a communication booth. Pat had a hard time looking at Ricky.

"Are you doing okay?" he asked. "You're handling everything?"

"Yes, it's all right to ask me if I have relapsed. The answer is no! This is no longer about me. I've got kids to think about and the life they are going to have. The Angelinis are representing you? How do we pay them? What do you want me to do?" Pat was all business.

"I don't suppose you'll believe me when I say I'm sorry for everything. I was really trying to give us a better life—better for you, better for the kids. I wanted you to have the best."

"I *had* the best when we were first married. I had you. That's all I wanted. I tried to tell you that so many times. You just never seemed to listen or care what I said. *You* had this grandiose plan for us. Granted you worked hard at it and granted it was nice but really Ricky, it was your plan. I never had a say in making it."

"If you were so unhappy why in hell didn't you leave—just get the hell out?"

"I didn't have the guts to then."

"Then? I suppose you have the guts now unless they're all rotted out with booze and—"

"I don't need to hear that from you. I came here to plan the next steps so I could tell the boys what's coming next."

"You don't tell the boys anything. Tell them I'm fine and I'm going to beat this rap."

"I'm not lying anymore to anyone. They know you're not going to beat this. You're not going to get away. They're not stupid. They know what conspiracy to smuggle in illicit drugs entails. They know what money laundering is. I kept telling you about being careful with those jerks in Italy. I kept saying to you that you are being used. *I told you so!*"

"Well, does that make you feel better? Are you feeling justified now?"

"I'm not sure what I'm feeling but I know I have the strength to make some changes in my life for the better."

"How's this for a change? Go get a divorce. Go make a better life for yourself since you've had such a bad one with me. Get out of here."

Pat reeled at Ricky's words. Silently she got up and walked away.

Cele saw her friend come out, pallid as a ghost. Both women were silent as they drove back to Queens.

"You going to be all right, Pat?"

"Yeah, fine."

Nineteen

Tapachula, Mexico 1977

Cathy's mission in the Mexican state of Chiapas was in Tapachula, not too far from the Guatemalan border. There was great poverty here. The population was mostly poor farmers, descended from Mayan Indians. The people hacked out a living on small plots of land or worked for the large coffee plantations. Yet there was a residual joy in the people who lived here. Life was hard but never so difficult that they could not smile.

Cathy felt at home here just as she did in Patzcuaro. She had been there five years and probably would be transferred soon to another mission, which needed her talents. She spoke Spanish plus the local dialect and her smile and personality made her an immediate favorite of the local population. In fact she had been visiting a parish instructing catechism when she was asked to come to the local medical clinic and help translate the visiting medical team's requests. Cathy pedaled up to the clinic and got off her trusty rusty bike. She could hear some fractured

Spanish from two young men who were directing the local men unloading a truck of supplies.

"OK, put *el boxo* in the second room on your *righto*, got that?"

The man nodded and carried in a large box. He was followed by some other workers carrying in equally large cartons. They were obviously going the wrong way much to the consternation of the young men.

"Hi. there." Cathy laughed "Maybe I can help? Exactly *where-o* do you want the *box-o put-o*? It's good to hear American spoken even if it's a little weirdo. How about them Yankees?"

The men breathed a sigh a relief. One of them spoke up. "Please tell them that those boxes go in the second room on the right and be careful with them because there are some medicines packed in them. I don't care much for the Yanks, being a true-blue White Sox fan myself. I'm Ed Hoffman."

"Hi. St. Louis Cardinals. Jim Custer."

"Nice to meet to you both. I'm Cathy Ferrara, uh, Sister Catherine of the Maryknoll Missions. Let me translate for you. *Cargar la caja con cuidado. Contiene medicina.*" In a matter of seconds the workers were complying with the new directions and the unloading continued smoothly.

"Are you doctors?"

"Not yet. Jim and I are med students who got shanghaied into coming down here for two weeks. After that if I last that long with this humidity, we go back to the States and work." He mopped his brow with his shirt.

"How do you stand this? I thought St. Louis was bad in the summer but this sucks," Ed commented.

"It takes a while but you get used to it. Some of Chiapas is highlands and while it's warm it isn't quite as humid up there. Just take it easy, drink lots of fluids and call me in the morning."

"That sounds like good medical advice. We learned that first day in med school, the part about calling in the morning. What do you do here, Sister?"

"We have a school and orphanage, a shelter for girls, a small home for the elderly and we used to have a clinic but now we send our sick people out to some of the other clinics here in the city. When I travel to the outlying regions I take a small medical kit with me for inoculations and very minor patch jobs. Who are the doctors..."

She was interrupted by the appearance of a tall, leggy green-eyed blonde who looked more like a model from Vogue than a health worker.

Cathy's eyes widened. "Wow!" she exclaimed.

The woman smiled and came over. "Hi, did I hear English spoken?"

"Yeah Doc. This is Sister Catherine from a mission here. She's been translating to the workers." Jim introduced Cathy.

The blonde smiled a picture-perfect even-toothed smile. "Great! Thanks, French was my language. I'm lost here. I'm Christie McGoff."

"Are you the doctor?"

"Yes I am. You look surprised."

"Well, uh, truthfully you look like you just stepped off a magazine cover."

"Oh pul-lease!"

The two guys laughed. One of them said, "Sister, you just blew it. Dr. McGoff is very sensitive about that."

"I'm sorry really. That was a, what do they call it in the States, a sexist remark. You'll have to forgive me but I've been away so long I forget to use the right terminology. If I hurt your feelings, I apologize."

"Apology accepted but as a penance for that remark could you ask the men to carrying in that autoclave very carefully and set it up in the treatment room. That's where we'll be doing some procedures. This clinic is awfully small and space is at a premium."

"Not a problem. Just tell me where you want it."

Dr. McGoff led the way with Cathy and the workers following carrying their precious cargo.

"Will you be staying long?" asked Cathy. "I'm not too proud to beg for some of our *povrecitos,* our poor ones, who are so in need of medical care. Can you see a few of them for me?"

"Sister, I would love to, really I would because I can see that there is a lot of work here but we already have a full docket and we haven't even set up yet. Our schedules have been planned for us. We start tomorrow and my fiancé and I will be here for a week or two, then some Seventh Day Adventist medical people will follow us. Please leave me your number and if there is any time off we'll fit something in."

"Well, I would need a little more time than just an hour or so. The people who live way outside in little villages are the ones who really need the help. The city people have access to some aid but it's those people who live far away who have nothing," Cathy pleaded.

"Okay Sister, I promise I'll try. You know I have a few Catholic friends and they told me about nuns and guilt trips."

"It works!" Cathy giggled.

"Somewhere in this mess, and I think I know where, we packed some Vita Pops. Lollipops with vitamins. Would you like some for the kids?" She left the room and Cathy heard her say to someone in the hall, "Honey, do you know which box we packed the lollipops in? I'm going to get some."

A voice answered her, then Cathy heard someone come into the room. It was Joe Dobek! Her heart stopped and she paled. The two looked at each other without speaking for what seemed like hours. Cathy looked down at herself. She had ridden her bike through some puddles. There was mud on her shoes and skirt. She knew she was windblown and sweaty. Nervously she smoothed down her skirt and brushed her hair with her hand trying to tame it. Joe broke the silence.

"How are you, Cathy?" he asked quietly. "I-uh-I never expected to find you here. How long have you been here?"

"Four... five years, Joe. I came here directly from Patzcuaro. It's good to see you. You are looking great."

"Thanks, uh, you're looking fine too."

That was the end of the conversation as both tried very hard to compose themselves after this surprise meeting. Christie walked back into the room with a plastic bag.

"Honey, this is Sister Catherine. She's a missionary. This is Dr.Dobek. Sister has been translating to the workers and she wants to know if we can squeeze in a visit to the outlying towns to see some patients."

Joe nodded but avoided looking at Cathy. "We've met already. Um, sure we'll see what we can work into our schedule. Just leave a place where we can get in touch with you." With that he walked out of the room very quickly.

"How about a Coke? And I brought some Cheetos down with me. That's my one addiction. We can split a bag and perhaps you can tell me about any one or two particular patients you think we need to see."

Cathy shook her head. "Thanks that's awfully nice and I haven't had a Cheeto in years but I have to get back and you have lots of work to do." Cathy was numb as she answered.

"Yeah, we do and we'll be in touch Sister. Do I hear a Brooklyn accent?"

"Queens. I'm surprised, after being away so long I thought that I had gotten rid of it. I guess you just can't take Long Island out of a girl."

Cathy couldn't wait to get out. She pedaled furiously until she reached her mission and quickly walked in without speaking to anyone. She went up to her room, sat down and tried to compose herself. It had been five years since she last saw Joe. He had asked her to come back with him to Chicago, to be with him through med school. Now he was a doctor and he was engaged to another doctor who looked like a model.

"I'm happy for him she said to herself. Then the tears started to flow and they would not stop. She heard the evening bell chime. It was suppertime and she was expected to be down to help serve the meal but she couldn't do it. All she could do was to cry. *I made the right decision then, I know I did but why do I feel like this... so empty. Why?*

There was a knock on her door. "Cathy?" It was another one of the nuns inquiring after her.

Drying her eyes, Cathy replied, "I'll be down in a minute after I wash up."

She went into the bathroom. She looked in a mirror and a face looked backed at her. She really never spent that much time looking in a mirror. Nuns weren't supposed to do that but here she was staring at herself. A tan face looked back, red-rimmed brown eyes, the beginnings of crow's feet from too much squinting in the sun, the short usually disheveled hair had some silver strands running through already. Suddenly she felt very old, much older than her thirty-seven years.

She splashed water on her face and dutifully went downstairs to help with supper. Evening prayers brought no comfort to her. She had this feeling of insignificance, without substance but most all of abysmal emptiness. These feelings would not go, no matter how hard she tried to pray them away. She forced herself not to go to the clinic where Joe was working. She was afraid of what she would do or say. Her downcast manner was noticed by all, especially the children who could count on her for fun and games. She withdrew from conversations with the other nuns who worked at the mission. A week went by and in the second week she got a message saying that time was available, if someone would come with her, to visit a few outlying villages. She prayed it would be Joe.

Eagerly, she was up early the next morning and got ready, paying a little more attention to herself. Her hair was freshly washed and she put on her best skirt, if one could call it that. The truck drove up from town and Christie McGoff got out. Cathy's face fell. She had hoped Joe would come. Christie cheerfully greeted her.

"We will go to three villages. One of them is about three hours away and we'll work our way back to here. The sisters suggested a few patients they especially think you should see. You have no idea how grateful we are."

Cathy got in the truck and there on the seat was a bag of Cheetos.

"I thought we'd share a bag and talk," said Christie. "It seems we have a lot in common."

"I don't know about that," laughed Cathy, "a beautiful doctor and a plain nun? We don't play in the same playground."

"Well, we do share Joe in a way," Christie said softly.

That took the breath out of Cathy who stammered. "Uh-well-well, that was several years ago and-and how did you find out?"

"Joe and I have been together for almost two years now and I'm getting to know him a little. He's not too talkative a guy so when he stopped talking completely I knew something was up. He told me about meeting you and everything. Actually I wondered about you long before I met you. I saw him the first day at med school and I knew right from the start he was what I wanted. He paid virtually no attention to me at all. At first I thought he was gay, then I thought he was married, and I thought he must have loved someone and it didn't work out. I was right. It took me two years of flaunting myself shamelessly before he ever gave me a tumble. I wanted to kill whomever it was who hurt him so badly. I never thought it would have been a nun."

Cathy didn't know what to say.

"There was never anything between us, I mean, physically of course. I was-am a nun but yes I did like him very much. What's not to like? He was fun, kind and wonderful with everyone. Being a nun doesn't mean you can't have feelings... you just don't act on them. I made a vow to God and I had to keep it. It was as simple as that."

"Well, I'm glad you did. I love him!" Christie stated that simply.

Cathy didn't say much about the matter after that. They talked about the cases that were awaiting them in the villages. There were five serious cases. One was a severely cross-eyed child who was doomed to a life of misery and taunts. There was a boy with a cleft palate who was three. How he lived so long was a credit to the loving care of his family who patiently fed him drop by drop. A young girl of ten had been burned as a child and now hideous scars marred her face and neck. There was a young pregnant woman expecting twins or triplets. A multiple birth with no medical attention was a death sentence for both mother and babies in such primitive conditions. Last, there was a teenager who had a deformed spine and since walking was impossible, he learned to scoot around. Christie was shocked as she examined the cases.

"You were right, there is such a need here. You could spend forever and still not make a dent. Most of these cases are beyond our scope of practice. If you can get the young mother to the town, we could make arrangements at the maternity hospital. The others will require extensive surgery. I don't know what we could do about those."

"Probably not much but thank you for trying."

Christie drove back and Cathy tried her darndest to keep the conversation light. As they came to the mission Cathy got out and thanked the young doctor profusely.

"Cathy, I do love him and I promise I'll take good care of him."

Cathy just smiled and waved good-bye. "Please do," she whispered.

The following days were no easier. Cathy tried harder than ever to forget about the past. Three more days and they would be gone... two more days and Joe would leave... tomorrow Joe and Christie would be gone and it would be easier knowing he was no longer in the same town.

There was a visitor one of the staff announced to Cathy. She walked into the office and standing there was Joe, dressed up. Cathy's heart hit the floor.

"I thought you had left already, Joe."

"Two o'clock this afternoon but I had to see you one more time. There is good news for you. Christie's family established a medical foundation back in Chicago. She comes from a long line of very wealthy physicians who have a sense of *noblese oblige*. They are very generous with their contributions. Christie asked for funds to help those people she saw. Arrangements will be made to provide for their surgery and recovery."

Cathy gasped, "That's incredibly generous and how wonderful! Thank you doesn't seem to be sufficient. I'm sure you had something to do with it."

"No, it was her idea entirely. She's really a good kid."

"I hardly consider her a kid. She's very beautiful and obviously smart and I know she loves you very much. I understand you're going to be married in two weeks."

"Yeah, that was part of the deal. She could have a huge wedding for her family but we had to come down and do some charity work first. I had no idea where you were and I was as surprised as you were when we saw each other."

"It was a shock!"

"You know Cathy, it took me a long time to get over you. I know we only knew each other for a week but in my heart I felt like you were the missing part of me and when we met I knew I had my other half in you. I felt complete. When I got my acceptance notice to med school I wished to God you were there with me to share in my joy. Do you know I actually rented a small place for us when I got back to Chicago? I was so sure you would come and join me. You never did." Joe stopped talking for a minute. "When I saw you this time the old feelings came back. I still feel the same. Cathy please, I would stop the wedding now. We could live together and have a good life. It's not too late."

Tears filled Cathy's eyes. "I... I... have to think about it."

"This time you have to think fast, my plane leaves at two. This time I want you to be there."

"What about Christie and your life together?"

"I like her so much. She's great and I don't know why but she thinks I'm great too. But she's not you! Men flock around her like bees to a honey pot. She would have no problem finding a replacement for me. Will you come?"

Cathy found herself nodding. She quickly walked out of the room. Going upstairs she went to the storeroom and found the small suitcase she'd brought with her. She put in her few possessions, then walked downstairs. She went into the chapel and knelt.

"I came to say good-bye. I'm leaving here. I've done a good job here and in Patzcuaro. I have tried to take care of your flock as You would want. But I want him. I want all the things that life with him will bring—love, marriage, children, a home. That's not so wrong is it? I feel so empty, so hollow. I need him to fill me. I'm sorry I didn't stick with you to the end."

Then she got up and left.

Cathy quickly walked across the compound carrying her suitcase. Children and people stopped to talk with her but she gently brushed them off. It was noon and she had two hours to get to the airport. What she would do when she got there, she had no idea. She didn't have any money or a ticket home but that didn't matter. Being with Joe did!

She heard someone call her name. Obediently she turned around. It was Sister Anastasia, the mission head.

"Cathy, are you going somewhere?"

"Yes, I am, I'm leaving, Sister. I'm heading back to the States. I have to go home."

"This is a surprise to say the least. Cathy, you never said anything at all to me. Why, all of a sudden? I don't understand! Did something happen... are you so unhappy here?" Sister Anastasia was truly shocked. This was so unlike Cathy.

"I've been happy Sister, five years and I have been happy. Really! But this time I can't let Joe go alone. I can't miss out. I've done a good job here Sister but now it's time for me to—"

"Does this have anything to do with the man who was here this morning to see you?"

"Yes! It has everything to do with him. I met him five years ago and he asked me then to return to Chicago with him. I told him no that time. I can't say no again. I'm sorry Sister. I hope you understand and will forgive me."

"It's not up to me to forgive you, Cathy. This is not a prison and you can leave at any time but have you thought carefully about it?"

"What's to think about?" Cathy answered impatiently. "He still loves me and wants me to return with him. We can have everything in life I have missed—marriage, a home, kids a chance at happiness."

Sister Anastasia nodded. "I can't argue with that! But tell me, can you be happy knowing that your happiness is based on someone else's sadness? Wasn't that lovely lady doctor engaged to him? Isn't that what she said when we met the other day?"

"Yes they are engaged but as Joe said it won't take her long to find a replacement."

"Have you prayed about this?"

"No I haven't. I'll pray later on for everything. Right now I have to get to the airport. The plane departs at two. I'm sorry, I really am sorry but I hope you understand."

Sister Anastasia shook her head. Tearfully she raised her hand and reluctantly made a Sign of the Cross on Cathy's forehead. Then she left without saying another word.

Cathy left the compound and got a bus to the center of town. From there she would hitch a ride to the little airport. From there she would be on a plane with Joe and on to Chicago and a new life.

Once in town she found hitching a ride was not as easy as she had hoped. It was one o'clock and she nervously paced by the square holding out her thumb. Finally a truck stopped and she explained she needed a ride to the airport. The driver agreed to take her. The truck rumbled along at a very slow pace. Cathy kept wishing it to go faster but the truck just wheezed along its way. Twenty minutes to two, the airport was in sight. Another five minutes until it pulled up to the front door. Cathy bounded out and headed for the airport's one ticket counter. There were not many travelers around. A clerk appeared at the counter.

"There is a flight that leaves for Acapulco at two. I am supposed to meet someone here. Have you seen them? They are *norte americanos.*

"*Ah, Si*! There were four of them but that's all. No one else had called for reservations so the pilot left earlier."

Cathy staggered back at the news. The plane left early! Without her! Oh God, what was Joe going to think? She told him she would come! She would be here!

"I'm sorry *Hermanita*, if we had known of another passenger he would have stayed until two o'clock. There is another flight tomorrow at the same time."

Cathy walked out of the airport in disbelief. She begged a taxi driver to bring her back to town, which he grudgingly did and from there she returned to the mission. She had no where else to go. The children saw her coming and a dozen of them ran to greet her. They were so happy she was back. Cathy, however, was not. Silently she railed against God. He was the one who delayed her departure so she didn't get to the airport in time. He was the one who didn't want to her to be happy. He was to blame. She returned to her old routine but without her customary gusto and enthusiasm. She went through the motions of working and praying but she felt nothing. Within the month, Sister Anastasia came with the news that Cathy was being recalled to the Motherhouse in New York. She was to leave immediately.

"I think it is best for you, Cathy. Everyone here will miss you terribly but I feel that this is the time for you to stop doing and start being. You need to reconnect with yourself and God and the only way to do this is to go on a spiritual retreat. I will pray so hard that you make a decision that is best for you. If you feel that you must leave, then so be it. You have been such a blessing to everyone. But please make this choice prayerfully not just on a minute's notice. God bless you!"

Twenty

Los Angeles, September 1977

Cele sat in her car at the Los Angeles bus depot, waiting for a bus from Phoenix to arrive. Cathy had phoned her a few days ago. It was a complete surprise that Cele welcomed wholeheartedly.

She had been in LA for a few months and she hated it. It wasn't just that she had to leave New York after selling what was left of her business. It was the feeling that she had been defeated by all that had transpired. The IRS went over her books with a fine-toothed comb and a magnifying glass trying to tie her in with Reno Roccollo. They had come up empty but that did her reputation no good. They didn't even send so much as a "sorry and you're in the clear" letter. Just a promise they would be checking on her in the future.

She had left for LA thinking she could start anew but luck did not smile on her so far. She worked in an upscale dress shop in Beverly Hills where she put her sense of style to good use. She quickly became a top salesperson. The bus finally showed up twenty minutes late. As she got out of the car, some underage street girls hit her up for change.

"Sorry fresh out."

"Bitch!" one of them responded as they went off to hit upon another person.

Cele and Cathy spotted each other and ran together for a quick hug.

"God, I'm so glad to see you," each told the other.

Cele drove straight to her condo and before long Cathy was sitting on a patio with a Margarita in hand. She told Cele nuns were permitted to drink Margaritas under special circumstances.

"Do you remember when we used to play Twenty Questions years ago? Let's play now. You go first," suggested Cathy. "I want to hear all about you."

"No! You go first. My twenty questions will probably run into two hundred and I will need more Margaritas before I'm done. It'll be more like a confession."

"Fire away!"

Cele scrutinized her friend closely. "Okay, here goes. You've been here almost an hour and you don't look like Cathy Ferrara. What have you done with her? You look like a hollow imitation. How's that for a start?"

Cathy took a sip of her drink. She couldn't swallow it for a minute. "That's probably because I'm not Cathy Ferrara anymore. I don't know who I am."

"Jesus!"

"I'm on my way to New York to the Motherhouse for a long retreat. I got permission to visit my Mother in Phoenix like I told you on the phone. After less than two weeks I thought it was time to leave. Funny, we ran out of things to say to each other after two days."

"How's she doing?"

"Life hasn't been kind to her lately. She's got some health problems and financially she's barely hanging on. She lives in a tiny two-bedroom single-wide in a trailer park and she has to work. She likes her job in a fabric store in a mall. Quite a comedown for a woman who once had three fur coats in her closet. My father really left her in a bind. When she went to sell the house, she found out that he had taken out a second mortgage to pay his gambling debts. By the time she paid off everything, she had about five hundred dollars left. You know just when I think I have resolved past issues with my Dad, I find out something like this and I hate him all over again. But what bothered me most was seeing Carol. She was so pretty. You should see her now. She's a scruffy-looking bleach blonde who lives with a guy who treats her like scum but provides her daily drugs. She's had two kids by two different men and several abortions. I saw her twice and the last thing she said was that it was all my fault. I should have bit the big one and married Nicky Torino so she and Mom wouldn't have to live in poverty. We could still be living in New York in our nice house and Dad wouldn't have had to leave like he did. Maybe I should have. Maybe I wronged Nicky."

"Oh for God sakes, Cathy! Has hindsight dimmed your memory? Marriage to Nicky and having Carmine Torino as a father-in-law! You know he was killed—gunned down by a Jamaican gang muscling in on his turf."

Cathy bent her head as she whispered a prayer.

"Girlfriend, what's really bothering you?" Cele asked solicitously.

"A spiritual crisis," replied a tearful Cathy. "I'm thinking maybe I shouldn't have been a nun after all. Maybe I had used the convent as a way to escape instead of facing everything and working it out and now it's come back to haunt me."

"That's not it! What else?" Cele was not going to let Cathy off the hook.

"I met someone and I fell in love."

"So what! Marry him for God sakes!"

"It was five years ago. He was down with a medical team. We worked together for two weeks, then he left. He asked me to come back with him to Chicago. I prayed about it but I couldn't. I took a vow and I couldn't break it. I got over it and went to Chiapas. I prayed for him every night like I do for all of you. Two months ago he came down with a volunteer group. He is engaged to a woman who has brains, beauty, and money I gather. She's a doctor, too, like he is. Joe said he still loved me and asked me to come back with him even though he was going to get married shortly. I said yes and I went to the airport but I was late—fifteen minutes too late. Fifteen minutes! That's what separated me from being with him— of having a home and kids with him. Fifteen minutes! I blame God. He could have helped me after all I had done for His poor people."

Cele was silent. She did not know what to say. She just let Cathy cry. Several Kleenex and some more Margaritas later it was Cathy's turn to ask the questions.

"How are you doing, Cele?"

"Surviving! I hate LA. It's so plastic but I had to get out and away from it all. You were right. I did hurt a lot of people by being with Reno. I don't blame him or myself. I knew what I was doing so I too have to pay the consequences. Lu found out and that was the end. Somehow Reno was deeply involved in a bunch of shady stuff, which was brought to light by Sal in a journal he was keeping. Reggie found it, turned it over to the FBI like a good citizen and all hell broke loose. You know it was Reno who fingered Sal... at least that's what Vinnie Perrini said." Cele looked up at the ceiling and blinked back tears.

"I don't know what happened to Reggie. She has vanished completely with the kids. In spite of my best efforts, I couldn't find them. The fallout hit Ricky as well because Reno was a partner in Rick's company that wasn't only dealing in plumbing supplies. Ricky is in prison too. I spent the last night with Pat before I left. She and I are the only ones left of the sisterhood who are speaking to each other, except for you. She's having a rough time but to her credit she's not drinking a drop. Sober as a judge. You know she always suspected that Ricky was involved with something. She told me that once at Sal's funeral. That's why she drank. So Sister Catherine, that's all the news fit to print. Reno, Ricky in jail; Reggie in hiding; Lu and Pat not speaking; me running out with my tail between my legs and you, the saint, having second thoughts about everything. What's going to happen?"

"We are being tested like 'gold tested in fire'."

"How biblical!"

"Once I watched an artist in Mexico make some jewelry. He fired up the metal, then poured it on and began to beat it into shape—pounding at it, re-heating it until he had made a beautiful shiny piece. That's what's being done to us maybe. Pounded and shaped and molded and we will be beautiful when we are finished."

"Bravo, beautifully said, but let me tell you something. It hurts to be pounded down."

Cathy and Cele stayed together for three days, then Cathy left for New York.

A few days later Cele ran into someone she had known in New York. The woman suggested a trip to Las Vegas because she knew someone who knew someone who knew everyone there and the person claimed there were plenty of opportunities in that desert town.

~ * ~

Cathy spent two months in the convent, two months of concentrated prayer and discernment. God and she made up. They were friends again. One of the surprises she had were several letters from Reggie to Cathy asking for her whereabouts and could she please get in touch. Cathy happily responded. In fact she wanted to get in touch with all her sisters, one by one.

~ * ~

Pat was in the kitchen when she heard the doorbell ring. She ran to the buzzer and rang it, opening the outside door. She could hear footsteps in the lobby and she ran down two flights of stairs. Cathy was coming up. Pat hugged her so hard and so long that Cathy grabbed on the railing for balance.

"You don't know how much I have wanted to see you and talk with you, Cathy. When I heard from Cele that you stopped in to see her I prayed I would get the same chance. Pat led Cathy up to her apartment.

"You're staying the night I hope."

"Yeah, Mother Superior let me out for good behavior." Cathy answered impishly.

The two women sat down for a long talk session, so long in fact that neither noticed the lasagna was well done.

"How are you doing Pat?" Cathy asked solicitously.

"You're using the same tone of voice that Cele uses every time she calls," Pat replied. "I'm not that fragile. I won't break and it's okay to ask me any questions. I'm very honest in my answers. I am doing well. I'm a recovering alcoholic and drug addict. I don't use the stuff anymore. I don't need it. My plate's pretty full with everything. I'm going back to school as soon as I can. I sold the house as we needed the money but this is a nice place and the kids are doing well. They were little the last time you saw them but they have heard so many Cathy stories they are eager to meet you. They'll be home later and so will my Mother. She's been a godsend."

"How's Ricky?"

"In prison, twelve years and he was lucky to only get that. The Angelinis put up another good defense for the Roccollo Mob," Pat said bitterly. "The boys go up with the Campiones every month but I don't. I don't want to see him at all. I'm still very bitter as you probably can tell about everything that happened. I'm trying very hard to put that behind and get on with my new life."

"I can't imagine how hurt you have been." Cathy said sympathetically.

Pat took a deep breath. "You have no idea. All those times when he lied to me about his involvement—all those times he called me paranoid when I told him my suspicions—he told me I was stupid and later on a drunk and there he was cooking up deal after deal with the Mob in Naples to bring in the stuff. I think I could have handled all that but then the crowning blow was the Lu business. Ironically that's what made me get well."

"The Lu business?"

"You mean Cele didn't tell you? She does keep secrets! Cathy, Lu and Ricky were having an affair at a time when I was very vulnerable. Yeah, I know I was drunk and stoned out of my mind but to learn that my husband and best friend were in bed consoling each other, drives me nuts. All I can think about was the two of them laying there laughing about me. In jail, he has the nerve to ask me for a divorce since as he put it 'my life with him was hell.' No! I most certainly don't go to see him."

"You have a lot of bitterness toward him!"

"You bet I do, Cathy. I know it's not very Christian. Forgiveness and all that but it still galls me. I cannot forgive him or her."

"Don't look at me Pat. I still struggle with that. I thought I had settled with my father and yet just recently when I visited my mother, I heard about everything he had done. You know she's living on a bootstrap and has for years because he gambled away everything. Once again I feel like I still can't forgive him and it has been years. I won't give you advice. I have none to give."

Their talk was interrupted with the arrival of Clara Damato and Anthony and John.

There were hugs all around and lots of joking about well-done lasagna. Pat seemed less tense with her sons around. They would be her salvation, Cathy decided. Early the next morning while Pat was in the shower Anthony came to Cathy with a request.

"Cathy, uh, Sister Cathy, I know you're Mom's closest friend and maybe you can help her. She refuses to see Dad in prison. I don't know what happened between them. I know only that he asks about her every time we go up but she won't even discuss it with us. She just slams the door on that one."

"Your Mom loves you guys more than anything and if she doesn't listen to you, what makes you think I will have better luck? Right now perhaps it's best to back off. When you get hurt so badly, you need time to heal your wounds. Until that happens you can't forgive because it's just lip service. Once time has gone by and the healing process starts, then you can bring it up. Until then, you and John will have to love both of them and be patient with both and an occasional prayer would help." She smiled. " Remember RICE—rest, ice, compress, elevate. Let your Mom rest, let her get back her self-confidence and self-esteem and compress her with hugs and elevate your wishes in prayer. It might work."

"Hey you two, is that a serious conversation I see going on?" asked Pat coming into the kitchen.

"No we were talking about RICE—rest, ice, compress and elevate when you get hurt." Anthony and Cathy smiled at each other.

~ * ~

Cathy's visit came to an end. She gingerly skirted around the issue of going on to see Lu, which she was planning to do next. She merely said Mother Superior had let her out for only so long.

"I love you Cathy." Pat was already teary-eyed. "Pray for me."

"Always, Pat. *Sempre come sorelle*," whispered Cathy hugging Pat tightly.

~ * ~

The taxi stopped in front of Lu's ranch-style house and very manicured lawn. Cathy got out and started up the walk. Halfway up, she saw the door open and screams of delight from Lu and Rosa.

"Oh my God, it's our Cathy," Rosa gave Cathy a huge bear hug and passed her on to Lu who hugged her equally tight.

"I can't believe you're here. God it's been so long. The last time you were here it was your party when you took your vows."

"Yeah it was, I bet you didn't think I would last this long. Come on, admit it, Lu."

"Let's put it this way, I was hoping you wouldn't last this long. I found some pictures of the party the other day and I have them out for you to see. There's so much I have to tell you, I hope you're prepared to stay a week. After supper or tomorrow, we'll drive to some of our old haunts. I think we can see Mrs. Tomasino, too. Ma told her you were coming. She's still sharp as a tack. Her first comment, 'She's still a nun?' She hasn't forgotten you.

Rosa poured wine while Lu got some snacks. Rosa nudged Cathy and whispered, "It's good you came, she needs you."

"How are you doing Mrs. R. I pray for you and Mr. R, too."

"I know that, you're our special angel. I know you wouldn't forget us. I'm doing okay."

She heard Lu coming to the room. "We'll talk later. I'll share you now with Lu. Lu, I'm going to make some zabaglione for Cathy. She always liked it. You got enough eggs or if not I'll run to the market, anything else you need?" With that Rosa left.

"You liked her zabaglione? God it's so sickeningly sweet."

"Hey, when I was a kid, I ate everything in sight including that. You look fabulous. You're even prettier than before if that is possible."

"Yeah, thanks." Lu spoke unenthusiastically at the compliment.

Cathy looked closely at Lu. "You're having a hard time aren't you?"

Lu dissolved in tears. "I look this way because that's all I have to do is concentrate on myself. I put everything on the outside because the inside is so rotten."

"Lu, how can you say that? You're not to blame for what happened. Your Dad made some bad choices that affected all your lives. He has to pay now. That doesn't mean he's totally evil. When I heard about... well, everything, I still couldn't believe it. Mr. R was and will be special to me. I think of all the good things he has done and I know what he did for my father—settling his debt.

La Sorellanza (The Sisterhood)   Barbara Wilson Wright

My mother told me when I visited her. My father would be dead probably if it wasn't for Mr. R. I will always remember that and I pray for him."

"Well you're probably the only one. Cathy, it was so bad at the trial. It's been over a year and I still remember sitting there and hearing all those things. I didn't know my own father just like you didn't know about your own dad—you know, his gambling and everything. I'm torn between wanting to hate him because of what he did and wanting to love him. Cathy, he won't see us. Not me, the kids, not my Mom or Junior. No one! He doesn't write or call. Nothing! Cathy, did you know about him and Cele? Did you know they were together since my wedding? That, I think, started it for me. It's been downhill from then on. Pat's drinking, Reggie... Jimmy leaving me."

"Jimmy's gone?"

"Oh, hell, yes. Thank God! That's the only good thing that happened out of this. He had been screwing around for years and I was the last to know. I didn't know about him, or about Cele and Pa. I knew nothing until it was too late. Am I that dumb or just blind?"

"Maybe neither, maybe you just loved them too much. After all you were a good daughter and a good wife."

Lu didn't respond. Finally she asked, "Have you seen any of the others, Cele or Pat?"

"Yeah, I spent a few days with Cele right when I first came back last year."

"You've been back since last year and you didn't let me know until now?"

"I came back late last fall and spent some time with my Mom in Phoenix. Then I stopped by with Cele for a few days. I have been on retreat for the past couple of months. I needed to work out a few things myself. I'm okay now."

"Now it's my turn to ask, what happened to you?"

"Oh, I guess I got tired and burned out. I started to blame God. I had second thoughts about everything—what I really wanted out of life."

"You mean like maybe you shouldn't be a nun. Heck, we all thought so years ago. For a while you were so sure that is what you wanted. I guess we change over the years. What we want at twenty is not what we want now. Look at me and Jimmy. God! I wanted just him. I was so happy when we got married. That was going to be heaven."

"You know your wedding was such a pivotal event in our lives. Each one of us was affected in such a big way by it. Think about it. Reggie met Sal, Pat met Ricky, Cele started thinking about your Dad and her business and me... well there was Nicky. That one event changed all our lives."

"Hey, speaking of Nicky, I gotta tell you about him. You wouldn't believe it if you saw him. He is so changed. Your know his father was killed, shot down in cold blood. Cathy, you won't believe the old neighborhood. Nothing is like it used to be."

"Neither are we, Lu."

Lu nodded in agreement. "Back to Nicky—you know when his father was killed we went to the funeral, Ma and me. After all, my father knew him! Hundreds of people around and Nicky comes up to greet us. He's lost about ninety pounds. He hugs me and Ma and says that he knows they did some things that were not right but neither Reno nor his father deserved ending up like they did. I was shocked. I've seen him a couple of times since then mostly at funerals. All the old folks are either dying off or moving away. Cele's family is the only one who still lives in the old neighborhood. One time he asked about you. He said do I still have that friend who was a nun and I said yes. He asked if you were really intending to be a nun at that time or whether it was just because of the circumstances, you know. I was so surprised I can't remember exactly what I said. Something about, well, you had a serious side that we never realized. Can you beat that? The guy actually turned out nice. I guess that goes to show you nothing is as it seems at the time."

"I'll add him to my prayer list."

"Cathy, did Cele say anything about what happened?"

"Yes, I think she's sorry."

"Well," Lu paused for a minute, "we all do things we are sorry for."

The conversation ended.

The next morning before she left Lu and Rosa took Cathy for a ride around the old neighborhood. The houses did not look as happy as they did when she lived there. Her old house was a bit run down not quite like the beautiful place that she thought it had been. *I guess it's like me.*

When the time came for the final good-byes Lu could hardly get through. She was crying so hard and she held on to Cathy forever.

"*La Sorellanza*, Lu, *sempre come sorelle.*"

"Will we be that again, Cathy, or is it over for us?"

"It'll never be over Lu, not for us."

Cathy returned to the Motherhouse that evening. There was a letter waiting for her from Cele.

Cathy,

I know this is your doing. I know you have been praying for me and it's worked. I'm in Las Vegas now and have been for a month. I like it and believe it or not I have a job with prospects for growing. Looks like you've got to stay in, Cathy. God listens to your prayers. Keep praying. If, however you should decide to get out, you will come here and together you and I will set Las Vegas on its ass... oops I mean, ear.

Love you,

Cele

Cathy smiled. Cele was right. I do belong in the convent and that is where I'll stay till the end, she thought. She felt peaceful, having said that. Mother Superior was delighted with Cathy's decision.

"Whenever you are ready Cathy, your next assignment will be Guatemala."

"I'm ready! On my way down there I would like to stop off in Florida if I may. I have one more 'sister' to visit."

"Oh yes, your friends, your *other* sisterhood. How did your visits go?"

"I have a lot of praying to do."

~ * ~

Cathy arrived at Reggie's house to the same enthusiastic greeting she had received everywhere. Hugs and tears and more hugs.

"You know you're the only one I wrote to," explained Reggie. "You're the only one I could trust not to say anything. I'm still so cautious."

"How are you managing?"

"Some okay days and some not! I still look over my shoulder all the time. Maybe eventually that feeling will go away. I get frantic if the kids are even one minute late. A month ago Anna asked me if she could go to the mall. We made arrangements to meet at a certain exit after. I forgot that there were two other exits from the store and I went to one and waited there. After a while I got hysterical. All kinds of thoughts were running through my head. She was waiting for me at another exit and she too got scared. By the time we connected we were both crying our eyes out. The people must have thought we were crazy as we hugged and cried in the mall. Cathy, I tell you honestly, I would never do this again. I honestly think I would prefer death to living this way. At least if we died, we could be with Sal again."

Cathy did not respond but continued to hug Reggie.

"Tell me did you see anybody when you were in New York?"

"I drove past the old neighborhood. It's changed. My old house looks a bit seedy. I understand Cele's folks are the only ones left there. I didn't see them."

"I suppose you saw Lu?" Reggie asked venomously.

Cathy was surprised by the caustic tone of Reggie's voice.

"What happened?"

"I don't imagine she told you. You know, Cathy, it was Lu who sold me out. She sold me out to Reno. I can't believe she was capable of doing that. She was my friend for God sakes! Why?"

Cathy was dumbfounded by this information. She just shook her head as Reggie went on.

"After I found Sal's journal I turned it over to the FBI. They had been to see me and talked with me about Sal's death. They too thought it was no robbery. I had to tell someone. This was just too much for me so I talked with Lu one time at lunch. She kept telling me not to trust them. Meanwhile it was her I shouldn't have trusted. She must have told Reno. Just a few days later I pull up to a stop sign. The kids were in the car with me. Two guys in front get out with guns and they were going to shoot me. One had a gun at Anna's head. Luckily, I was being followed by the FBI and they shot one of the guys. Immediately they took us to a safe house. We couldn't even go back to our home. Not ever! I had laundry in the dryer. I had sauce cooking on the stove. I haven't ever been back. They packed up everything and arranged to sell the house. The kids and I lived in secret for almost three months. Cathy, I hate Lu so much right now. I can't even think of her without wanting to puke. She totally ruined my life and my kids' lives too. You have no idea what evil I have wished upon her. I regret they didn't kill Reno just as he ordered my Sal to get killed. I'm consumed with this hatred! I'll never get over it."

"No, not right now. You're still in too much pain but someday you will have to make peace with yourself."

"I'm not into this peace and forgiveness."

Cathy shook her head. "It will take years."

"By the way did you know your father is supposed to be here someplace in Florida? Do you know where?"

"No, I don't think my mother knows either. I thought I had forgiven him long ago but when I see the way my mother has to live because of him, the old feelings still take over and look how long it has been! But eventually Reggie you will have to come to terms with this for your kids. They will have to learn forgiveness from you."

"Well not for a hell of a long time! You know what I miss a lot. The fact that I can't write or talk with Pat or Cele. I can't even contact them. The sisterhood is dead, Cathy. It won't ever come back."

"Perhaps it will someday. I believe in miracles."

After a few days Cathy took off for Guatemala where she would spend the next seven years.

Twenty-one

Las Vegas, 1984

It was a day as hot as only Las Vegas can be in late June. Cele had been working inside an air-conditioned room. She was putting the final touches of some Fourth of July costumes. Her eyes ached from looking at thousands of red, white and blue sequins. She got into her car and turned on the air-conditioning full blast. She made her way onto the parkway and headed home. She had been in Las Vegas for seven years and in the biblical sense they were seven years of plenty. Cele came to Las Vegas with an acquaintance and wound up staying. She had found her niche. She was back, designing costumes for showgirls instead of dresses. This was fast-paced work well suited to her level of energy.

Her condo in Vegas was her refuge from the heat as well as the activity. She came in and flopped on the sofa with the daily mail in hand. There were the usual ads, a bill or two, and a letter addressed to her from the Angelini Brothers Inc.

"Jesus, after all these years what do they want?"

She opened the letter and began to read.

Dear Miss Benedict,

We got your address from your parents. They said you have been living in Las Vegas for a number of years. Great town! We took our wives there a couple of years ago and we had a fabulous time. I wish we had known you were there because we would have looked you up.

We have some sad news to share with you. I hope you don't mind us telling you. Last month Reno died in prison. He had cancer.

Cele re-read that part again and again. Reno was dead! She crumpled the letter in her hand and from her body came a sorrowful cry. Reno, her Reno, the man with whom she was passionately in love for all those years, was gone. While she had gotten over the end of the romance, he was still very much a part of her. Every man she knew since then she would compare to him and usually they were found lacking. None whom she had met had the powerful effect on her that Reno had. No one came close to his vitality, his zest for living, his passion and his skill as a lover. Sobs and tears overwhelmed her. She felt herself not being able to breathe. Getting up from the sofa, she paced the room calling out his name.

"God, Reno I loved you so. Did you ever realize how much? You were everything to me and now I have nothing, nothing of you. Why wouldn't you let me have your baby? At least now I would have something of yours. I wouldn't have cared what people said."

The tears fell unabated. Finally Cele sat down and took the letter and smoothed it out. She continued reading it.

> *He was diagnosed a couple of years ago but refused any kind of treatment. His son claimed the body and brought him home for burial in the family plot. The funeral was quiet and private by the family's request. However we felt that you would want to know.*

> *We hope we did the right thing by telling you. If ever there's anything we can do, please let us know. We plan to visit Las Vegas again soon. Maybe we can meet you and talk about the old neighborhood that has gone to hell. Things don't ever stay the same.*

> *Sincerely,*

> *Vic and Angelo Angelini*

Sleep did not come to Cele that night or for the next few nights. There were times she felt she was going mad with grief. *I've got to talk with someone.* Immediately she decided to get in touch with Cathy. Cele called the motherhouse in New York and somehow got an address of the mission in Guatemala City. She sent a telegram asking Cathy to get in touch immediately and sure enough a few days later she got a call late one night from Cathy. For the first few minutes Cele could only sob and it was not until

Cathy reminded her that she was paying for this call that Cele was able to speak.

"He's dead Cathy, Reno is dead!" and the tears began again.

"I'm sorry Cele, God rest his soul and I will pray for him daily. No matter what, he was still one of my favorite people in the entire world and I think only good thoughts of him. How are you holding up?"

"I'm not Cathy. I'm losing it badly. I can't sleep or think about anything but him and our life together such as it was. I regret so many things but mostly that I didn't have the guts to say the hell with the world and the hell with whatever people thought and just be with him."

"I can only imagine how you are feeling, Cele, but truthfully Mr. R. never would have permitted you to do that. You know that! I know how deeply you loved him. You told me that many times but while he may have loved you too, he would never have allowed you to disrupt his world. It would have ended sadly for you. He would have ended it. That's just the way it would be. I warned you so often about getting hurt. What are you going to do?"

"You mean, like go crazy?"

"No, you won't but you need to put some closure on this."

"Like how?"

"I don't know... maybe write to Lu and Mrs. R. You've got some apologizing to do, Cele. That will help as a start."

"Repeat that again, you want me to apologize to Lu and Rosa!"

"Yes, yes I do!"

"You're crazy Cathy, you've been out in the sun too long. Why would I ever do that?"

"Because your actions hurt someone probably very badly. Mrs. R. did not deserve that. You need to tell her you are sorry for the hurt you caused. She too has got to come to some sort of closure and this might help her as well as you."

"What are you bucking for—sainthood?"

"No but try it. I bet you will feel better after even if you never get a reply. What else will you do? Cry a river? Think about it. Love you. *La Sorellanza.*"

"*Sempre come sorelle,*" replied Cele not really meaning it.

A month went by and Cele was still grieving. *Damn you Cathy, why do you do things like this to me?* One day out of desperation Cele sat down and wrote a terse three line letter to Rosa Roccollo.

Dear Mrs. Roccollo,

> *I am sorry to learn of your husband's death. I want to apologize for the hurt I caused you. Please pass on my condolences to Lu.*

Sincerely

Cele Di Benedetti

Cathy had been right. While she did not get a response, Cele did feel better. Later on she wrote to Cathy to tell her.

Dear Cathy

I did what you told me. I'm putting it to rest. The only thing I still regret is not having something of Reno's to remember him by. Believe it or not I toyed once with the idea of having his child. I don't think he would have been happy about that. All I have left are some memories. They don't comfort me.

Cathy responded with an idea.

Cele, have you ever given thought to becoming a mother. No, I'm serious. You have so much love to give. Any child would be so lucky to have you as a mom.

You are generous, kind, talented and fun and no matter how much you protest that kids don't like you I bet you would be totally great. It would be the world's best-dressed child that's for sure. Think about that and I will start praying for that too.

"Oh God Cathy," said Cele when she read that. "Save your prayers for something else."

~ * ~

Lu tore open the letter from Guatemala. It was from Cathy. Even though Lu didn't like to write, she found great comfort in pouring out her soul to Cathy. Even from three thousand miles away, Lu thought Cathy seemed to understand.

Lu,

I'm worried about you. This is the second letter I have gotten from you and you still seem so depressed. Now it's time for a boot in the butt so if you're not in the mood for a lecture, throw this letter away now.

Lu, you are very pretty... you always were. I would have given anything to have looked like you. Beauty is a gift, capitalize on it. Why don't you go into the beauty business? Put what you know how to do and apply it to others. Show others how they can be more beautiful. I bet women would flock to you by the hundreds. You can tell them that true beauty comes from within but the outside counts too. You said in your letter you were not smart. I don't believe that for one second. Your father was smart and you must have learned something from him about business. Remember the lemonade stand we did for the Missions in grade school? We had no business on our street. Your Dad comes along and says, "Advertise, change the location, make people want to buy your drink." We made signs, moved to the Boulevard and we made ten or twelve bucks Remember? Your Mom had to go to the store for more lemons. She probably spent more than we made. You could do something if you put your mind to it. Now get off your size 6 ass (yes I said ass) and move it in the right direction. No reason why you can't have both beauty and brains.

Love you Lu. I think of you a lot, my sister. La Sorellanza. Pray for me as I do for you.

Lu got up and poured herself an iced tea. She sat down again with Cathy's letter. A business? Yes it was true while her father never discussed his business at home he did make comments about other people's businesses. Usually they were negative. At least she would know what not to do. She never thought about it but her father must have had some business sense. The more she deliberated about it during the next few days, the more excited she got at the prospect. Maybe a business gene was buried somewhere in her body. She'd show them that she was more than a pretty-faced ex-Mafia princess.

Twenty-two

Guatemala, 1985

The bus ride from Guatemala City to the little town of San Ignacio was six hours long. It felt like twelve hours as the rickety bus chugged along at forty miles per hour on downhill runs and wheezed at twenty miles per hour uphill. Most of the trip was uphill. Sister Cathy Ferrara was in the country for about seven years now. She loved Guatemala because of its beauty of both land and people.

In 1985, this was a country in turmoil. The ruling class of people owned eighty percent of the land. Poverty was prevalent everywhere, the country's infrastructure was abysmal. Education and health care was scarce especially for the indigenous population. Worse yet was the presence of army-backed right wing death squads who roamed the countryside at will, murdering and torturing anyone whom they perceived to be a dissident or guerilla fighter. Bodies appeared at the roadsides, often mutilated beyond recognition, to serve as a warning to the population.

Sadly, the US government was backing this regime financially. It was not a good time to be here but this was also a place of great need. Cathy spent the first part of her trip quietly praying. The next part was amusing the small children aboard who were restless and the last part she spent rocking a crying baby so the poor frazzled mother could get some rest. At last the bus reached its destination and Cathy gratefully got off with her bags. Sister Philip was there to greet her.

"Cathy, it's so good to see you. How are you? Did you have a good trip?"

"The question is, Sister Phil, how are you? How's the leg?"

"I don't know why people make such a fuss. In the end we are all going to die and all this hubbub is for nothing."

"Yes I know, but dying from a gangrenous wound on a diabetic leg is not the best way to go."

"Oh, and how would you like to go?"

"On a beach, at sunset, sitting in a chaise lounge, in a modest nun-like bikini, with a box of chocolates in my lap and a Pina Colada in my hand. That's the way to go."

The elderly nun burst out laughing. "Oh, Cathy, be serious."

"You're right Phil. Skip the Pina Colada, too sweet. Make it a Margarita instead."

"I hope you get your wish, Cathy. You always make me laugh. You are so full of fun. Come, you must be exhausted from that trip. Come rest up and we will visit and I can issue you orders for the next week."

"Mais oui, mon general," Cathy saluted and followed the nun to the mission building. On the way some teenage boys stopped her.

"Okay, *Hermanita Cassie*," they couldn't pronounce the "th" sound, "we play basketball?"

"In a few minutes, I have to speak with Sister Philip but then I will come out and I will beat you."

"Cathy, rest up first. Let me fill you in on the news while I make us some tea. Then you can tell me why I am being called back to the city."

~ * ~

Sister Philip reluctantly left the little mission the next day and she vowed she would be back as soon as possible. She issued Cathy a whole list of things to do. Sister Philip was a revered elderly nun. She had been here for decades and was actually more at home in San Ignacio than anywhere else.

"I'll be back shortly. Don't forget the altar boy practice later today and the girls' choir this evening. I have been bringing a little food to the Alvarados sisters every few days and—"

"I promise I'll take care of everything. You promise to get yourself looked after. *And* when you get back, you may be in for a surprise. I'll have everything done just perfectly."

"That sin of pride will cost you several extra rosaries tonight."

"Oh, Phil, I'm so far behind on all those extra rosaries, it'll take me forever. Have a good trip, get well, come back soon because I will have to be in Guatemala City in about two or three weeks if all goes well. Say a prayer for this special intention and mail this note for me. Here's the address. I want it to go off immediately. This is my special intention." Cathy handed her a soup label on the back of which she hastily wrote a letter.

"Last thing before I leave, there's been talk that the Army is on maneuvers in the hills by Paquin. Be careful. We don't want any incidents or run-ins with them. We have enough troubles without them."

After promising for the twentieth time that she would attend to everything as instructed, Cathy hugged the old nun and returned to the mission. Altar boy practice, yes, girls' choir, yes, but first a game of basketball, *yes*!

The week passed quickly. There was enough work at the mission to keep many people busy—classes to teach, clinic work, gardening to keep a supply of food, visiting the sick and elderly, although here in San Ignacio if people lived to fifty or beyond, that was a miracle. There were rudimentary health care classes. Simple things like hand washing, bathing, wound care and she didn't forget basketball. Working with the young was Cathy's forte. It was a case of mutual adoration. No matter how tired she was, she always found time to play or set up some kind of game. Nun or not, Cathy was fun!

A week later Sister Philip had not returned. A letter from the mission in Guatemala City stated that the elderly nun needed an extra week to fully recover, then she would be sent back because she was "driving us nuts" as the head of the mission wrote. The mission also sent some supplies and a part for a pump.

The little pueblo of Paquin had gotten a well installed in the center of town. This made life a little easier for the villagers as they no longer had to travel some distance just to get water for their daily use. The old pump had died and here was a replacement part. Cathy made up her mind that the next day or so she would take the old mission truck and deliver the pump herself. One of the villagers could help and she could install it. Cathy was very proud of her mechanical skills.

The next day brought some disturbing news. Some young men came to the mission at night. They told stories of an army raid on a few mountain villages. The army they said was looking for guerillas but somehow they hid and got away. Cathy was worried. Paquin was up in the mountains but it was a sleepy little village whose inhabitants were more concerned with farming their tiny plots of land than in fighting. She determined to go up and check on their well being. The next morning, cranking up the mission truck and praying for one more trip out of it before it went to truck heaven, Cathy left, water pump and tools in hand.

It was almost noon when she arrived and even before she drove into the dusty little pueblo, there was an ominous foreboding feeling. The silence was what she noticed first. No stray dogs barking, no children running about, no women at the stream washing clothes, no villagers waving as she drove past their huts. A chilling feeling ran through her. She entered the tiny square where her worst nightmare came true. Four army trucks were parked at right angles so they made a square. In the middle of the square in the hot sun sat many of the villagers, their hands on top of their heads. There was no place for her to turn the truck around. Some soldiers walked out of a house holding a dead chicken. They signaled for her to stop and get out.

"I'm Sister Catherine from the mission in San Ignacio. I came to deliver a water pump. What's going on? Who is in charge?"

The soldiers did not expect to find an American here in this place. They looked at each other not knowing what to do. The soldier carrying the dead chicken hid it behind his back.

"I will tell my sergeant that you are here, *Hermanita*. You had better stay here."

The soldier left and returned in a few minutes.

"The sergeant says you are to stay in one of these houses until the lieutenant or captain come."

"But what's going on?" demanded Cathy. "Why are those villagers sitting under guard out in the hot sun. What's happening?"

"Please go *now* into that house and stay there. Do not come out."

Cathy went into the little house. It was a one-room adobe covered hut. The one room acted as a living room, dining room, kitchen, and bedroom for a family. She went in and sat down her ears straining to hear anything. She waited for a half-hour. No one came so she ventured out and went to the next house. It was empty. The next one was also empty. She went to the last hut on what passed for a street. Behind it were some woods.

Going inside she found six children huddled together. A young girl around thirteen was trying to soothe the terrified youngsters.

"*Hermanita*, the soldiers came this morning. They took some men away," the young girl explained tearfully. "Then they came back and took all the others and put them in the plaza. My mother told me to take some of these children and hide. I can't find my sister. I'm afraid to go out and look for her. These children are crying and I'm afraid if they make too much noise the soldiers will hear and come back for us."

"No, you did right. You did exactly what your mother told you to do. All right children, let's play a game. Let's see how long you can go without making a sound. I have my watch and the one who can be the quietest will win a prize. Ready?" Cathy put her finger to her lips. She got up and went to look out the back at the woods nearby. If she could get these children out and to the woods they could hide until the soldiers left.

She walked to the front door and peered out. The coast was clear. No soldiers were visible.

"That's wonderful *ninos*," she said with a smile, "I'll have to give all of you a prize because you are all so good. Now listen to me. We are going to tiptoe out of the house and go around to the back. Then, quick as a lizard, we are going to run into the woods and hide. Of course there can be no talking while we are running, otherwise you'll lose."

She motioned to the children to line up. Picking up the smallest, she headed for the door and went out.

"Hold it right there. Where do you think you're going?" Two armed soldiers were walking toward the group.

"Please, let these children go. Let them run into the woods. They won't hurt anything. They are so young. Have some mercy on them. I'll stay here."

One soldier was tempted to let them go but the other ordered them to stay. Two more soldiers came up to join them. They talked among themselves and one, the fat young man, motioned the group back into the house. He went in also.

Cathy sat down on the floor and the children gathered around her. She pleaded some more with the soldier but to no avail. He just kept eyeing the youngsters.

Finally he said to the young girl. "How old are you?"

The young girl refused to answer. She just looked down at the floor.

"Hey *chica*, I asked how old you were. Answer me!"

"Thirteen," she answered almost inaudibly.

He shrugged. "That's old enough. Get outside. The rest of you stay in here. You come out and I'll kill you."

He stood up and laid his weapon down on the floor and motioned to the girl to go outside.

Cathy was livid. "You can't do that. She's a child. What kind of perverted monster are you? For God's sake, leave her alone. Think of *your* sister."

The soldier snickered. "I don't have a sister." Then, grabbing the young girl by the hand he headed for the door.

"No!" screamed Cathy. "No!"

She ran for the door and blocked it.

"Get away, bitch, or you'll get some when I'm done. Then I'll share you with my other friends and after that you'll never want to be a nun again."

He laughed at his joke. Cathy launched herself at him. He pushed her away so hard that she landed on the floor.

"I can do it here, no matter."

He grabbed the girl tearing at her blouse. He leaned her over the little table. Cathy saw her chance. The doorway was clear.

"Run children, quickly into the woods. No noise and you'll win a prize."

The children sprinted out the door and she herded them toward the woods. Then she returned to the house. The soldier had unzipped his pants. He held the young girl by the hair and forced her head back. With his free hand, he fondled her breasts and moved to kiss her on the mouth. His fat lips puckered up. Cathy ran in and threw herself on him jumping on his back.

"Nina, run!" she commanded and the girl leaped off the table and headed for the door. The soldier was trying to get Cathy off his back but she held on with a firm grip around his throat.

"*Ayuda me*, help me, Manolo, help," he yelled.

He slammed backwards into a wall and that caused Cathy to lose her grip. She slid off and on to the floor.

"Fucking bitch," he snarled, "let's see how you like this."

He jumped on top of Cathy and tore at her dress. She fought back kneeing him in the groin. He howled in pain and rolled off. His gun was on the floor. He grabbed the barrel and swung it at her, stunning her. Cathy lay motionless.

"Manolo," the soldier yelled again for his friend. He was not able to stand because of the pain. His friend appeared at the door.

"Get me up," he snarled. "I'll teach that bitch a lesson."

Manolo helped the fat soldier to his feet. Then he reached down for the gun and pointed it at Cathy. Before Manolo could stop him, he fired his gun at point blank range. Cathy's body jolted as the bullet entered her shoulder. Blood quickly flowed out of the wound.

"Jesus, God, what the hell did you do? You shot her, you imbecile." Two other soldiers ran up.

"Who did you shoot?" one asked.

"He shot the *gringo* nun."

"Christ, we were looking for her. The captain wanted to interrogate her. What are we going to tell him? Go on, get out of here."

"She attacked me. That whore jumped me and attacked me. I was just tying to protect myself."

All the soldiers left the hut. Cathy moved a little. The floor underneath her was covered with blood. She put her hand to her shoulder to stem the bleeding. Looking around the room she saw that no one was there. Good she thought to herself, the kids got out. They made it. She crawled to the doorway leaving a trail of blood along the dirt floor. She was getting very faint. *"Come on Cathy you can make it, come on."*

She crawled out of the door and lay there too weak to go on.

Down the street the soldiers were running toward the house. There was an officer with them. He quickly surveyed the scene.

"You fucking idiots," he screamed at the soldiers. "You created an international incident. You shot a *norte americana*. How the hell am I supposed to report this?" He grabbed his pistol and beat the offending soldier with the handle. Turning back he looked at Cathy who was on the ground outside the hut.

"Bring her here," he ordered. Two soldiers ran and dragged Cathy by the arms to the middle of the street. Cathy moaned in pain.

"She's still alive. We've got to do something." The officer thought for a moment.

"Go back to the truck, get one of the guns that we captured from the guerillas," he ordered one of the men. "She's as good as dead now. We might as well finish the job."

Cathy opened her eyes slightly. She looked at the growing pool of blood. She had one more thing to do.

"Daddy, it's all right. I forgive you. I'm sorry it took me so long."

The soldier came back with a rifle. The officer took it and fired two shots into Cathy.

"Take her out into the woods. Leave her there. The animals will do the rest. Take the truck far away and burn it." The captain turned around and left with one last command. "Make sure there are no witnesses."

The soldiers carried out their orders. No one noticed that Cathy Ferrara did not die as she wished. She did not die in a chaise lounge by the beach with a Margarita and a box of chocolates. She died on a muddy street in Paquin, Guatemala, fighting for the rights of others.

Twenty-three

Lu, accompanied by her daughter Caroline, stepped out of their car at the parking lot at the Maryknoll Sisters Motherhouse in New York. They had come for the memorial service for Cathy. Lu looked around. The last time she was here years ago was when Cathy took her final vows as a nun. Now she was here for a funeral Mass. They walked across the parking lot to the chapel. There were already several nuns outside talking quietly. As Lu and her daughter approached the chapel door a nun greeted them

"Good Morning! I'm Sister Agnes. I was, or I should say, I *am* a friend of Cathy's."

"Good Morning Sister, I'm Lu—"

"Oh I know who you are. You're Luisa Cianci. Cathy described you perfectly. You were one of her sisterhood," Sister Agnes said with a smile. "I'm so happy to finally meet you."

"How did you know?"

"Well there's not a whole lot of entertainment at some of the missions we serve. Cathy talked constantly about her friends and the good times you all had. I got to know you pretty well. Luisa, Pasqualina, Regina, Celestina, she said it was like reciting a litany of Italian saints."

"I'm afraid the only saint among us was Cathy." Lu bit her lip in an attempt to keep from crying.

"Not really, we are all called to be saints. Anyway I'm glad to meet you and put a face with each name. Is it true you put a glass full of tadpoles in one nun's room?"

"You did what, Mom?" Caroline asked, laughing.

"Yes, well, I only went along. It was Cathy who planned it along with another friend. There were five of us. We've sort of lost touch with each other over the past few years."

"I'm glad you could come. We have saved the front—"

That was as far as Sister Agnes got. She stopped and looked over Lu's shoulder at a long stretch limousine that had pulled up. "Wow! Would you look at that! They're going to have to park that at the bus stop."

The front passenger door opened and a man in a uniform got out. He opened the back door and a woman exited. She was dressed in a smart black suit, a black straw hat, and stiletto heels. Everything about her said "high fashion." Even the nuns standing by the chapel stopped their conversations to look. The woman gave some instructions to the man and began to walk up the stairs.

"That's got to be Tina Benedict," said Sister Agnes.

"If you don't mind we will just go in and have a seat," said Lu pushing her daughter toward the door.

Sister Agnes walked down the steps to Cele.

"Good Morning, CelesTINA." she said with a laugh.

"Cathy used to call me that. You have the inflection right. I used to hate it. She did it to annoy me. I'm Tina Benedict. You must be Sister Agnes. Thank you for notifying me about this. I wouldn't have missed it for the world."

"I'm glad you could made it. After all you have done for Cathy and her missions I knew you would want to come. It's almost time. The Sisters are getting ready to process in but I'll show you to a seat. We have reserved the front rows for her friends."

"Is Mrs. Ferrara here?'

"No, serious health problems prevented her coming from Arizona but she sent some stuff, pictures of Cathy. Let's go in."

Sister Agnes led the way and started down the center aisle. Cele touched her arm and whispered, "I'd prefer to sit toward the back. It's been a while and I'd feel more comfortable here." She pointed to an aisle seat halfway up.

Cele sat down and looked around. There were a lot of empty seats up toward the front. She was looking for a familiar face or two from the old neighborhood. There were none she recognized. There was a redheaded lady in the front row but she didn't look like Carol Ferrara, Cathy's sister. She gazed at the front altar. There on the side was a small display of pictures. Cele could make out a baby picture, First Communion, high school graduation and a picture of Cathy the nun. It must have been a recent one. The same crinkly eyes when she smiled, the same *cat who ate the canary* expression on her face.

"Thanks Cathy, thanks so much for everything." whispered Cele.

The music began and the sisters entered the chapel two by two, singing a favorite hymn. It was a joyous song not one that would be associated with a funeral. The service began with the same prayers she had learned with Cathy so many years ago. Cele was surprised by the fact she remembered them. *It was like riding a bicycle. Once you learn, you never forget no matter how long it has been.*

Toward the middle of the service Sister Agnes approached the altar, bowed and stepped up to the pulpit.

"In the name of the Father, Son and Holy Spirit, I welcome you here to the celebration of the life of Sister Catherine Ann Barbara Ferrara, she was a Maryknoll sister, missionary, martyr and my friend. We entered formation together so many years ago I have lost count and we served together in Mexico. Sister Cathy was not supposed to be a nun. When she came the first day, she and I were partners. We assembled and walked to the chapel together. All I could smell was cigarettes, alcohol and cologne mouthwash."

There was laughter from the congregation.

"From that moment on I knew life with Cathy would be very interesting to say the least. Her nickname was "Foxy Ferrara.""

More laughter.

"Cathy holds the record for the number of times she broke Grand Silence in a month. Fifty two times. Not bad for a month that had thirty days. She chewed gum, belched at will, and once caught a fly in chapel by slamming her prayer book shut after the fly landed on a page."

The chapel convulsed with laughter.

"I learned years later that she came within a centimeter of being asked to leave and I'm ashamed to admit I too wondered why she was allowed to stay. There was nothing nun-like about her. In fact she was so bad, she made the rest of us look good, so our novitiate was easy. She is proof that God has a sense of humor and she is proof Our Lord looks deep within each of us. He looked into Cathy's heart and liked what He saw. He saw fun. He saw laughter. He saw dedication to duty and He saw a love of people. Cathy said she loved because she was loved. She was an 'all for one and one for all' person. This she got because she was part of a sisterhood of friends from her youth who inspired and supported her throughout her life."

Lu wiped her eyes with her hands while her daughter patted her on the arm.

"At this time I should like to invite members from the congregation to share a happy or funny story because this is a celebration, a party for Cathy."

From the front row an elderly nun stood up with assistance. She walked to the front of the altar, bowed and faced the people.

"I have to admit also that Cathy was not our number one choice but I was struck by something she said during her admitting interview. When asked why she wanted to become a nun, she replied, and I can remember that clearly to this day, 'Because I love people.' The rest of us probably said 'because we love God.' You know God is easy to love. We all love Him but sometimes we find it hard to love His people. Cathy did!"

The nun sat back down and another one took her place with a funny story. Sister Agnes came back to the pulpit.

"There are some friends of hers here. Perhaps one of them would come up and share a Cathy story with us."

No one stood up.

"Ms. Benedict, how about you?"

Cele almost fell off the pew. She vehemently shook her head but Sister Agnes waved her up. Cele walked up the aisle to the altar. She felt very uncomfortable up here.

"Umm, I'm Celestina Di Benedetti and I was a friend of Cathy's. I was with the group of girls who drove her up that first day. We were the ones who plied her with booze, uh, liquor, and cigarettes and we took bets on how long she'd last. We did not want her to come to a convent. We felt she belonged with us. There were five of us. We called ourselves *La Sorellanza*. That means The Sisterhood in Italian. Cathy was always very proud of us. She would lead us in this cheer and at the end she would raise her hand and we'd yell '*La Sorellanza*' and the response was '*Sempre come sorelle*' always like sisters, which we were. We were quite a group. If you rolled us into one person it would be the perfect woman. One was very pretty, one was very smart, another was just the sweetest girl ever and Cathy, she was the most fun. I am very happy to have been Cathy's sister and friend."

Cele's voice quivered and broke. She could say no more. She had to sit down. She walked away from the altar and started back to her seat. The red haired woman in the front seat stood up. "*Sempre come sorelle*," she said.

Cele froze. My God, who could that be? Could that be Reggie? She walked back to her seat as another woman stood up. She had salt and pepper hair and was gaunt and tired-looking. "*Sempre come sorelle*," she said almost inaudibly. Cele barely recognized Pat. She looked about sixty instead of mid forties. Pat nodded at Cele. Cele sat down in shock. *Oh my God, Cathy arranged one more meeting of the sisterhood.* Trying not to be obvious, Cele looked around. Was Lu here too? She couldn't see anyone who resembled her.

At one point the congregation was asked to offer each other a Sign of Peace. It was a hug or a handshake. Cele bolted up the aisle and ran toward Reggie. Both women hugged and held on to each other. A minute later they were joined by Pat and there was a three-way group hug.

The people in the front row squeezed closer so the women could sit together for the remainder of the service.

"Mom, why don't you go up there and be with them?" Caroline poked her mother. "You were one of the sisterhood."

Lu did not respond and did not move from her seat. She stared straight ahead.

Just before the service ended, Sister Agnes waved to the celebrating priest. She had one more message to share. She was tearful as she faced the people.

"One of the sisters just conveyed me the message. You know those six children that Cathy saved? They testified against the militia. They wouldn't have survived there. We feared they too, would have been killed. The United States government has just granted them political asylum and they will be joining us in Florida in a few days. Isn't that wonderful news? Cathy's job on earth is done but she's just beginning her work from heaven."

The people in the chapel applauded and the concluding song was sung with joy. It was a celebration, as Cathy would have wanted. The service was over. Cele, Pat and Reggie stayed in their seats still hugging and crying and hugging some more. Sister Agnes came over.

"Isn't that the best news? We are so happy because we worried about the future of the children. Cathy is still taking care of things." She smiled through her tears. "There is a small reception area in the back of the church. Would you like to go there? I'm sure you all have plenty to share with each other."

Arm in arm, the three women walked to the back. Sister Agnes led the way, then closed the door.

"God I'm so happy to see you. You look great! How are you? How are the kids?" Hugging each other again and again, the three women talked all at once not listening for answers.

"Wait a minute, hold it," Cele said, "Twenty questions, remember we used to play that!

"Let's do that now. Reggie, you go first."

"Well my name is Margaret Flaherty now. Please can you call me that?"

"Margaret Flaherty? Why did you pick that name?"

"When we got into the witness protection program, we had to choose new names. It had to be completely different from the one we had. Not even the same nationality. The only thing I could think of was Irish. That's the opposite of Italian. I don't know why I chose it. I don't even like Margaret but it popped into my head. The red hair goes with the name. Anna Catherine chose Cara and you wouldn't believe what name Sal Jr. picked. It's awful but he likes it. It's Howard!"

"Howard?" Both Pat and Cele said in unison.

"How are the kids?" Pat asked.

"Fine now. It was tough but we made it through and they are doing beautifully. They're great kids. How are Anthony and John?"

"Wait a minute, we haven't finished with you." Cele said. "What are you doing, where do you live, how are your folks?"

"OK, I am a travel agent. We live in Florida and the folks are getting older but they're fine."

"A travel agent? You hate to travel! You didn't even want to go away on your honeymoon." Pat remembered Reggie's reluctance so many years ago.

"Yeah but I've gotten better now. I still rather stay at home but I've got to work so this is fun. I take several trips a year, mostly to the Caribbean since I'm the expert on it in my office."

"Can I ask this next question? Are you married?" Pat looked at her questioningly.

"No but I am seeing someone. We've been together sort of for the past five years. He's from Cuba, came here as a kid. He's an accountant who worked in the same building as I did. He lost his wife to cancer. We may or may not get married but lately I think maybe we will. I never thought I'd marry again after Sal. I didn't want to. Losing someone is so hard but you know being alone is hard too. The kids like him. He's a nice man. Are my twenty questions up because I have lots to ask of you guys."

"Reggie? How—" Cele started to ask.

"Please, my name now is Margaret. I've gotten used to it and I still have to be careful."

"All right Marge. How did you find out about Cathy?" Cele asked.

"Oh, I've kept in touch with her over the years. She was the only one I could write to. She helped me so much right from the beginning. I had a lot of... stuff... I had to work through but she stuck with me. In fact she stayed at the house a couple of years ago before she went down to Guatemala this last time. We talked for three days straight about everything and everyone. Through her I kept track of you. I just had to come today. I had to see you even for a short time. I have missed you so much. Sister Agnes, the one who brought us here, said she found my address in Cathy's things. That's when I heard."

"One more, then it will be Pat's turn. What about Lu?"

"I don't know if I can answer that. I was looking for her in the church. I didn't see her. You know in spite of everything, I... uh... I sincerely hoped to see her. Okay, that's it for me. My twenty questions are over. Now it's Pat."

"Fire away, I'm ready"

"Same thing, who, what, where, how, when."

"First of all I'm fine. I am a recovering alcoholic and drug addict. Those days are over for me. Looking back I can't believe I was so stupid but I'm through kicking myself in the ass. I've done well. I'm strong. I did go back to school and I've gotten my bachelor and master's in psychology and I am enrolled in the PHD program. I'm about one third finished and—"

"Oh my God, how great!" screamed Reggie, "you did go to college like you always wanted to! How wonderful!"

"That's terrific!" said Cele. "Now I can brag about my friend the psychology doctor. Pretty soon we'll see you on TV. *The Dr. Pat Hour.*"

"Yeah sure! What if no one calls in and I'm sitting there in front of the camera waiting for the phone to ring."

"Not to worry, Regina-Margaret and I will call in a hundred times. God knows I've had enough problems I could discuss. I wouldn't have to make any up. So, where are you living, how are the kids, your Mom and Ricky? How's he? Are you divorced?"

"Boy, you sure do get down to basics, Cele. You always did. I live in Washington Heights and I've been there for years. I got a real nice apartment on Cabrini Blvd. It's big and it was just perfect for the boys and me. I had to sell the house, as you may or may not know. Defense lawyers aren't cheap and it took a lot of money. My mom lives near by and guess what? She went back to school too. Sixty-three years old and she's a sophomore. The kids are good, busy with their lives. Anthony's in computers and John is a sophomore too. He marches to his own tune. Do you know Reggie, not too long ago he asked about Sal Jr. You remember they were only a few months apart? Out of the blue, he asked." Pat paused for a minute. She knew what she had to say next and wanted to choose her words carefully.

"As for Ricky, well, we are separated and have been since that time. I don't know if you knew this Reggie, but the fall-out from Reno's trial hit Ricky also. Reno was a silent partner in Abbodanza Supply and after his trial, the Feds took a real close look at the company. Well, the company went down and Ricky was arrested and though the Angelinis tried, he was still convicted of laundering drug money and conspiracy. He is in prison for twelve years. He'll be out in another couple of years for good behavior. I really thought hard about getting a divorce but I decided with a lot of help from counseling not to. We made life hard for each other. I brought some heavy baggage with me when I married him and he had a lot too. You know I didn't see him for years. I made the boys go, of course, but then Cathy said 'Enough. You won't get completely better until you face him'."

Pat remembered her conversation with Cathy several years ago. At that time she was still full of bitterness and nowhere near ready to forgive. Cathy kept encouraging her. "It took a while but eventually I did and I got quite a surprise. They can take classes in prison you know and Ricky was taking psychology classes also. We're kind of building on that knowledge. I go up once a month or so depending on my schedule. The boys are happy about that. So, we'll see. I too kept up with Cathy. She didn't ever mention seeing you Reggie but I knew she did and I know she kept up with you, Cele. I found out about Cathy through Mom. She read it in the newspaper and called me. I cried like I hadn't cried in a long time." Pat sniffed and wiped her eyes. "I got Cele stories from her. Good and bad ones."

"Yeah there were quite a few of those but lately I've gotten boring."

"That'll be the day when Cele is boring," laughed Reggie. "Alright, tell us a few good stories but start with the bad ones first."

"Well, I-uh, well, you know now about Reno and me. I can't say much about it except that I really did love him at the time and when he died in prison I took it bad. I haven't decided whether I was blind to everything or I just didn't want to know. Hindsight is so much clearer. I know there was never any future with him but I just couldn't give him up. When I would go to Lu's house sometimes I just wanted to run out. I was ashamed but... Eventually Lu found out and we haven't spoken in years. I regret that. Anyway the business, of course, went kaput and I left town, tail between my legs. I went to LA but didn't like it so when I visited Las Vegas I stayed. I got into something really great. I do free-lance costume design for the showgirls and it's going great. I'm as busy as I want to be. But now for the good part, I'm a mother!"

"Oh Cele, my God, I'm so happy, *we* are so happy for you."

"Cele!"

Both women grabbed and hugged her.

"You didn't gain any weight! Did you get stretch marks?" teased Reggie.

"Don't forget varicose veins. I got some with John and they never went away. So are you married or are you a single mom? By the way was it via artificial insemination or did you do it the old-fashioned way and with whom and when?" asked Pat barely able to conceal her glee.

"I did it the easy way, no stretch marks, no varicose veins and I certainly am not going to get married! I adopted and I have three kids—two boys and a little girl."

La Sorellanza (The Sisterhood)   Barbara Wilson Wright

"It was Cathy's doing. About four months ago. She'd been after me for years. Once I got kind of down and I mentioned it to her. There really is something to this biological clock. I mean I was back in business, doing well financially, I was seeing this guy, older, very wealthy and we talked one night about getting married. I would have been wife number four. The heck with it I said. We are still friends, if I get horny I can always go to him but anyway I told this to Cathy when I was down in the dumps. She decided I needed kids and she never let up. She badgered me all the time until I finally gave in. I didn't think she would act so fast but as soon as I said, 'well I'll think about it,' she writes back and says she found the family for me. The kids just came into the orphanage. Their parents were killed by the military. She said they needed a mother and I needed them. She was right. They have made such a difference in my life, I can't believe it. Wait, I brought her last letter with me." Cele dug in her Bill Blass bag and pulled out a soup can label. Cathy had used the back of it as writing paper.

Cele,

A quick note, everything is all set. My good friend at the embassy, Bob McCormack, assured me he will personally hand carry all the paperwork to each agency for approval and signatures. In just a little while you'll have your kids. You're going to love them, Cele. I told them that soon there will be a surprise in their life. They are great. Two of them like to paint and draw and the little girl loves to dress up. She's always putting on a flower or something. You'll be a wonderful Mom and just think—no morning sickness. Love you Cele. La Sorellanza, Sempre.

Cele mopped her eyes. "I can't get through this letter without crying. This was the last time I heard from her. The day she died, that afternoon I got a call from this guy who said everything was set. I was to come down in about a week with the money. This adoption was costly. You have to pay everybody and their uncle but I didn't care. Cathy would pick up the kids from the orphanage and meet me in Guatemala City. Of course, we didn't know anything was wrong at that time. A few days later, I called him to check on some last minute details and he told me Cathy was missing. She had not returned to her mission for several days but they were doing everything they could to find her. I called back every day for two weeks but there was no news of her. Finally one night he called. They had found the truck she had driven, then some villagers showed them where she was. The army just dumped her in the jungle but when some people found her, they buried her."

Reggie, Pat and Cele hugged and cried for a few minutes, then Cele went on with her story.

"I found this out when I went to get the kids. One day Bob called me and told me to come down immediately. I had one day's notice to get ready. I arrived at the airport around one. By three that day I was in front of a judge with the money in hand. He offered condolences but I silently damned all of them to hell. By five I was back at the airport. We got the first available flight out of there. We got to Mexico City and arrived in LA that night about eleven. The kids were exhausted but I just couldn't stay one more day. I was so angry." Cele paused and put her hand on her face.

"You know Cathy is buried in her mission village. I paid for the funeral. They said she would have wanted that. I wanted to bring her body back here but maybe it's better. Oh, she was right, those kids are great and we took to each other language barrier or not. They learned 'McDonald's' in one day."

"How old are they and what are their names?" Reggie asked.

"Ramijo or Ray as I call him is almost eight. His brother, Miquel, is six and the girl is three and a half. She is Kayla. They were Indians, probably Mayan. They picked up English almost overnight. I bought every Disney video I could get my hands on at Target and—"

"Target? You're joking. You shop at Target?" Pat asked incredulously.

"Yes I do and I shop at Wal-Mart, too. They have the best prices on toys."

"Well Margaret, we have lived to see everything now. Cele, shopping at Target. God, do you remember the days when she wouldn't even shop on lower Fifth Avenue because those stores weren't classy enough? Cele, at Wal-Mart! Will miracles never cease?" Pat teased.

"Oh knock it off! I do conventional things. Jesus, I just sold my beautiful Las Vegas condo and bought a house in the suburbs. It's got four bedrooms, a yard and a pool and I've joined the Mom and Tots play group."

"I'm just kidding, Cele. Like Cathy said, you'll be a great mom. Speaking of moms, have you talked with Mrs. Ferrara? How's she doing?"

"Yes, I did. I called her about, you know, where Cathy should be and she agreed also about Cathy staying down there. Typical Italian momma response. She says she has her own special angel in heaven now. I understand she's not feeling well but she sent those pictures of Cathy for this service. I'll call her when I get back. Well, anymore questions?"

"I have one. Can anybody play?" It was Lu standing at the door.

There was uncomfortable silence for a minute. Then Reggie always the group sweetie walked over to Lu. Lu's eyes misted with tears. Of all the girls it was Reggie who came first. Reggie, the one she had hurt the most.

"Hi, my name is Margaret Flaherty. I am a friend of Cathy's."

"Sure," said Cele, "come on over and play. The rule is you have to tell the truth or you have to eat a bug if you lie."

"I already ate one. You and Cathy made me."

"Did not!"

"Yes you did! I know, I had to eat it."

"For your information it wasn't a bug. I found this teeny tiny little stone and Cathy rolled it in dirt and we shoved it in your mouth. How are you, Lu? You look good as usual."

"Hi, Lu," said Pat. She made no attempt to go over to her.

"I didn't want to come in. I've been sitting in that chapel with Caroline and I heard you guys laughing. Caroline made me come, saying this was for Cathy. More than anything right now I want to see all of you but in view of everything I can understand if—

"It's over Lu," said Pat. "All that crap is over and we have survived. You know in a way we were all victims, victims of centuries of garbage. The Mafia, the Mob... you know what I am speaking about. It was always there, always a part of our lives but we never said anything about it. We never said anything about the octopus in the living room. It was just part of our lives. We tiptoed around it but we could never tell anyone it lived in our house. I've done a lot of thinking. I had plenty of time to do so. Think about it. We lived together. Thank God we liked each other because life would have been very lonely. We were isolated from others. Truly we were. Did you ever have a Polish or Greek friend? Could you ever date someone other than a neighborhood guy? Could you ever tell anyone what your father did for a living?"

"No, not me! I wanted to go to the prom with Tanya Grigoriev's brother. He was so cute, blond haired, blue-eyed. My father had a shit fit," Cele said, "Either I went to the prom with one of our guys or not at all. At the last minute I asked Bobby Vincio. I hated it. That's why I fought tooth and nail with my parents to let me go to the fashion school. I slaved for two years working two jobs so I could get enough money. Thank God I was able to win a scholarship. I thought I had gotten away from that but obviously I didn't."

"I didn't know that, you never said anything to any of us." Reggie said sympathetically.

"I couldn't talk about it." Cele said shaking her head.

Lu said, "One time my father and I were at Johnson's Shoe store. I was picking up some shoes for tap dancing class. I remember seeing someone from that class. She was getting shoes too. Her mother was with her and I introduced my father. She said how nice it was that my father could come with me to get them. I said my father was a businessman and that's why he could take the time off. Later in the car my father was furious with me for telling strangers what he did. I was never to say anything about the family again. You're right Pat, as I got older I just chose to ignore it."

Pat said, "It wasn't until after everything happened that I found out the circumstances of my father's death. I was always told it was a car accident. He was a getaway man for the Mob for God sakes. He died as a result of a shoot out. When I finally got up the nerve I asked my Mother about it. She said she was sworn to secrecy. Her support came from the Mob and she had to keep quiet about it. Ricky too had to keep his activities quiet. We could never talk about business other than 'How was your day dear', and yet we enabled this to go on by our passivity. We were brainwashed in a way."

"Yes but we didn't know better. That was normal for us," Lu interjected. "All my life it was the same, 'we stick with our own kind. This is how we survived in this country,' my father would say. We stuck with our own and helped each other against the *pezzonovante*, the establishment. Thank God it's different for my kids."

"Cathy helped me to see that Lu. It took a while but eventually I came to understand what she was saying. I know now you had to tell your father. It would have been disloyal to him to know what I was doing and not tell him. That is such a strange code. It's almost feudal." Reggie-Margaret said.

"Yeah it is but then understanding where it came from it makes sense. Sicily as beautiful as it is, is still a feudal society. The rich have everything and the poor eat dirt. They adopted that code even though it ruined many of their lives. It goes on from generation to generation. Loyalty, silence, an eye for an eye. I just can't believe we allowed this to take over our lives." Pat shook her head.

Lu addressed her remarks to Reggie. "Reg-uh, Margaret, I really didn't mean to betray you. I swear to God Almighty I was worried that you were being taken in. I thought maybe they were taking advantage of you and that somehow you would be hurt. I-I can't say I'm sorry often enough. I can't tell you how I felt when I sat in the courtroom and heard the things I did about my father. It's a horrible thing I did, Margaret but not nearly as horrible as knowing your father, a man whom you loved, was responsible."

"The funny thing is I still think of him as Mr. R, the man who was always there for us." Reggie said. "Kind, generous, funny. Maybe that's how you should remember him too."

Pat nodded in agreement. "That's kind of what I tell my guys. You get rid of the octopus by not perpetuating it to another generation. As I said it's over, let's put it to rest. Each of our lives has been affected by it. My father died because of it, Cathy was practically sold by her father, Reggie, your husband was killed, Lu, your father was a part of it, he and Ricky went to prison because of it, Cele you too. Enough! *E finito!*" Pat spoke intensely.

"Amen to that, Pat." Cele squeezed her hand. "Marge, how long are you staying here? Do you have to go back right away?"

"I'm going back to the city and flying right out tonight. I came yesterday and Sister Agnes put me up in one of the guestrooms. I really can't stay, in fact, please don't say anything to anyone especially in the old neighborhood.

I'm sure by this time nothing would happen but I have to be careful."

All the women nodded.

"Sure thing kiddo, I have a limo courtesy of my rich friend. I can give you a lift because I want to get back to the kids. I'm leaving today too. Motherhood is calling."

"Lu, did you know Cele is a Momma and she shops at Target and Wal-Mart, can you believe it.?"

"Yes I heard that outside the door."

"Wait, wait, we haven't played twenty questions with Lu. Your turn and this time I will make you eat a bug for real if you don't tell the truth. What are you doing? How are the kids, your Mom? Are you seeing someone? I know about you and Jimmy. Cathy mentioned it. Sorry!" Cele said.

"Don't be sorry. I'm not. Yes, I'm dating. I don't like it much. Things are so different these days. Cele, I'll have to ask you for advice. My mother is too old and I'm too embarrassed to ask Caroline."

"Sorry girlfriend, I'm doing my playing in a sand box these days. I'm not so good with advice."

"Caroline is with me. She drove up. I just couldn't do this alone. Jimmy Jr. is in grad school and Ma is fine. Speaking of fine, so is Mrs. Tomasino. She's in a nursing home in Bayside I think. Ma visits her once in a while. True to form, she's running the place. She's eighty-seven and she knows everyone's business there. I'm in business too, legitimate, believe me. I went to beauty school, then opened a small chain of salons. Discount Beauty Shops, high fashion, low price. I have four of them. It seems I have a head for business. I'm not as dumb as I thought. Cathy pushed me into doing this."

"Cathy pushed all of us into doing things. She always did! You were never dumb, Lu. Ricky said I may have been the studious one of us but you were smart. I'm glad for you. What's with Jimmy Sr. these days?" Pat said.

"I haven't seen him in over a year and the kids haven't either. I know he's on his third or fourth Miss Tits. He works for a used car lot. Nothing like in the old days but he gets by. I didn't ask for alimony or child support. I just wanted out. Ma sold the old place. The neighborhood had changed so much that she didn't want to stay there. She bought herself a cute townhouse and she went to beauty school, too. Sometimes, when she's not the social butterfly, traveling, going on cruises, she will come and help me out if one of the operators is ill. She's very fussy about whose hair she does. She only works on ladies her age and they love her. They claim she is the only one who does hair like it used to be done. I don't really see too many people from the old neighborhood, maybe some at funerals that's all."

Lu paused for a minute trying to get courage for what she wanted to say next.

"Uh, I got say this guys before I lose my nerve. I'm really sorry for everything, for the hurt I caused each of you. She stopped. "Cele, I know he loved you, he told me so and my mother knew all along. She wasn't—well, she felt sorry for you most of all. She got your letter a few years back."

Cele stared down at the floor not daring to look at Lu's face.

"Pat, I'm sorry. I didn't do it to hurt you. I was hurting so much myself, I just didn't—" Lu stopped, she couldn't go on. Tearfully she looked at Reggie and just shook her head. Reggie came up and took Lu's arm and the two women just stood silently. Cele cleared her throat.

"Marge, we really have to go. If you tell me where your bag is, I'll get the guy to pick it up. Listen, why don't all of you get in the limo with us. We drove Cathy up together. Let's drive back together this time. I know there's champagne in the frig. We can share a toast. Can Caroline drive herself back to the city? If not, the footman or whatever you call him can drive your car back and she can come with us."

"I'll ask her but I have a feeling she'd rather go off on her own," Lu answered.

"My bag is already packed. I left it at the guesthouse. I'll go get it now and meet you in front," said Reggie.

"Pat, will you come or did you drive?"

"No car. I don't drive anymore. I took the train up this morning, then a cab here. I would *love* to come with you."

"OK, Doctor." Cele put her arm around Pat's shoulder. "That has a nice sound to it, 'Dr. Pat Campione'!"

"Thanks but it will be Dr. Pat Damato."

~ * ~

The women walked out of the side room. The chapel was empty now except for one nun who was praying. The sun was shining through the stained glass window behind the altar. The light was soft and ethereal, almost heavenly. Cathy's pictures were still up on the side of the altar.

"Let's go up," whispered Pat. Let's go up for her."

Arm-in-arm, the four women walked up the aisle to the altar. They stepped up to the side. For a moment they were silent, then Cele softly broke out with their old cheer.

"Holy Smokey, Crimin' Crokey,

Look out world while we do the Hokey.

Shake those buns, shake those booties,

In all the world no sweeter cuties."

She stopped. Her body shook with sobs.

Reggie raised her hand. "*La Sorellanza!*"

"The Sisterhood!"

Pat and Lu and the sobbing Cele responded, "*Sempre come sorelle!* Always like sisters!"

"Group hug, come on everyone," said Pat and took Cathy's picture off the stand. She held it while the girls put their arms around each other and hugged.

"*Yeah!*" They whispered loudly.

The nun who was praying just smiled.

Meet Barbara Wilson Wright

I've been so lucky, as this is the second book I've had published. "Not bad for an old broad," I laughingly tell my friends. The first book, "A Life Hidden" won the Golden Wings Award from Wings Press.

I'd like people to know you're never too old to try anything. All you need is the desire and be willing to work to achieve your dream. I'd be happy to encourage anyone... just write me:

barbara @bwwbooks.com

***VISIT OUR WEBSITE
FOR THE FULL INVENTORY
OF QUALITY BOOKS***:

http://www.wings-press.com

*Quality trade paperbacks and downloads
in multiple formats,
in genres ranging from light romantic
comedy to general fiction and horror.
Wings has something
for every reader's taste.
Visit the website, then bookmark it.
We add new titles each month!*